WICKED
RUIN

SE 7 EN SINNERS

S.L. JENNINGS

Wicked Ruin
Copyright © 2017 S.L. Jennings

ISBN-13:978-1977646101
ISBN-10:1977646107

Cover Design: By Hang Le
Editing: Siren's Call Author Services
Proofreading: Kara Hildebrand
Formatting: Champagne Book Design
Photography: Mika Reyes Photography
Models and Creative: Maud

WICKED RUIN

PROLOGUE

I HEAR THEM BUT I CAN'T MOVE. I CAN'T SCREAM. I CAN'T call out to them.

No. Stop. Don't do this.

Don't do this to me. Not again.

I'm drowning.

No. I've already drowned.

I was held under water when I was just a young girl. A baby who had never known what it meant to be wanted, to be loved. I stayed under too long, and I woke. I surfaced as someone else. *Something* else.

They put me in those wicked waters again, and I knew I wouldn't surface as I did before. I would not resurface a second time.

But I did.

I woke up in that water. I was reborn in that water. I was

changed. But somehow, I was the same. I was me, yet I wasn't.

I was the me before her. Before Adriel.

One went in.

Two came out.

One died.

So that two may live.

Kill one to save a million.

He knew. He always knew.

ONE

LEGION

H IS BLOOD WAS FIRE IN HIS VEINS.

Molten lava that singed his nerve endings and kindled his cells into ash, only for those delicate, microscopic flecks to reform and mend themselves whole again.

No. Not whole. Stronger. Indestructible.

He had been remade into the monster he once was. The monster he had tried to flee for centuries. He had surrendered his power to escape the lost souls that had haunted him for millennia, serving as his own personal horde of poltergeists.

And now…the souls had found him and they were angry. Their voices were a chorus of violent hisses, whispering seductions of malice and carnage. Blood. They begged for blood. And they would not be appeased until it stained every inch of the damp stone walls of this underground tomb.

Dread hangs heavy and thick in the air, an almost palpable plume of darkness swirling around the small, trembling figure swathed in a ratty hooded robe.

"What have you done?" His voice is as ice cold as death.

"It's…it's true," the woman simpers, her words barely audible. "You're him. The Legion of Lost Souls."

"What have you done?" Each word is a stab wound to the woman's flickering courage.

"I-I released you. So you could save my daughter." The mention of her estranged child releases a snarl from his lips, tight over razor sharp fangs. She shivers at the sight.

"Where is she?" Each word trembles the ground beneath her feet.

The frail woman manages to answer, "He took her. He promised he wouldn't hurt her, but… The sanctuary. They took her to the sanctuary." A sense of urgency lights her sullen eyes. "Please, you have to hurry…before he kills her! There isn't much time."

Legion looks towards the heavy concrete door, his supernatural hearing picking up footsteps from several yards away. There are many of them—at least a dozen. His gaze goes back to the woman that birthed Eden, only to attempt to murder her time and time again. He steps forward. Killing her would be a kindness compared to the fate she will face for freeing him. But she did so, knowing full well she would be struck down, to save her child. The very same child she had cursed as an abomination, a scourge on her life. Why?

There is no time to ask. Not when the retched stink of

death fills his nostrils with every inhale. He can feel her in his blood, a mystical pull that draws on his power, leading him to her. But first, they will fall. All of them. Every fucking creature—human or otherwise—that had a hand in her torment will fall at his feet in immeasurable agony.

Each heavy footfall to the door is a warning—an omen. When he steps into the hall, he simply waits, the sweet taste of rage on his tongue and the exhilarating surge of promised violence tingling his palms. He blinks, thick, black lashes kissing his cheeks, and revels in the feel of his swelling power. For centuries, he had been content with the tiny fraction that had sustained him enough to survive. Just a miniscule drop so he could hunt and kill those that had been touched by the Devil's influence.

He had missed this terrible power. Missed the way it called to him, taunted him, enticed him. He missed the smell of their putrid fear as his enemies laid their eyes on his hulking frame. He missed the sounds of their racing hearts just before he reached into their chest cavities and turned their most vital organs to pulp.

The closer they got, the more excited—the more utterly alive—he felt. Each step towards him and their impending execution filled him with a dark thrill that sang in his blood and throbbed in his newly made bones. It wouldn't be long; he'd make it quick. No time to enjoy the sounds of their mangled cries or the feel of their limbs writhing in unspeakable anguish. Their deaths would be merciful, which was much more than they deserved for what they had done. What they had taken from him.

The second the first wave of agents enter the long, stone

corridor, they pause at the sight of the massive beast yards away. Their hesitation is their misstep, and Legion merely smiles, sensual lips pulling over sharp fangs, before he catapults them into sheer horror. Just a beat of silence before their screams echo through the hallway along with the sounds of ripping flesh and gurgling blood.

He doesn't even have to lift a finger. The lost souls know exactly what to do, and they always do their job well. One by one, the agents crumple into mangled heaps onto the cold ground, befallen by their own blades. Just a whisper of possession is all it takes to drive the strongest men mad. And with fury and vengeance pumping in his veins, Legion needed even less than that.

The screams barely last sixty seconds before dead silence greets him, and he is one with those merciless souls once again. They sing him sweet nothings, each dark note laced with promises of death of destruction. *This way. Come with us.* He coasts across the corridor on a cloud of carnage, led by his insatiable bloodlust, only pausing to note the state of his undress. What's left of his clothing are mere tattered rags, torn to shreds by an angel venom-tipped whip, courtesy of Alliance thugs. And when they had worn that to frayed, limp threads, they opted for silver-plated brass knuckles.

His wounds had since healed, but he would never forget their faces. The way they laughed and cheered with pride, spitting in his eye when Legion refused to give them the satisfaction of a reaction. And when they had grown desperate after hours of torture, they had whipped out their pathetic little cocks and pissed on him. All in the name of their Lord and Savior.

Bullshit.

They would pay. For taking Eden. For attempting to degrade him. For making a mockery of his Father. They would all pay.

He snatches up a pair of pants, boots, and a jacket off the biggest of the fallen soldiers. He would've been considered huge by human standards, but to Legion, he was no more than a pissant.

He didn't bother with weapons—he didn't need them. The souls that now inhabited him had been trapped for centuries, and they had plans for any and every one who had ever wronged him. They would not be silenced. And what they wouldn't do, Legion had particular…gifts…that allowed him to manipulate other creatures into doing his bidding.

With long strides, he clears the hallway, only to find himself faced with another. He follows without hesitance, the ghosts that had internally haunted him leading the way. To human eyes, they were invisible and silent unless they intended otherwise. But to his kind—to the demons who prowled in the shadows and the angels that hid behind their self-righteous rules and traditions—they appeared as wisps of black smoke with eyes of raging fire. They wrap themselves around their master in protection and possession, awaiting his command. He could dampen their appearance, veil them within himself, but right now he wanted them out in full force. Let them see. Let them all see what he had become. Let them gaze upon him in terror before he ripped their throats out.

Legion finds himself at the foot of a narrow, winding staircase. He can smell candles burning on the floor above. Patchouli, clove, lavender, and something else. Conjuring scents. He takes the stairs three at a time, only to come face to face with half a dozen armed guards, all wearing various shades of shock.

Legion flings his power out, not even bothering with possession. The men crumble to the floor, their bodies seizing in horrifying pain as their blood turns to boiling acid in their veins. They don't even have the chance to scream in agony before their vocal cords are liquefied, which is exactly what Legion was aiming for. He still has the element of surprise on his side, and if the voices echoing in his skull speak the truth, he'll need it.

He steps around the bodies of his victims at the top of the stairs, their faces mutilated with oozing blisters that stink of pus and rotting flesh. Moments ago, he may have felt remorse. He wouldn't have reveled in their suffering, even if it were deserved. But that was when there was a shred of humanity left in him. When he was actively seeking salvation for all the pain and destruction he had caused so many centuries ago. When he was wracked with guilt and shame that ate him alive every time he took a life in order to serve what he thought was the greater good.

That seems so long ago. As he harnesses his simmering temper, the smell of death at his back, the greater good is a distant memory. There is only one thing he lives for, only one thing that fuels his ire: Vengeance.

That internal tug that seems to grip his joints and muscles pulls harder, the feeling urgent, desperate. It's her. She needs him. And as much as he'd like to storm into the sanctuary and unleash his rage on every foe that stands between him and Eden, the cloying scent of angel venom hangs heavy and thick in the air, as if it's been manipulated into a mist that sizzles the surface of his skin. He doesn't even feel the burn. No doubt, it's a diversion tactic, meaning that whatever is on the other side of those wooden double doors is the very thing he so desperately seeks.

There is one of him, and at least three angels on the other side of those doors. Even at full strength, he would fall, but not without taking one or two with him. They knew this, which is why the sanctuary doors were so sparsely guarded. They'd let the humans die for their noble cause, so arrogant to believe that he could be subdued enough to give up on her.

Or maybe this was their plan all along. Remake him into the beast he once was, surrendering all hopes of redemption. Scatter a few meaningless human lives in his path just to prove he's nothing more than an inherent monster. And lead him right to his execution, using Eden as bait.

No matter. He wouldn't turn his back on the one person who kept him tethered to this mortal realm. The single, solitary ray of light in a dark, cold void that was now his soul.

It would surely be a fight to the death, but he would die for something he believed in—for someone he believed in. He would give up eternity so she could live a long, human life, free of the influence his ilk had bestowed upon her. She deserved that much, even if his existence was scrubbed from her mind. Even if he never felt the brush of her silver hair against his chest as she molded her body to his under the veil of midnight. Or watched the way her big brown eyes grew wide when Jinn prepared all her favorite foods. Or spied those secret moments when she was sprawled out on his bed, headphones on her ears, and her nose in a book.

He would die with discontentment and longing in his heart, but it was worth it if it meant she had a shot at a real, meaningful life.

Legion takes a deep breath, the angel venom in the air singeing his lungs. He fell from Heaven for the one he thought he loved, only to find he was manipulated by Lucifer and his unquenchable thirst for power. He rose from Hell to rid the world of his brother's treachery, turning his back on his true nature in a quest for salvation. And now, he would fall again. He would fall for something much greater than he and the Se7en ever anticipated. He would fall for the silver-haired girl who set his world aflame, the girl he was originally sent to assassinate.

He would fall for love.

He's on the move, fists tensed at his side, jaw locked in steely concentration. The doors open on their own accord, barely a blink of his power. The overwhelming stench of those conjuring candles assault him, and the mist of angel venom that coats his skin burns a little more with each step forward.

And he stops.

The sanctuary is empty, filled only with the sickly sweet honeysuckle scent of his former brethren. Tendrils of black smoke dance atop dozens of pillar candles as they've just been snuffed out seconds before.

He's too late. Those guards weren't put in his path to stop him, or even lead him into a trap. They were sent to distract him, as if his captors knew his bloodlust would be too all-consuming to ignore. As if they knew the beast in him would take pleasure in their gruesome deaths.

Still…that pull, that yank on his insides has him striding

towards the ornate altar, towards the white marble basin that's situated before a ten-foot tall wooden cross.

It's not until he clears several rows of pews before he realizes he was wrong about one thing, and just for a moment, just for a shuddering breath, he pauses, frozen in place between the echo of two faint heartbeats.

The sanctuary isn't empty.

For in that space where he currently existed, where he was bound between heaven and hell, two bodies lay at the base of the marble basin.

Eden.

And Adriel.

TWO

EDEN

THEY SAY DEATH IS PEACEFUL.

Quiet.

A supposed reprieve from the strife and suffering that Life has so generously bestowed upon us.

I wanted to believe that. Sometimes at the risk of my own mortality. I wanted the Earth to swallow me up and nestle me in the downy-soft embrace of that promised paradise, freeing me of the rust and piss-stained shackles of poverty and abandonment. An afterlife devoid of pain and loneliness, full of light and love.

I wished for it as a little girl who hadn't even lost her first tooth, or kissed her first boy. I wished for it as a young woman who had yet to have her first epic love.

I wished for Death the way I wished for a family. The way I wished to belong to someone—anyone—who would have me.

Death is a lie. A fallacy. Death is a fast-moving cancer that infects and destroys all it reaches. Just a touch is all it takes. Then it's all you can taste…all you can smell.

It aches in my bones and rasps in my ears. Its mangled, spiny fingers scratch up my spine.

I feel Death all around me. Violent, retched, gruesome.

Death is here.

Hello, old friend. Glad you could make it.

I wake up in a room I don't know, wearing clothes I've never seen before. I'm stiff, but not sore. My mouth is dry, but not uncomfortably so, and I don't taste blood as I'd expect. A flavor that I've grown all too familiar with these past few months.

I blink against the dim light streaming from a nearby lamp, allowing my eyes to adjust to my unfamiliar surroundings. Vibrant jeweltoned fabrics, draped ceilings, and ornate gold lanterns, reminiscent of Moroccan opulence. Each detail is ecstasy to my eyes.

I sit straight up, faster than I intend to. The last thing I remember is…

That tiny, bare cell. Sitting with my father.

Pain.

The images come flying back to me with lightning speed, flashes of blinding light and sound and unbearable agony. I squeeze my skull between my palms, willing it to stop, or at the very least slow, so my sleep-addled mind can process it all.

I remember. I remember taking Rev's hand. I remember feeling like my brain was being blended into pulp. I remember that voice…that voice that spoke a language that was too beautiful and melodic to be of this world, yet I could understand it. And I remember knowing that I was going to die.

And I did.

I'm dead. And this…this must be the afterlife.

"No," I rasp, shaking my head. "No, this isn't right. I wasn't ready. I can't be dead." My heart pounding in my ears, I lower my shaky hands from my face and take a deep, steeling breath. "I can't be dead."

"And you're not."

The sound of her voice—so sultry, ebbing on erotic—is so jarring that I actually yelp. I hadn't even heard her open the bedroom door, as if she merely manifested out of thin air.

The Watcher crosses the room with all the grace and allure of a belly dancer. She dons her usual floor-length sarong and bra top, both in shimmering peacock colors. Much more modest than the sheer, jeweled number she wore the night we met. The bright hues against her olive skin and jet black severe bob make her look like an exotic goddess. She comes to the side of the bed and sits down, her movements lithe yet deliberate.

Out of shock and confusion, I stutter, "What…what's going on?"

"You're not dead," she smiles slyly, a secret on her fuchsia painted lips. In fact, you're more alive than ever. But you know that, don't you?"

She's right. I do feel alive. I actually feel…good. Like myself, but not. *More.*

Still, I ask, "What are you talking about?"

"You've been out for nearly three days, Eden. A lot's transpired in your slumber."

Three days? I've been asleep for *three days?*

How did I get here? And why am I here? Better yet…

"Where's L?"

"He's around," she replies with a dismissive wave of her hand. "He was here for some time, but he's been otherwise occupied…all things considered."

She's purposely being dodgy, as if she wants my mind to go to that night of her party. She wants me to remember the way she was able to manipulate L into kissing her in front of me. Not just kiss her. Worship her with his mouth. As if the mere taste of her was an intoxicating tonic that made him forget that I even existed.

"What am I doing here, Irin?" I demand, the memory chilling my tone.

She laughs, flicking a lock of hair behind her ear, completely adorned with blue and green jewels. "Get dressed and come find out for yourself. Washroom is over there," she nods towards a door across the room, "and drawers and closets are stocked. You're welcome, by the way."

"You're welcome?"

"Yes. That's what one usually says after they're thanked for quite literally saving one's ass. Didn't those wretched public schools teach you anything?"

Stunned, I don't respond. I don't feel like playing games, especially the ones Irin has in mind. And I'm still stuck on the *saving my ass* part.

She reads the confusion on my face, wholly amused, and repeats, "Get dressed. The others will be just tickled that you're awake." She claps her hands and pulls them to her bountiful cleavage.

"Others?"

"Oh yes. They've been waiting."

Without any more explanation, she rises to her feet and heads for the door, hips swaying with hypnotic seduction. I silently watch her overly theatrical exit, afraid of what truth could be waiting for me on the other side of that door, yet anxious to find out what happened to me.

I expect to be a bit shaky on my feet after being out for three days, but when I slide out of bed, I feel...solid. Strong yet feather-light. Even my walk feels different, as if someone else guides my bare feet across the cool hardwood.

Eager to assess myself in the mirror, I dash to the bathroom, fully expecting to see someone else's reflection looking back. But it's me. Bewildered brown eyes, a silver mess of bed hair, and chapped lips, but me all the same. But even with the evidence very clearly staring me in the face, something's off. I feel it. Not wrong—no. Just...different.

Realizing I'm not going to get any answers by ogling myself, I step out of my borrowed silk nightie and turn to the claw-foot tub to draw myself a much-needed hot bath. The water is heaven on my skin, and I'm tempted to spend an hour luxuriating in the suds. But first...answers.

As promised, the wardrobe is stocked. However, Irin failed to mention that it was with only her clothing. Well, clothing that she would wear. Sarongs in every color, pattern, and fabric. Midriff-baring bra tops studded with jewels and lace, several sheer enough to expose nipple. Even Hell had better offerings than this.

I end up settling for a black sarong with a scalloped hem and a matching bell sleeve wrap top that hits above my navel. It's the least obscene thing I could find, yet it still leaves me tugging at the shirt to cover more skin. I luck out with the shoes; Irin has so kindly included several pairs of satin flats, embellished with colorful beads and gemstones. Very bohemian and actually pretty damn comfortable.

After attempting to tame my matted hair, I leave the solace of the beautifully exotic room to seek out what I so desperately need: answers. I've never been in this part of Irin's mansion, so I follow the hallway to a huge space outfitted with dozens of plush lounge chairs and giant pillows along the walls. There's a stage and bar backlit with a soft red glow. I remember…this was the main area designated for the party I attended. And at the bar, propped on a stool, sits a drop dead gorgeous boy with bronze skin and dark, alluring eyes. He's slender, almost feminine, yet fit. His lush, black hair hangs to his bare shoulders, accenting his straight, elegant nose and bowed lips. He wears only a short white sarong, barely long enough to cover his boy bits, and sandals. The young man, who can't be older than seventeen, smiles brightly, and gracefully slides off the stool to approach me. When he stops before me, a smile still gracing his lips, I notice that his cheeks have been brushed with a gold shimmer, and he may be wearing eyeliner and mascara. That, or he has the thickest, most amazing lashes known to man.

"Hello, Eden," he greets with an accent I can't quite place. "I'm Kairo. It's nice to see you again."

Again? I'd like to believe I would have recalled this beautiful creature, but the last time I was here, we were surrounded by stunning men and women. Plus, I was impaired, to say the least.

"Irin asked me to show you the way to her quarters, just in case you don't remember the way."

He extends the crook of his willowy arm to me, and after a few seconds of quick contemplation, I hook my hand to his elbow. What else am I going to do?

"I hope you found your accommodations comfortable. And the clothes…did they fit ok? I had to guess," Kairo comments, leading the way down an opposite hall.

"Yes. Thank you," I reply quietly. I don't have the heart to tell him that while the room is beautiful, I'm not a fan of the fashions.

"Irin tells me that you were held captive by the Alliance of the Ordained. I'm terribly sorry. I hope you weren't injured."

"I wasn't."

"Good. From what I hear, they can be ruthless brutes. We don't see their kind often. They find our way of life baseless and depraved."

Judging by what I can remember from the last time I was here, I can understand why. Homosexuality, promiscuity, intoxication…something tells me Irin has no qualms about sins of the flesh under her roof. In fact, she encourages it.

Before I know it, we're standing before a set of exquisitely carved doors, encrusted with gleaming red jewels and gold accents. And in the center of each door is an intricately designed eye made of sparkling black diamonds. The Watcher's lair.

I take a deep breath. The last time I was here, I fled with humiliated tears burning at the backs of my eyes. I'm in no mood for Irin's narcissism and mind fuckery, but she has information, meaning she has the upper hand. And according to her, she saved my life. And if I remember correctly, Irin never does anything without reciprocity. She'll expect something in return. Something I'm not sure I'm equipped to offer.

Like the first time I faced these striking doors, they open on their own accord. And what I see nearly makes me break down right then and there.

They're here. The Se7en.

Phenex, Jinn, Toyol, Andras, Cain, Lilith, and...

Legion.

My lips part and my mouth dries. The words are choked from my throat, and I struggle to swallow. He's...so much more gorgeous than I remember. Like it hasn't merely been three days, but weeks. Months. And although it's impossible, he seems bigger, taller. Even his hair seems darker and those gray eyes brighter as he regards me closely, his lethal gaze crawling up and down my scantily clad body. He is every bit as brutally beautiful as I could imagine. And while I could stay frozen in place like this, our eyes locked in silent battle, my mind immediately goes to...

"My sister. Mary."

"She's here. Safe," Cain answers from where he stands on Legion's right. I realize that the Se7en are all either sitting or standing beside each other on one side of the room. As if they're on guard. That's when I look to the other side of the room, and that wretched knot of emotion throbs once again.

Sitting on the far end of the giant sectional is Crysis,

looking a bit worse for wear with his arm in a sling and a bandage on his head. And next to him sits one of the most stunning creatures ever created.

"Niko?" I rasp through the golf ball sized lump in my throat.

"In the flesh, baby," the young warlock smiles lazily, smoothing the lapels on his dark suit. He stands to make his way to me, and I meet him halfway, nearly crumbling into his chest when he wraps me in his arms smelling of sea and spice and an impending storm.

"I thought…I thought you were gone," I murmur into his jacket, biting back sobs.

Niko kisses the top of my head. "Oh, you'll have to do more than that to get rid of me."

With glossed eyes, I look up at him, refusing to hide the vulnerability that shines so painfully within them. "How? And how did you get here?"

Niko pulls away only to wrap an arm around my shoulders. A hint of hesitation on his brow, he looks to Irin who says, "There's much to discuss…much for you to learn. Come, Eden. Sit."

I let Niko lead me to the sectional to a space between him and Irin. He handles me carefully, gingerly, as if I'm a life-size porcelain doll. Maybe he's stronger here, and he's afraid of hurting me.

I glance over to where the Se7en are stationed and notice that they each regard me carefully, yet none of them say a word. And Legion…three days ago, he had me pressed against a cold, damp brick wall in an alleyway as he pumped inside me just feet away from passersby. And now he acts as if I'm not even here. What happened? What am I missing?

"Eden, a lot has transpired in the past few days," Irin begins. "What's the last thing you remember?"

"I don't know." I shake my head, urging the foggy memories to come forth. "The Alliance. They took me…took us." I whip my head to Crysis who sits slightly slumped forward on the far end of the couch. "What happened? My father…they captured you, too."

Crysis nods, a lock of blonde hair falling over his eye. I notice that it's puffy and yellowish with a fading bruise. "We were ambushed outside the diner. They knew somehow—the Alliance. They had been trailing me. I couldn't block them. My abilities were nullified."

"They hurt you." Sorrow twists like a knife in my gut. Of course, they'd torture one of their own.

Crysis shrugs. "I've had worse."

"You should've seen him when I found him," Niko adds, his crystal blue eyes going wide. It must've been bad. Nephilim have accelerated healing and superhuman strength. What had they done to Crysis? The cuts and bruises, the busted up arm… I've never seen him look so mortal.

"How? How did you get here?" I ask Niko. Last I saw him, he was dying, and I was forced to abandon him to save myself. I'll never forgive myself for leaving him. The image of him fading right before my eyes still haunts me.

Niko winks a mesmerizing blue eye. "Courtesy of *you-know-who.*"

"What else do you remember?" Irin interjects, steering the conversation. Apparently, she's leading this little meeting, and playing catch-up is not on the agenda. Still not a peep from the Se7en, which is more than a little disheartening.

I swallow, forcing my memory to dig back to that cold, dim room. "My father had me locked in a cell. He came to me. Told me he would make everything better. He said he would release me from the life I had been cursed with and give me one where I could be free of..."

I look to the end of the sectional, to where the Se7en refuse to meet my gaze. Their coldness is a stab in my heart.

"Demons," a low voice rumbles.

Legion lifts his head, eyes glowing with silver fire. His expression is stern, detached. It reminds me of that first night in his room—him sitting in the shadows waiting for me to wake up in his bed. Counting my breaths, calculating which one would be my last. I remember feeling fear I didn't even know existed. At that point, I wanted to believe he was just a man, but I think even then I knew he was something else. Dark. Dangerous. Deadly. He was all those things. But when he pinned me to that bed and paralyzed me with the starlit stare to conjure the intruder of my soul, I knew he was something more. I *felt* it.

Now, as his glare shackles me to my seat, locking my bones and muscles in place, I feel it again. That inexplicable fear. And the notion that he is again something more.

He looks away, releasing me, and adds, his voice grave, "Your father offered you a life free of demons. And you accepted."

"No," I shake my head, realizing the reason behind his coldness. "Yes. It wasn't like that. I only said that so he wouldn't hurt you."

"Hurt me?" He snorts.

"Yes. I knew he had you, and he told me he had Crysis. I said whatever he wanted to hear to get you both out of there."

"We know," Irin chimes in. She reaches over to gather my hands in her much smaller ones. The gesture is almost motherly. And considering what she is, and what she's capable of, I know I should pull away and accept this farce for what it is. But I can't.

"What next, E?" Niko questions beside me, moving in closer. I'm not sure if it's for comfort or protection.

"I don't know. That was it. That's all I remember."

"No, it isn't," Irin accuses. "There's more."

She's right. There is more. But the memory of that head-splitting pain physically makes me ill. Just the thought of that agony, as that haunting voice echoed in my brain, makes the room spin. My vision goes blurry. My mouth fills with the taste of blood and bile. I can't go in there...that dark water. I can't breathe under there. It's too cold. Too deep.

"I know," Irin whispers. "I know."

I look up at her with tear-filled eyes, urging her to say what I can't. Begging her to finish the story of my death. She's already seen it, I can tell by her rare, solemn expression. Maybe she felt it too.

"He took your hand, and there was unspeakable pain. Pain that split you in two and left you maimed and bleeding. Then he spoke in a voice, a language, you'd never heard before. A tongue not of this world. But it wasn't you he spoke to, was it, Eden? It wasn't you who he called out to right before you blacked out from the torment."

I will myself to respond, but the memory of that pain is still too fresh in my mind. I can feel it again, nudging me to that dark place…to that pool of never-ending blackness.

"No, it wasn't," a sweet, sing-song voice answers for me, drawing every eye to the entranceway. The woman who stands there, dressed in gleaming winter white from head to toe with a crown of fiery red hair, is quite possibly the loveliest, most ethereal creature I've ever seen.

She steps forward, her silk gown whispering against the hardwood, and stops just feet away from where I sit. Pale, sea-foam green eyes fall on me, and for a moment, I think I feel myself being pulled away from that dark place. And that un-shakeable fear is replaced with a sense of…peace.

"It wasn't you he spoke to, sweet Eden," she smiles reas-suringly. "It was me."

THREE

I KNEW WHO SHE WAS THE MOMENT I HEARD HER VOICE. And still I sat there, staring up at her, my face pinched in confusion. Because if she's here, then that means I wouldn't be. I would be truly dead, in every sense of the word. And now that I'm no longer Called, I would no longer be under the protection of the Se7en.

Which explains everything.

"Adriel, I'm glad you're feeling well. Please join us. We're just getting to the good part," Irin says, releasing my hands to wave towards the space between Nikolai and Crysis. Away from the demons.

I look to Legion, my vision blurry, but he won't meet my eyes. No. Of course not. He's staring straight at Adriel, his long lost love. A love that led to his fall from heaven. A love that drove him to spare my life just so he could have a tiny taste of it once again.

I can feel myself breaking. No, not breaking. Desiccating. Like all my vital organs are slowly, painfully, shriveling and dying. My chest aches with an unending hollowness that makes me shiver. I wrap my arms around me in defense, trying desperately to ward off the creeping doubt and betrayal. But it's too late. I'm falling into a deep pit of despair without anything—anyone—to grasp onto. No one is coming to save me. I'm going to fall and fall until I hit rock bottom and shatter into oblivion.

I'm not needed anymore. Legion has the one he's always wanted. They're together again, and all his interest in me is null and void. No wonder he won't look at me. And when he does, it's with contempt and disgust. I was nothing more than a placeholder. A distraction from the longing he coveted for her—for Adriel. And now that I am no longer her surrogate, I am nothing more than a lowly, inconsequential sack of blood and bones.

"I, uh…" My voice is trembling so violently that I can barely get the words out. "Um, uh. Excuse me."

I go to stand—to flee—but Nikolai gently grasps my arm. "No. Stay." His expression is so earnest that I nearly crack into sobs right then and there.

"Yes, Eden," Irin chimes in, an amused grin on her face, despite the distress marred on mine. "Stay. There is so much more to learn. Adriel?"

She turns to the unearthly beauty. Only Nikolai separates us, and it's not enough. Just days ago, we inhabited the same body—my body—and I just wanted her gone. I have so many questions—*Why me?*—yet I can't speak. Hell, I can't even look at her, resigning to stare at an imaginary spot on the floor, just to keep the tears at bay. Thankfully, Kairo takes it as his cue to distribute drinks—mimosas—and I gladly accept.

"I suppose I should start from the beginning," Adriel says to the room. "Billions of years ago, I fell in love. It was a deep, all-consuming love that was not meant for me. Or him." She looks to Legion. I'm not brave enough to see if he returns her gaze. "It cost us both greatly. He chose to fight. I chose defeat. And I've regretted it every day of my existence since."

"Is there a point to this little trip down memory lane?" Crysis grumbles, wincing. I could seriously kiss him right now.

Adriel soldiers on, ignoring the Nephilim's snide remark. "I wallowed in my shame and sorrow for centuries, wishing I could take it back. Wishing I could find atonement for my misdeeds. That opportunity arose twenty two years ago."

That gets my attention and I turn to stare straight at her, perplexity hanging heavy on my brow. I get where she's going with this, but what does her regret and search for redemption have to do with me?

"His thirst for vengeance was unquenchable. It drove him to distraction, consuming him in a way that had become self-destructive. But it had been so long...so I didn't realize what he was doing until the deed was already done. I didn't have a clear picture of his motives at first, but once I did, I knew I had to act."

"Wait. What are you talking about?" I ask, my tone incredulous.

"Eden, you were created as a means of revenge for my sins. Mine and the one you now call Legion. Uriel, my mate, wanted to punish us both for our transgressions. So you were birthed to be wielded as a weapon. How you would be wielded is still unclear."

"Uriel?" I'm not sure why the name sounds familiar, and I definitely don't understand what it has to do with me.

"Uriel always felt like an outsider. He looked up to the others, the older, more revered of the Seraph, even to the point of envy. So when we betrayed him, he took it as more than a personal offense." She turns to speak right to Legion. "I believe he and Lucifer conspired the rumors that you forced and defiled me. I would have never said that. Uriel wanted to destroy your reputation. Lucifer wanted you desperate enough to act in anger. For that, I am sorry, Samael. So truly, deeply sorry."

"Don't call me that." The words are just a rumble in his chest.

"I'm sorry, Sam—"

"I said, don't call me that!" L roars, forcefully enough to rattle our flutes of champagne and orange juice. Reflexively, Cain and Phenex, stationed at each flank, tense and step closer to him.

Even from feet away, I can feel Adriel's trembling. I don't blame her. There was rage behind those words. And pain. Not just any pain either. The kind that you can feel all the way down to your bones, and no matter how you try to sooth the ache, it never ceases.

I've seen Legion pissed before, but not like this. The fierce conviction in his tone, the bite of betrayal in it...something is different between them. Not just history. Something soul binding that will forever connect them.

"I...I. I apologize... Legion." Adriel stammers. She

plasters on a pained smile that doesn't meet her soft green eyes. "As I was saying, when I realized that you could be hurt in all this, Eden, I had to do something. I…fell. Not a true fall from grace, but it was enough so I could inhabit your body. But because of what you are, I could not fully possess your soul. You are much stronger than you could ever imagine."

"What I am?" I frown.

"That, and what your father is. There's never been anything like it."

"My father's a renegade street preacher who kidnapped me," I reply flatly.

"Your father is Seraph," Adriel retorts, her tone sharp. "Uriel didn't inhabit Joshua's body. Uriel *is* Joshua. He took a human form, courted your mother, and purposely created you. And he stayed on Earth, kept close to you, to keep your true identity cloaked with forbidden magic."

"My true identity?" I scoff, rolling my eyes. "What the hell are you talking about? There really is no mystery behind being an unemployed cashier."

Adriel shakes her pretty little head. "Eden, you have no idea, do you? Uriel is one of the most powerful archangels in history. Which would make you…" She lifts a slender brow.

"Nephilim," Crysis answers after I refuse to utter the word.

Nephilim?

No fucking way.

I can't be. I'm not strong or inhumanly fast. And the only supernatural gift I had was forced on me by Adriel. And now that she's no longer inhabiting my body…shit…

This doesn't make any sense. Some of the most beautiful,

most cunning, most dangerous creatures to have ever walked this earth are inside these four walls. And I am nothing like them. Sure, I've always felt different, like I don't quite fit within society's standards. But that's what poverty and pain does to you. It alters your very being, molding you into a savage hell-bent on survival. Yes, I've always been a survivor, even when giving up would have been so much easier. I never understood what I was surviving for.

"I know you believe it was my influence, or even an effect of the Calling that gave you certain abilities. But in all honesty, it was you, Eden. That was just a small sample of what you can do—a fraction of your power. The bit that Uriel could not dampen. I only inhabited your soul to keep him from hurting you. Or worse."

I look to the Se7en, who don't look the least surprised. Accusation and betrayal are etched in my face. "You knew?"

Legion is stoic, yet his lips twitch with his unspoken confession. It's Phenex who speaks. "Eden, we only just learned this days ago, upon our arrival here. Had we known, we would have never…" For the first time, Phenex looks uncertain. His honeycomb eyes shift to Legion then to Ariel then back to me.

"You never would have taken me in," I finish. My wounded glare falls on Legion, and I speak to him and for him. "You never would have touched me."

Because not only am I not like them, I am the daughter of his sworn enemy, the offspring of hate and betrayal and vengeance. It makes sense now—their coldness, their distance. How can they care for me when I am a physical reminder of everything they despise and hope to kill?

I look down at my hands and turn them over, the same

hands that held him, stroked him, worshipped him. The same hands that reached out to him after the Alliance thugs, led by my father, hit him so hard that I felt it in my teeth. What I am now is what I've always been. This shouldn't change anything but it does. It changes everything.

"You must understand, Eden," Phenex continues, following my line of vision. "Nephilim have a natural predisposition to their own kind. We understand if you feel…differently… about us, now that the cloak has been lifted."

I meet those guarded golden eyes, once full of so much warmth and understanding. Phenex was the first to show me kindness. Lilith was playing a role, but it was Phenex who wanted to protect me, wanted to care for me. He was my friend.

"Do you feel differently about…me?" I retort, my voice shaky.

"No," Phenex answers earnestly, and I believe him. I need to believe him.

I don't know what I am, but the girl I was three days ago—the girl that went into that black water and drowned—she's still here. She still hurts. She still bleeds. She still loves.

"Ok," I nod. "I don't feel differently either. Nothing has changed."

"While that may be true," Adriel begins, cutting into the tension, "there was another reason I felt the need to intervene. One that we all underestimated. Lucifer."

"So he knew too." It's not a question. I'm not even surprised anymore. If anyone would want in on a devious plan, it's him.

"Is there anything Luc doesn't know? Nosy fucker," Cain

snorts. It seems like they've all relaxed a bit, now that I've declared that nothing has changed. Still, they watch me closely, as if at any moment I could fly off the handle and do my father's bidding. Whatever modicum of trust we had before has been fractured.

"He knew something, I'm just not sure what. But once Uriel realized that I fell to protect you from him and Lucifer's influence, he resorted to unwarranted violence to get me back."

I heave out a frustrated breath. All this, for what? For who? I didn't ask for any of this. And it's Adriel and Legion's indiscretions that nearly got my sister killed. It's their actions that led to her boyfriend, Ben's, death, along with dozens of others. How is that fair? In what fucked up universe is any of this ok? My dad is a psychotic archangel with an ax to grind. And my pseudo-stepmom, who jumped into my body, had an affair with my would-be demon boyfriend?

Fuck outta here with that nonsense.

"So what? Uriel set this all up to trap L? And to get you back? Well…you're back, right? I don't know how—or why—but you're back, and I'm no longer needed in all this shit. Uriel has what he wants. So why am I here?"

Adriel looks to Legion for aid. Her savior. Her knight in shining-fucking-armor. Not even millennia have altered their connection.

"When I found you—both of you—," Legion begins, his deep timbre causing my bones to shiver, "I wasn't sure if you would survive. The extraction is fatal to humans, but you… you are not human. And I needed to make a choice: hunt them down, or stay with you."

"We got there shortly after L found you," Toyol chimes in. "Once they subdued Crysis, their surveillance failed. Something they hadn't counted on when they tried to take him out." He tips his head at the angel-human hybrid, a sign of respect. "The trail was cold. But they knew we would come for you, and that's exactly what they were hoping for. They wanted us away from home."

Home.

The Seraph were counting on drawing them out so they could attack their home. *Our* home.

"Sister," I rasp, my eyes going wide.

"I got her out of there in time. I swore on everything that I am that no harm would come to her, and I meant it," Cain assures, stowing his snark and brashness. He strokes the dark hair on his chin, his expression pinched in contemplation. I know he means every word, and I give him a grateful nod. Honestly, I don't give him enough credit for his devotion to her.

"Unfortunately, the Seraph still retrieved what they were looking for," Phenex says. "The Redeemer, one of our oldest and most sacred relics. It's also the weapon that can permanently wipe out the existence of demons."

Shit. A world without demons. That's exactly what that psycho was rambling on about. And while Uriel apparently has a hard-on for one demon in particular, I'm sure he has no qualms about taking the rest of them out too.

"Which is why we're here," Toyol chimes in. "The Watcher's home is hallowed ground. No blood can be shed here, so we're safe. Until we get the drop on where the Seraph is, and what they plan to do, we need to lay low and come up with a plan."

"That's not all…" Phenex adds. "He also has your mother."

"My mother?" I had forgotten about her involvement in all this. But of course she'd be with them. She helped them lure me, promising a fresh start for us. I've hated her for so long for what she's done to me, but I never stopped loving her. I never stopped hoping that she would get better and we could be a family again.

"She was the one who…released me," Legion utters. Everyone goes completely still and silent. Not even the sound of an exasperated huff from Crysis or the clanging of one of the many gold bangles that adorn Irin's wrists.

"Released you?" I ask, cutting into the tense quiet. "She broke you out?"

"No. Yes. She…released me." Seeing the confused pinch between my eyes, Legion grips the hem of his shirt and drags it over his torso.

My mouth goes bone dry. My heart stutters in my chest. Tan, smooth skin is etched with whorls of black ink from his collarbone to the defined V that tapers into his jeans. But there are no scriptures of salvation. No tribute of what he once was before his fall from grace. Not even the dark feathers of the Se7en symbol engraved over his heart. Instead, a fiery beast with uncanny silver eyes that seem to shimmer on his muscled skin—a dragon—is intricately carved over his entire chest and abs. In its mouth, caged by razor sharp fangs, is a blood red ruby. It's hideous. It's beautiful. It's a complete replica of the pendant Nikolai gave him before we were pulled out of Hell. And I know exactly what has happened to him, and why he looks even bigger, ever darker, and more deadly than he ever seemed before. He isn't a demon assassin anymore. That doesn't even begin to sum up the extent of the terrible danger that stands before us.

"L is dead. Samael is dead. I was remade—reborn into what I was before. The very thing I've hated and rebelled against for centuries. *The great dragon was hurled down – that ancient serpent called the devil, or Satan, who leads the whole world astray. He was hurled to the earth, and his angels with him.* However, the great dragon was not called the Devil, as man believed. He was called *Legion*.

"I am the Legion of Lost Souls. And I have risen once again."

FOUR

I RIN DECIDED WE ALL NEEDED A BREAK AFTER SO MANY pivotal revelations, and I couldn't agree more. But I didn't want to be alone. Not after finding out what I am. Not after learning what Legion is. It's all too much to digest at once, and I need some semblance of normalcy. Just a small remembrance of my life before all this.

"I was wondering when you'd wake up," Sister smiles when she spies me in the doorway of her suite. She's still hooked up to IVs and bandaged, but she seems to be in good spirits, which is exactly what I need right now. Apparently, Irin was gracious enough to provide all the necessary equipment to help her heal, and I couldn't be more thankful to her for that. She even has an on-site physician for her round-the-clock care, which has been a huge help considering that Phenex is needed more than ever by the Se7en.

I nearly run to her side, yet resist the urge to gather her in my arms. She still has a long way to go, and I'm not sure if I have superhuman strength or what. She's endured so much, and I would kill myself if I hurt her even more.

"How are you feeling?" I question, looking for any signs of harm during the attack on the Se7en's headquarters.

"Good, actually," she beams, her eyes going wide with excitement. "Did you know there is this mystical balm that actually accelerates healing? It's made from angel blood and some funky herbs, but holy crap, it's good. Costs a grip too, but Cain insisted when Irin suggested it. I can't even tell you how awesome he's been. All of them, actually. And your friend, Nikolai? Wow, girl. Wow. Seriously, men should not be that pretty. It's not fair."

I smile at her infectious positivity. Still the same, old Sister, prattling on a mile a minute. Nothing will ever break her, and it inspires me every day. "Well, actually, he's not a man. He's a warlock. A prince too."

Sister shakes her head. "Not. Effing. Fair."

"Tell me about it. You should see his brother, Dorian."

"He has a brother?"

"Yeah. He's the king of their kind."

"Welp…that's it." She gives a wave of a bandaged hand. "Both ovaries have just exploded. I'm barren. Or pregnant."

We laugh together, and it feels so good to not think about all the crazy shit I was just woken up to, even for a moment. Just two sisters talking guys and being silly. Just being *human*. Although, only one of us can honestly take that title now.

We chat for nearly an hour about everything and nothing, keeping the conversation light and optimistic. Sister, once again, is blown away by the existence of otherworldly creatures, and the opulence of Irin's mansion. I have to admit, Irin is loaded. I can't figure out exactly what she is—and truthfully no one has—but she must be very old to have amassed such wealth.

"I was afraid...when they came," Sister admits, her eyelids getting heavy. Her body is working overtime with the angel-blood infused healing balm, and the morphine drip doesn't help either. I wonder if *my* blood could help her. Or even Adriel's. But there's no way I'm asking her.

"Everything's ok now," I smile, trying to muster up some optimism.

"And when they told me...what happened to you. I wasn't sure if you would wake up. No one knew for sure at first, because humans aren't supposed to survive whatever they did to you. Irin said you just needed time...that your body needed to adjust."

I school my features, desperately trying to give nothing away. "Did she say why I needed to adjust?"

Sister lays a gauze-wrapped hand on mine. "I know you're not like me. I've always known. And now that you're here, and you're breathing, and you're alive, I know that my suspicions were true. And that makes me love and admire you even more."

I don't have the heart to lay it all out for her, to tell her that I'm not deserving of her admiration, and barely deserving of her love. Not when my father created me to be a weapon. Not when I've hurt people and lied and cheated and *killed*. I can't blame what I've done on Adriel. I can't even chalk it up to the Calling. It was all me. And now that I'm no longer cloaked by whatever magic Uriel used on me, who knows what I'm capable of.

I open my mouth to tell her just that, but she's already drifted off to sleep. Maybe it's for the best—a sign from God. I'm sure He knows my truth would only hurt her even more.

With a kiss on her forehead, I whisper goodnight and turn to leave her to rest. Cain is standing in the doorway. I don't even know how long he's been there.

"She looks good," I say, swallowing thickly.

"She does," he answers, his eyes going to her sleeping frame. "She's getting stronger every day. Phenex says the scarring will be minimal too."

I nod. "Thank you…for getting her out of there. And for taking care of her. I know your priority was the Redeemer, but I can't tell you how grateful I am that you chose her."

Cain nods back in response. "Not as grateful as I am that she chose me." His gaze goes soft as he sidles up to her other side. "We can and will get the blade back. But her… Her life is much more precious than a piece of sharpened steel."

And although I suspected it before, realization finally hits me like a ton of bricks. Cain loves her. The scarred, vicious Demon of Murder is in love with my sister. And oddly, I wouldn't be upset if she felt the same. No one would protect her more fiercely than him. And now that she is fully immersed in a world that is so unstable and uncertain, she's going to need him. Especially when I'm not here.

Without another word, I exit the suite, leaving Cain to watch over my sister as she sleeps. I want to ask him about Legion and Uriel, and what we're going to do, but I can't. Not here. I won't disrupt the bit of peace he's found in her.

I'm still too restless to go back to my room, and after sleeping for three days straight, I don't think I could sit still even if I tried. And being left to my own thoughts is definitely out of the question. So since it looks like we'll be staying here for a while, I decide to explore Irin's massive estate. The halls seem to always be filled with a flutter of activity, mostly from Irin's staff, whose uniforms seems to consist of little more than underwear and short, colorful sarongs. Beautiful boys and girls parade seductively, each one stopping to happily ask if I need anything. I can tell that they enjoy being here, and probably literally live to serve. None seem older than twenty either. I don't know if they're immortal, like Irin, and stay young and gorgeous through magic, or if their employer just likes jailbait. I wouldn't be surprised if it's the latter.

I stumble into what seems to be a study. No. I can't even call it that. It's a library. Dozens upon dozens of shelves are filled to the brim with volumes marked with numbers. Years. They're labeled with years. These are The Watcher's recordings, dating all the way back to the beginning of time. Holy shit.

I run my fingers over the leather spines, not even knowing where to start. The Watcher is said to have seen everything. How many mysteries of this world has she documented?

"I can't tell if Irin is the most efficient historian in existence, or just the ultimate voyeur."

I turn towards the voice, and smile, my eyes automatically filling with happy tears. Nikolai strolls over to me from the doorjamb, as smooth and graceful as ever, wraps an arm around my waist, and kisses the top of my head. Affection is so easy with him, as if it's the most natural thing in the world.

And it doesn't hurt that his scent of sea and spice is as intoxicating as his beauty.

"Can you imagine the shit we could learn in just one of these?" I say. "What's the real deal with the Bermuda Triangle? Is the Loch Ness monster real? Where's the Lost City of Atlantis? We could create Unsolved Mysteries on Steroids. We'd be famous."

"I don't know. I kinda like not knowing everything. The Divine only knows there's enough shit I wish I could unsee. Plus, I'd be afraid of learning too much about myself in the process."

"Why?" I ask looking up at him. I feel him shrug.

"Would you want to read about all the shit you've done? All the shit you've tried to forget about? I've been alive for over a century, and I was a ruthless deviant for most of that time. I guarantee some of history's greatest tragedies were caused by my kind, if not personally by my hands. I don't want to be known for those faults."

I nod, understanding completely. I've only been alive for a little over two decades, and I've done enough foul shit to have an entire book dedicated to me. I don't need to be reminded of all my mistakes.

We stand in silence for a beat, gazing at the stacks, before I ask, "Did you know? In Hell…did you know what I was?"

"I suspected, but I wasn't sure. I knew you weren't fully human though."

"Why didn't you tell me?" I don't even hide the tinge of hurt in my voice. I don't have to with him.

"Because you weren't ready to hear it. You were fractured when I met you. I didn't need to add to that. Not when I needed you to be strong."

He's right. I was a mess when we first met. If he had told me that I was anything else other than a girl who had been dealt a shitty hand, I probably wouldn't have believed him. Then doubt would have eaten me alive. I know Niko did what he thought was best, especially with not having any concrete evidence. It would have just added to my confusion.

We stroll through the library until we stop at a huge mural, the twin to the one in Lucifer's study. The Rise and Fall of Humanity, starring the demon my heart aches for, Legion.

"You ok?" Niko asks, knowing exactly who and what consumes my thoughts.

"I don't know. He's...different. I can feel it. I felt it the moment I stepped into that room. And now that I'm different too, he won't even look at me. And when he does, it's like all he sees is Uriel."

Niko shakes his head. "It's not that. I think he's just... afraid. That you can't see *him* anymore. The Legion of Lost Souls is not just a demon, Eden. He is many. That has to be some seriously fucked up shit to deal with. And maybe he's struggling with holding on to who he truly is."

His words bring me the comfort I so desperately need, and I nestle into his side. "Geez, why couldn't I have just fallen for you? Demons are complicated as hell."

"Because you have a warrior's spirit. And warriors live for the fight." He pinches my hip, making me squirm. "Besides, you couldn't handle me. I'd shatter you to pieces, and you'd be coming back, begging me to do it again."

"Arrogant dick," I jibe.

"What was that about my dick?" he shoots back.

I chuckle, giving him a playful elbow to the ribs. "I still can't believe you're here."

"Same here. Seems like Mr. Hellfire has a thing for you."

"So Lucifer really sent you? Why?"

Niko shrugs. "Said he wanted me to help you and the Se7en. Though I'm not sure what he thinks I can accomplish."

"Is it permanent?"

"Not if I don't succeed."

I turn to him, my eyes bright with excitement. "Oh my God, Dorian and Gabriella…they have to be beyond happy right now."

His gaze drops to the floor. "I haven't told them."

"What? Niko, you have to call them. Now! They were devastated when you didn't come back with me. I know they want to see you."

"No, E. I won't involve them in this. It's too dangerous. And if I fail…" He shakes his head, dispelling the thought. "I can't get their hopes up only to watch them suffer again. They have my nephew to protect. I won't be the cause of any more strife."

I get it, although it kills me. "You will succeed. We will succeed. And you'll be with your family again. I promise."

Niko smirks, his ocean blue eyes dimming with unnamed emotion. "Pretty words from such a pretty girl." He kisses my hair again and we resume inspecting the mural.

"You rescued Crysis. How?"

"He was chained up in some underground cell, drained of most of his blood, barely alive. Lucifer sent me straight to him, as if he knew he needed to be saved. Had I not been there, the Se7en would have never found him."

"That's strange," I murmur.

"What is?"

"That Lucifer would want to help a Nephilim."

"Well…he helped you, didn't he?" I look up and frown at Niko, not out of annoyance, but out of confusion. Plus I'm just not used to considering myself as something other than human. "Don't get me wrong, Luc is as self-serving and narcissistic as they come. And every move he makes is calculated and deliberate. But I think…I think he saved Crysis for you."

My frown deepens. "For me?"

"He knew you'd need help; you'd have questions. Crysis is your friend, and after finding out the truth, you'll need as many of those as you can get. He is your kind…your family, in a sense. He can help you tap into your gifts and strengthen them. And if this comes to a fight—which I believe it will—you're going to need him."

Again, I know he's right. Even though he's considered young for an immortal, Nikolai has proven to be insightful and wise beyond his years. His friendship is everything to me, and I am so incredibly thankful that Lucifer saw fit to send him, even if it is for his own selfish reasons.

The gauche sound of my growling belly makes us both break into chuckles, so we decide to seek out sustenance. After Hell, I'm over formal dining, so we simply pop into the kitchen where Irin's staff is cheerily prepping.

"Is there anything we can do for you?" a lovely young woman asks sweetly. She is wearing a scarf around her breasts, fashioned like a halter top, and a long sarong with a high slit.

"Um, I was hoping we could get something to eat?" I ask, feeling uneasy with so many eyes on me.

"Of course! What would you like?"

"Some cheese, crusty bread, and a bottle of red would be perfect, my dear," Niko answers smoothly, causing the young woman to blush bright red. I roll my eyes. Charming bastard.

"Of course. Coming right up."

Niko's indelible charisma scores us a gorgeous charcuterie board and the best wine I've ever tasted. We sit cross-legged on one of the many chaise lounges in the party room, noshing and chatting. Well, he sits cross-legged. I've got my feet tucked under me, thanks to my obscene skirt.

"I swear, I think Irin is just teasing me. Why do Lilith and Adriel have a regular wardrobe, while I'm prancing around in concubine clothes?"

"Now, if I was a different guy," Niko begins, tearing off a piece of crusty French bread, "I'd tell you that you look damn delicious and to just go with it. But since I am your *fairy-fucking-godmother*, I'm going to tell you to ask the staff to bring you what you want. They love it when we request stuff—it's weird. Like, they get off on servitude. They'd probably bust a collective nut if you asked them to replace your entire wardrobe."

Duly noted. I make a mental note to track down Kairo and give him a list of Eden-approved clothing.

"Well, fairy-fucking-godmother, can I ask you something? And I want you to be completely honest, no matter how much you think it'll hurt my feelings."

"I don't know how to be any other way."

I take a deep breath and slowly let it out. "Now that Adriel is back, do you think Legion…" I can't even say it without my face going hot.

Niko lifts a brow. "Do I think they're fucking around?"

"Well, I wasn't going to say *that*, but yeah."

"No. Do I think she wants to? Probably. But do I think he's trying to rekindle that flame? Not at all. He spends all his time with the Se7en. Training, plotting, counting his eight pack. When we first arrived, he sat by your side for hours, silent and still as a fucking statue. Not even a twitch of emotion. He'd just watch you. And when he wasn't doing that, he was in the gym, fucking shit up. I don't even think the guy has slept."

My brow furrows with confusion. "Why would he sit and watch me sleep for hours, yet not even speak to me now that I'm awake? That doesn't make any sense."

Niko takes a long sip of wine, contemplating his next words. "Look, E," he begins, setting down his glass. "I shouldn't be the one telling you this, and I feel like a fucking narc for doing so, but I want you to understand. After Legion was reborn, he was filled with so much rage and hatred. And fear… fear that he would lose you. He… Well, let's just say that anyone who stood between him and you was promptly and gruesomely discarded. I think that might be fucking with him a little bit. I mean, how could it not? He's spent centuries trying to do the right thing. Now killing is second nature to him. And it may be hard for him to accept just how much he relishes it."

"So? What does that have to do with freezing me out?"

"You're half angel, baby. And you fell for him when he was a demon seeking redemption. All hope of that is lost now that his true self has been released. Maybe he's afraid you won't be able to forgive him for what he is. Maybe he's struggling with forgiving himself."

I nod, tearing the bit of bread between my fingertips into tiny shreds. "God, I hope you're right. Because I know she wants him…but if he wants her…"

Niko's hand goes over mine. "If he does, then he's a damn fool. And he doesn't deserve you, human, Nephilim or other."

A small, sad smile curls my lips. "Tell me again why I didn't fall for you first?"

Niko returns the sentiment before stroking my cheek. "You're only half angel. Too fragile."

FIVE

TWO BOTTLES OF WINE LATER, AND I'M DRUNK.

Being out for a few days really does a number on my tolerance, so I kiss Niko goodnight after he walks me to my room.

"Sure you don't need help getting out of those clothes?" He wags his eyebrows playfully.

"Oh, sweetie." I lightly slap his cheek. "I can't handle you, remember?"

"I'm reevaluating your mortality." He smiles lazily.

"Let me know how that goes." Then I close the door in his face, feeling more than a little proud of myself. Niko is gorgeous. *More* than gorgeous. But he's my friend, and it seems like I have a good shortage of those these days. Besides, anything that would and could happen between us would be purely physical. His heart belongs to another...the one that keeps him tethered to his morality. Amelie. And I could never betray her, although I've never met her. She's the reason why he's here, fighting for good. She keeps him connected to the humanity that he thought he had lost.

Sleep comes easier than I expect, and soon I am drifting into a distorted dreamscape. The noxious smells of fragrant burning candles mixing with the cloying scent of honeysuckle. Bone-chilling black water that soaks through my clothes, digging into my skin with its frigid claws. Flashes of bright, blinding light that burnmy retinas until my skull aches. I can't breathe, and every time I try to scream, black water fills my lungs. I'm choking. I'm sinking. I'm drowning.

Then came the pain.

Like I was being sawed in two. I felt my bones break, my tendons tear. I blacked out from the intensity of it, only to wake in even more agony and pass out again. I couldn't even cry, could barely think. I just knew that I was dying, and I welcomed it. I wanted it to be over. I needed to be free from this torment. My sister would be sad, but she would find happiness again. And Legion…he would understand. Where ever he was, he'd survive this and move on.

A hand grips my arm, and I feel myself being dragged from those murky, freezing depths. Oxygen. I need oxygen, but I can't open my mouth. I'm paralyzed with cold, with pain.

I hear muffled voices, shouting, but I can't make out whom they belong to. It sounds like…chanting. Then behind my eyelids, I detect another blast of brilliant light. I can feel its warmth against my skin, like concentrated sunshine. I want to move closer to it, let it thaw my frozen frame, but my nerves are still numb. I gather all the strength left in me to no avail.

I want to cry out of frustration, but even my tear ducts have been rendered useless.

Oh God…I don't want to die. I take it back. My sister needs me. Now that Ben's gone, I'm all she has left. And the Se7en…they tried so hard to keep me safe. All their sacrifice can't be for naught. And Legion. I can't die without telling him how I feel…without telling him that I love him. It may not mean much to him, but he has to know that he, and these past months, has meant everything to me.

But it's too late. The light dims, inviting in the biting cold of darkness. There's a scuffle near where I lay, frozen and dying, like someone collapsing. No one is coming. I'll die alone, just as I was meant to. Just as I should have back in that dingy convenience store before I knew what it felt like to have something—someone—to live for.

When I stir awake, the sheets twisted around my legs, I reflexively reach out beside me, expecting to feel a hard, hot, masculine frame. But there's no one there. The pillow is as cold as I felt in my dream.

No. Not a dream. A memory.

That black water, the blast of celestial light, those chanting voices. I remember it all. But it's not adding up. Something just doesn't make sense to me. Uriel wanted Adriel back, so why didn't he take her? Why leave her there? Hell, why leave me there, if he planned to use me? Surely I can't be the only one who's pondered her presence.

I jump out of bed and get dressed, anxious to talk to someone. I know I can trust Niko implicitly, but he knows about as much as I do when it comes to the Uriel-Adriel-Legion love triangle. Talking to the Se7en would prove difficult when they're so uneasy around me. So I decide to take Niko's advice and seek out Crysis. He's Nephilim, like me, and he may know something he's not revealing. Did he know Joshua is Uriel? I don't think so, considering he was nearly killed for his involvement with me. But he knows more about angels and their motives than I do.

When I question one of Irin's staff on Crysis's whereabouts, the young man cheerfully offers to lead me to the fitness room, which is underground. And when I say fitness room, imagine Gold's Gym on crack. Wall-to-wall, state of the art equipment, more weights than I can count, heavy and speed bags, and a raised platform dedicated to boxing and mixed martial arts. And right in the middle of that platform is a shirtless, sweat-slickened Legion facing off with Jinn and Toyol. Unlike him, his opponents are armed—Toyol with his blade and Jinn with a long wooden staff. However, Legion's massive, clenched fists may as well be twin sledgehammers.

It only takes a moment before they all notice me. Lilith stills the speed bag she had been pummeling. Andras slows his swift pace on the treadmill. And Phenex sets down a stacked weight bar he had been bench pressing. The only one who isn't glaring is Cain, and that's because he isn't here and most likely at Sister's side. I'm a walking freak show, and I've never felt so out of place, even when I thought I was the lone human surrounded by supernatural creatures. It's like there's a flashing neon sign hanging over my head, boasting that I'm the closest thing to the angel that they're all training to kill.

I can feel Legion's eyes pressing into me as I cross the room and head for the free weights, where Crysis is working on strengthening his busted arm. It's been less than twenty-four hours, but he looks better. The swelling has gone down in his face, and he seems to have gotten a little color back. Unlike the Se7en, he doesn't stop what he's doing to gawk, as if he's not even surprised that I've come to him.

"Actually, I expected you to come to see me much sooner," Crysis remarks as I approach. He takes in my shock, then my annoyance, and adds, "Sorry. Force of habit. The connection is a bit amplified now that you're uncloaked. I'm going to have to teach you to shield yourself."

"You can do that?" I ask, sitting on the bench beside him. I want to embrace him and tell him how glad I am that he's ok, but there are too many eyes on us.

"Yeah. It's not too difficult, but it definitely comes in handy when dealing with angels. How are you holding up?"

I look around the room. The Se7en have resumed their activities but with less gusto. As if it's all a front for eavesdropping. No doubt they can hear every word we're saying.

"Good. Well, as good as can be expected. I still have so many questions."

Crysis snorts. "I'd be disappointed if you didn't. I was born Nephilim. Anyone else in your situation would've lost their fucking shit already."

"Yeah," I reply distantly. Little does he know, I'm doing my damnedest to hold it all together. "Maybe. I'm still processing."

"Well, shit. Ask me anything. You're the first of your kind, but maybe I can fill in the blanks."

"First of my kind?" I frown.

Crysis blots his sweat-beaded forehead with a towel and whips it over his shoulder. "Your father is Seraph. That's like a super angel, meaning they're held to a higher standard. None of them have ever procreated with a human. But of course, your *boyfriend* would know that. Maybe you should ask him to explain it to you."

A low growl sounds from the other side of the gym just as Legion springs to attack Jinn, blocking his staff with a bare forearm.

"Yeah…I don't think that'll happen," I reply, my voice low.

Crysis smirks, knowing good and damn well that Legion's growl was for him. "Oh? Trouble in paradise?" he antagonizes.

I roll my eyes and shake my head, refusing to respond. Legion has gone through a huge transition, and while my feelings for him haven't changed, I can't say that I truly know him anymore. I'm not about to risk a potential confrontation just because Crysis is feeling petty.

"Look. If you want my help, meet me later. I'm kinda anxious to see what you can do too."

I make a face. "See what I can do?"

"Like I said, you're the first of your kind. Every Nephilim's gifts manifest differently, most of them influenced by their angel parentage. You've gotta be able to do more than look pretty and bitch about your shitty love life."

I flip him the bird and turn on my heel, putting a little extra attitude in my strut towards the door. In all honesty, I'm curious too. I hadn't even thought about what extra abilities I might have now that Uriel's cloak has been lifted. But I'm not about to admit that to Crysis. Seems like being betrayed by the Alliance and coming close to death has done nothing for his humility. Not that I'd expect it to.

I find myself back in Irin's library, intrigued by what could be contained in those volumes. I find the book marked for the mid-1990s. What if my conception and birth were detailed in here? I mean, I don't want the gory details, but what if there were clues as to what Uriel had in store for me? Or how he came to Earth and met my mother? Was it really Lucifer's seduction that made her go crazy, or something else?

I'm flipping through the handwritten pages, my eyes consumed with the details of events I had only read about in dated articles. It's not just American history either, meaning there's a lot to scan through. And while there's no mention of Uriel yet, I find that I have a ton of ground to cover.

I'm so consumed by my research that I don't even realize that I'm not alone until I hear the clang of silverware. I spin around to find Adriel setting down a tray on a small, round table.

"I thought you could use some breakfast," she smiles sheepishly, sliding the tray to the middle of the table.

Well, this is awkward.

This woman has been inside me for most of my life. Yet, she is a stranger. I don't feel connected to her. I mean, exactly what is she to me? My friend? My guardian angel? My boyfriend's overbearing ex? And being the girl that I am, devoid of any kind of filter, I don't hold back.

I close the book I'm reading and cross my arms in front of my chest. "What are you doing here?"

Adriel looks down at the tray filled with freshly baked pastries, juice, and coffee. "Oh. I thought you might be hungry after—"

"No. What are you doing *here?* I remember…I remember when they pulled you out of me. If Uriel wanted you so badly that he would risk killing his own daughter, why are you not with him?"

Adriel nods, looking down at the tray. She takes a seat and pours herself a cup of coffee from the carafe.

"After they pulled you out, I fought them. With everything I had, I fought to protect you. Uriel could have easily overpowered me, but he didn't. Instead, for some unknown reason, he and the others fled. I passed out shortly after that."

I can't even dispute that. I remember that warm, blinding light. That had to have been her. And the feeling that someone had collapsed beside me. I remember that too. But it still doesn't explain why Uriel fled without taking his beloved mate.

I reluctantly take the seat across from her. I hate to admit it, but I am hungry. And that coffee smells divine.

I begin to pour myself a cup, and I ask her straight up, "Are you here to spy on us?"

Adriel actually looks affronted. "No. Absolutely not. I would never… I would never do anything to put you or anyone else in danger."

"Then why are you here?" I question again, taking a cheese danish from the bread basket.

She tips her head to one side. "I don't think I understand what you mean."

"I mean, are you here because you want to help us defeat Uriel? Or are you hoping to rekindle what you once had with Legion?"

And there it is. That little flicker of shameful truth in her seafoam green eyes. It lasts only half a second; she's perfected the art of deception. But she can't fully conceal the gravity of her feelings for Legion. Because love that intense, that all-consuming, is impossible to deny.

I should know.

I nod, my lips pressed in a knowing grin, and lean back in my chair. She knows I'm privy to her little secret. How could I not be? When I could literally feel the magnetism between them yesterday. Hell, everyone within a mile could. What they had was enough to make them both fall from Heaven. Adriel can claim she did it to protect me all she wants, but it was Legion she was protecting. It was Legion she was compelled to rescue.

Adriel sips her coffee, her gaze penetrating, unflinching, just as mine. She sets down her cup and clears her throat. "You have to understand:I loved him before any measure of time existed. Before your world was even a speck of dust floating amongst the stars. Love like that cannot simply be summed up into words. It is infinite."

"So you still love him," I say flatly.

Adriel shakes her head, but answers, "It's not that easy, Eden. He is a part of me, even now. What we had..." She smiles, her eyes flicking upward, as if conjuring a distant, happy memory. "It's not something I could help, even if I tried."

"So is that why you're here? To win him back?" Flaky danish is pulverized to mush between my fingertips.

"No." She lifts her chin proudly. "I can say that honestly. Samael—I mean, Legion—made his choice. I would never stand in the way of that."

"Yeah, well, I'm not so sure," I mutter, casting my eyes downward.

Before I can stop it, or even anticipate it, Adriel reaches

over and lays a hand on mine, forcing me to meet her soft expression. "He does care for you. I can see it. Even as he is now, you are the one who consumes his every waking thought. You are the one he's fighting for, even if he's fighting himself. You have to believe that."

I glance down to where her hand rests on mine, hating myself for finding comfort in her touch and in her words. Fuck. She's his ex. She still loves him. And she's nice as hell, and I'm pissed that I want to like her. I have to respect her honesty, and truthfully, it makes sense. I may never understand the bond between two angels, but I know how I feel about Legion. And it's unshakeable, even if he's avoiding me. Even if he never wants to speak to me again.

"You have to admit," Adriel begins, pulling her hand back to grab a scone. "It's not surprising that I was able to inhabit your soul so easily. You and I aren't so different from each other."

"How do you figure that?" I raise a skeptical brow.

"Well, aside from having similar taste in men," she shoots me a teasing grin, "we both know what it feels like to experience tragic loss. I didn't just lose a lover during the rebellion. I lost brothers. Sisters. And for a long time, I lost my way. I felt dead inside…without purpose. At that point, I was just surviving. And when Uriel took his leave to this world, I thought, *finally.* A reprieve from him constantly breathing down my neck. I had been waiting for the other shoe to drop for centuries, and then…it did. He created you. And then when Lucifer intervened, I knew I couldn't just sit around and wait for things to happen. I had to step out on faith and do something."

I shrug a shoulder. "I don't know about faith."

"Of course you do," she replies cheerfully. "Faith is what kept you alive for this long. Not me. Faith is what let you trust a houseful of demon assassins and accept them as your family. You may not have faith in a higher power—not now at least—but you had faith in them."

"Isn't that—I don't know—sacrilegious to your kind? You're an angel. They're demons. Aren't you all sworn enemies by nature?"

"Are we?" She tips her head to one side. "When we all want the same thing—to protect the ones we care about? When all we want is to preserve life, human or otherwise? Remember, Eden…even the Devil was once an angel. One of the most beautiful and talented of all, I might add."

At just the mention of him, I roll my eyes. "So I've heard. Wasn't he the one who spread that vicious rumor about Legion, just to get him on his side?"

"He was," she nods.

I frown, confused. "And yet you speak of him with fondness?"

"Forgiveness is powerful, Eden. It is a gift, not for the one who so desperately needs it, but for you. I've made my peace with what Lucifer did. He was in a dark, desperate place. He did it, not to hurt Legion, but because he loves him. Selfishly and sometimes foolishly, yes, but he loves him all the same."

I shake my head and mutter under my breath, "Fucked up way of showing it."

Adriel chuckles at my crass words. "I can't disagree with that. Lucifer has always been…impulsive to a fault. But in essence, his greatest sin was curiosity. I don't agree with his methods, but I can understand how doubt can make you do destructive things."

I don't even know what to say to that, so I busy my mouth with chewing a bit of pastry. The way she talks about Lucifer considering what he's done…what he's still doing. How can she be so thoughtful? So forgiving? Everything about her seems so…gracious and warm and kind. Which makes insecurity creep into my already muddled headspace. How can I compete with that? With her? I'm a mess, even on my best days. I'm irrational, vindictive. I don't automatically see the good in people. If anything, it's just the opposite. I expect people to hurt me. I anticipate disappointment right from the jump.

And now I know why Legion fell for her. And I can't understand why he would ever have any interest in me.

Adriel is everything I am not. With her flowing red hair, soft, feminine features, and unblemished milky skin, she is the picture of purity. It's not enough that she's compassionate and emotionally more mature than I'll ever be. No. She has to be physically perfect as well.

"The Se7en will be planning to head out for patrol in the next couple days," she informs me, breaking me out of my self-deprecating reverie. "There are reports of a rise in destruction and violence in the city."

My eyes go wide with worry. "Is that safe? With the Seraph still out there with the Redeemer?"

"There are risks, yes. But humans are dying. And your mother…"

"She could be in danger too." I hadn't considered the thought that Uriel would harm her. He was her husband, even if it was all a lie. She loved him, and when he left, it literally destroyed her. I never realized that he could be planning to finish the job.

"When are they leaving?"

"I'm not sure," she replies. "Legion is calling a meeting this evening to discuss the details."

"I want to be there." Up until this point, I had always felt like one of them. But now...fuck. Maybe they don't want me in on their plans. Tough shit. My mom is involved, and if anyone should be fighting to get her back, it should be me. Even if she didn't do the same for me all those years ago.

Adriel nods, noting the urgency in my tone, and gracefully stands. "I'll let you get back to your research." She dips her towards the volume I had been flipping through. "Start with the early 1990s. That's when your parents met. If there are any clues about what Uriel has planned, you'll find it before your birth. As you know, he left before then. He would have no reason to stick around after conception."

Hearing those words sends a pang of rejection to the hollow of my chest, but she's right. Phenex told me the act of conception was deliberate. Uriel would have no use for me until much later. Until now.

I watch Adriel leave the room, still on the fence about her presence, yet oddly comforted by it. I don't know if it's because her angel blood calls to mine, or if she's that convincing, but I do know there's no way she should be privy to more than me when it comes to what's going down in my city. Especially since I'm the one at risk of losing more than anyone else.

SIX

Aftern a run in with Kairo to request a more practical wardrobe and a visit with Sister, I head to the gym to meet up with Crysis.

I'm nervous. I've hardly given any thought to what abilities I might hold, and since I know virtually nothing about Uriel, other than the fact that he's a sociopathic piece of shit, I'm not sure what I'm genetically predisposed to. Shit, if my ability to bend the wills of humans is any indication, what else could I be capable of? And should that power be contained or unleashed upon the world? Self-control has never been my strong suit. Maybe I'm better off not knowing.

But I can't think like that. Not if I'm to help get my mom back. Not if I'm to survive whatever fresh hell awaits me.

So I'm on the raised platform fashioned like a boxing ring, earbuds in, blasting Kendrick Lamar's "HUMBLE," and

59

pretending like I'm not freaked the fuck out about tapping into my dormant Nephilim traits.

Crysis enters the empty space and smiles at me, the gesture too cunning to be encouraging. "Wasn't sure you'd show."

"I told you I would," I reply, a bit perturbed with his skepticism. I pull out the earbuds and put down the borrowed iPod—another request I had for Kairo.

"So you're cool with this?" he questions, setting down his water bottle on a bench. He slides off the sling that supports his busted arm and climbs onto the platform.

"Cool with what?"

"The whole Nephilim thing. Seemed like you had more of a penchant for doom and gloom."

I roll my eyes. "Nothing's changed."

"But hasn't it?"

Before I can respond, he strikes, launching a right hook for my jaw. Some inner instinct kicks in and I catch his fist in my palm, barely registering the power behind it. I'm so stunned by my body's swift reaction that I don't even see his left arm swing out, sending his fist straight into my stomach.

I crumple, catching myself with shaky palms against the ground. "The fuck…" Cough. Gasp. "…was that?"

"Your reflexes are good," Crysis remarks. "Good but not good enough. Now, get up."

"Fuck you," I spit.

"Maybe later. Get the fuck up, Eden."

My arms tremble as I struggle to push myself up. Saliva collects in my mouth, the telltale signs of approaching vomit. Deep breaths. I blink away hurt, frustrated tears, refusing to admit weakness.

"Good girl," Crysis notes, as I climb to my feet without an ounce of grace.

"I'm not a fucking puppy, and I'm not your girl," I grit, letting his condescension fuel my ire. "Don't do that shit again."

"You think your opponent is going to announce when they'll strike? This isn't a movie, Eden. No one is delivering long ass monologues before they kill you. You need to be ready."

"I fucking know that," I bite back, my voice hoarse from the blow. And I do. I need to be ready to fight. And I'm not talking meet-me-after-school type of fighting. I need to be prepared enough to potentially take on an archangel. An ancient being billions of years older and infinitely stronger than me.

Fuck.

I get my legs up under me again, not 100% stable, but not quite shaking like a leaf, and put my fists up in a defensive stance. Crysis laughs like the asshole loon that he is.

"And that's supposed to do…what?"

I raise my fists higher, blocking my face. "I'm not about to let you kick my ass all around this gym."

He drops his hands, completely confident that I couldn't possibly get the drop on him. "Baby, had I'd been full blood angel, let alone Seraph, your ass would have been kicked five minutes ago. You think they're battling with brute force?"

"Then why the hell did you hit me?" I shout with all the might my hoarse voice can muster.

"Because quick reflexes are just as important as your other abilities. But since you want to play it that way…"

He lunges towards me quicker than any human could

detect, yet somehow, I sidestep him just seconds before his fist collides with my face. Holy fuck. He's really hell-bent on hurting me. I'm smart enough to know not to let my guard down so I swiftly pivot, so that he's facing away from me, and shove my foot into his lower back with the intention of catching him off balance. Unluckily for me, he anticipates the move and catches my foot.

"Good," he remarks before pushing me back with enough force to send me flailing onto my ass. "Now get up and do it again."

I push myself up, my body protesting with the effort, but make it to my feet. Before I'm even steady, Crysis strikes again with a right cross, but I'm ready. I block the blow and push him back, delivering a swift jab of my own to his chin.

"Good," he remarks, rubbing his jaw. "But I know you're planning to attempt a left cross, then a right elbow to my temple. Then while I'm off kilter, you're going to try to sweep my feet from under me, getting me on the ground. You may be able to block my punches, but you can't block your mind. So either way, you're fucked, Eden."

Shit. He's right. I slowly lower my fists, watching intently as he does the same.

"So what are you saying?" I pant. "That I'm essentially playing a losing game?"

"I'm saying that you need to stay two—no five—steps ahead. Be just as physically strong as you are mentally. There's no way you're evenly matched to a full blood angel, but you have the element of surprise. They don't know what you can do."

Hell, I don't know what I can do, but again, he's right.

That's the upside to Uriel abandoning my mom after planting his deadly seed. He doesn't know how his genes have manifested in me.

I nod at Crysis, hands on my hips as I catch my breath. I'm out of shape, and it shows. I can throw hands when I have to—and I've had to a lot—but full on combat? I'd collapse in the first five minutes.

Crysis sees it too, and says, "I want you in this gym every morning, doing cardio. Then we'll do some weight training and work on your fighting skills. After that, we'll dig into your mental capabilities. And when you're not in here, I want you in that library, looking up everything you can about Uriel."

"Yeah. Sure." I suck my teeth. I know I need work, but there's no way I'll be ready in time. We can't hide out here for too long before the Seraph start sniffing around.

"It's not gonna be easy; I can promise you that," he replies, noting my discouraged expression. "But we'll give it our all, ok? I just need to know that you're committed to this."

A nod, and I raise my tight fists in response. "Let's go again."

We spar well into the afternoon until Crysis insists we rest and work on flexing my other muscles. I'm grateful—I can barely stand and have taken more blows than I've landed. Crysis doesn't even look like he's broken a sweat, yet I'm drenched, winded, and dotted with bruises that are already purplish and angry. I refuse to complain—I hate that I'm limping over to a nearby bench, clutching my side to ease my sore kidney. Crysis claims that I'm stronger than he expected for a beginner, another gift from dear old dad, but I don't see how when he literally just kicked my ass.

"Drink," he demands, handing me a water bottle. I do as I'm told, gulping down its entire contents. I unceremoniously swipe the back of my hand over my wet lips and chuck the empty bottle at my feet.

"So what now?"

"Now…creep into my head."

"You know I can't. You can block me."

"That was when you were cloaked. Come on… dig in there and bend my will."

I take a deep breath and pause for a long blink, conjuring all my concentration. When I release my mental reel, flinging out that invisible hand towards Crysis's consciousness, I'm momentarily stunned at how easy, how *good* it feels. Like stretching a sore muscle after an intense workout.

"Good," Crysis remarks, feeling my influence gently press into him. "Keep going."

I push a little deeper, but I'm met with resistance. Like he's pushing back. I shove harder, that unseen hand balling into a fist. Sweat beads at my temple and I grit my teeth. I punch the barrier blocking my path, but it's like running head first into a brick wall. My ears are ringing and I taste blood in my saliva.

"It's just like physical combat, Eden. You can't just walk right in. Fight me."

With a grunt of frustration, I focus on molding my invisible hand into something more menacing. A spindly claw with four-inch talons? No. Crysis is steel and stone. A sledgehammer. A wrecking ball. Each one is met with a harder, thicker barrier, hardly putting a crack in Crysis's shield. And every time I collide into it, the throbbing in my skull becomes more intense, the taste of blood more potent.

"Think, Eden!" he barks through clenched teeth. "Stop trying to be something you're not. Think."

"I am!" I choke out, blinking through angry tears.

"You're not. You can't beat them at their own game. You aren't stronger than them. You're not faster than them. What *are* you?"

Fuck.

I don't know what I am. I've never known. How the hell am I supposed to figure this shit out now, when my skull is on the verge of shattering and my eyes feel like they're being ripped from their sockets. I can't hold on, but I refuse to let go. I won't let failure ruin me. I will make it. I will survive.

I'm a survivor.

I've had to hustle, scheme, and fight my way through life. I've had to go to the darkest places inside myself to ensure my city did not make me a statistic. I am a product of my environment, and within it are the dirtiest, most predatory creatures on Earth.

I steel myself, clutching the sides of the bench until my knuckles ache, and mold myself into a serpent. A long, black snake with beady, red eyes, thin enough to slip through the fissures of Crysis's shield. The moment I think of it, I spring into action to avoid revealing my plan before it unfolds. I can feel his awareness on me, and just before he can block, I slip through a crack.

I'm inside his head. Not the staged area he let me penetrate when he was pretending to be Christian, my blind date. But the real Crysis, the Nephilim member of the Alliance who was nearly murdered by his people for daring to fight against tyranny.

It's dark but warm, almost comforting. Peaceful. I've only felt this sensation when Adriel touched me, but this is different. I taste it on my tongue, sweet and refreshing like citrus, replacing the metallic tinge of blood. Its tangy scent fills my nostrils, and I'm reminded of the beach in June. Something brushes up my side, soft, sensual tendrils of velvet, leaving behind the essence of sunshine.

And then I'm pushed out. Not just pushed. Catapulted. Crysis threw me out of his head.

"What was that?" I gasp, reeling back.

Crysis swings his leg over the bench and climbs to his feet. "That's enough for today."

"Wait…you touched me in there. How is that even possible?"

"I said that's enough," he spits harshly, moving towards the exit. "We'll pick up again tomorrow."

I rise to follow after him. "Crysis, can't we just talk about…"

And that's when I notice him.

Legion.

He's standing in the doorway of the gym, his face shaded in shadow and his eyes glowing with molten silver flames. He tracks every step Crysis takes until he brushes past him. Then his gaze falls on me.

For a while, we just stare. Just breathe. Just exist.

"Are you hurt?" he asks, his voice low yet there's an underlying note of concern in his words.

I shake my head slowly, almost afraid to scare him off. "No. I'm fine."

He enters, his steps measured, as if he's just as worried

about scaring me too. "I went to your room. You weren't there."

"Yeah." I take a shaky step towards him. "I've been in the library…researching." I give a nervous smile. I don't know why I feel so uneasy around him. Days ago, he was deep inside me while I bucked and begged him for more. Now, I'm afraid to say the wrong thing.

"And you're training."

"I need to learn how to fight and harness whatever weird abilities I may have. Now that I'm…ya know…"

"Nephilim," he answers for me. There's no malice in his tone, but I can tell the word feels like a cuss on his tongue.

"Yeah. That." I shrug. "Crysis thinks I could be some type of super Nephilim, since my fath—" I swallow down the word. "Since Uriel is Seraph. I just don't know anything about him, not that I'd want to. But if I can at least learn how to fight, I could be helpful…in rescuing my mom. And getting the Redeemer back."

I'm rambling. I literally cringe at my inability to close my damn mouth. Or at least change the subject. Legion has barely said two words to me since I woke up. I can think of about a thousand other things I'd rather we be talking about.

"Is that what you want? To fight with us?" he asks. A few more steps forward.

"Yeah," I nod. "If it means we're all safe. Of course, I'd fight with you." I move until just a couple feet separate us, the closest I've been to him in what seems like forever. "I would fight *for* you."

He shakes his head, but his silver eyes warm with a familiar emotion. It's the first sign he's shown me that part of him— the part that showed me such gentleness and passion—has remained, even with his rebirth. The man I grew to care for so deeply that just the mention of his name would steal my breath is still in there. He's here with me. Maybe he never left, despite what he feared.

"I would never ask you to do that," he says. "But if that is what you want—"

"It is. It's what I want. You all have risked so much for me, and finally, I don't have to be some helpless damsel. Hell, I don't want to be. I don't want to stand on the sidelines while everyone sacrifices. It's my fault you're all in this mess."

"No." He shakes his head and casts his eyes downward. "It's my fault. My indiscretions drove Uriel to madness. If I hadn't deceived him, he would have never entered your world. He would have never courted your mother in a quest for revenge."

"And I would have never been born," I add.

I am the product of Uriel's rage and hurt. A constant reminder of weakness and betrayal. How difficult it must be for him to have to look at me and be forced to relive that part of his life.

He doesn't say anything to dispute my claim because he knows it's true. I would have never been conceived had it not been for Legion's lust. No, not lust. Love. In some fucked up roundabout way, I am a result of Legion's love.

His love for Adriel.

I know he can sense where my thoughts are headed, because he runs a hand through his dark hair and says, "I just wanted to see how you were adjusting."

"I'm fine," I lie. I can't be fine. Not when there's so much distance between us.

"Good." He looks like he wants to say more, and I'm internally begging him to. Instead, he nods once and turns on his heel in retreat. Leaving me to stare at his back, missing the way it felt under my fingertips—smooth and hot and hard as stone.

I gather my iPod and what's left of my pride, and head to my room. As I'm rounding a corner, I get a glimpse of that same chiseled back, so muscular even under his fitted tee. I should stop this being timid shit. This man...a few days ago, I was able to call him mine. Why does that have to change? And if it's his feelings that have been altered, he should be able to tell me so.

I break into a power walk to catch up but stop dead in my tracks.

He's not alone.

I dip into an open doorway, my face hot and my palms sweaty, and listen in on their hushed conversation.

"You look tired," Adriel says, her voice soft. The same voice she used with me.

"I'm fine."

"Are you sleeping? Eating? You know...if you need me, I'm—"

"I said, I'm fine."

A beat of silence. A rustle of fabric.

"I missed you. Every day for a millennia, I ached with longing."

"Adriel..."

"I can't take back what's been done, but know that nothing has changed. At least not for me."

Another strained silence.

"I've changed." His voice is so quiet, it's almost a whisper.

"Not to me…"

"Don't."

"Sam—Legion. Can't you feel this?"

"I said, *don't.*" He heaves out a heavy breath. "Look, I have to go."

"Later?" There's hope in her voice.

"Yeah, sure."

I don't breathe until the sound of his heavy footfalls diminishes down the hallway. Then I let the blood red rage flood in.

I said I would fight for him.

I fucking meant it.

SEVEN

I ARRIVE AT IRIN'S SITTING ROOM DRESSED IN JEANS, combat boots, and a sweater, ready to do battle. I haven't been able to focus on anything since those moments in the hallway, too consumed with doubt and anger after witnessing Adriel try to seduce Legion. All that faux reassurance from her, and I believed her. I'm not only pissed at her conniving, two-faced behavior, but I'm also pissed at myself for letting my guard down.

"You ok, E?" Niko asks after kissing me on the cheek.

"Yeah."

I head to the far end of the sectional and plop down unceremoniously. Crysis is already here, successfully avoiding eye contact since our awkward episode in the gym, along with Irin, whose presence is confusing considering she's adamantly neutral. She instructs her staff to start distributing glasses of wine and spirits. Good. Alcohol. That'll certainly ensure I keep my shit together.

Niko raises a knowing brow and sits beside me. "Uh oh."

"Uh oh, what?" I sneer.

"You've got the look of a woman with a score to settle."

I start to lie, to tell him that he's wrong, but then Adriel walks in, the perfect picture of virtue and elegance in another floor-length silk gown. The fabric is an iridescent white, and her hair is pinned up, showing off her slender neck. Any and all attempts to hide my contempt are DOA.

Niko snorts a laugh at the murderous expression that no doubt is etched on my face. "Yeah. You seem *totally* ok."

When the Se7en file in a moment later, Legion leading the pack, I still haven't released my fury. But the fire currently burning a hole in my chest turns molten, and my rage morphs into something else. Hurt. And jealousy.

He could've set her straight, and he didn't. He could have told her that his sleeping habits are none of her damn concern, and he didn't. At any point in that torturous conversation, he could have told her to kick fucking rocks because he doesn't want her, and he didn't do that. No mention of me, or what I thought we had before all this shit went down. Instead, he promised her *Later.* He left the door open for more.

I don't even know how to take that.

His earlier actions had shown that he had no interest in continuing any type of relationship with me, but then that moment we shared in the gym... I saw him. I glimpsed the man he was, the man I know he still is deep down. At least I wanted to believe I did. Now I'm not sure if I ever really knew him at all.

At that moment, Kairo comes to us with glasses of wine. He gives me a wink when I take mine then sashays to a hidden area while another one of Irin's underlings—a svelte, leggy brunette wearing nothing more than a bikini top and a short sarong—tends to the Se7en. I don't miss the way Adriel's soft green eyes track her, just as mine do.

"Let's begin," Legion announces, the booming bass of his voice immediately drawing everyone's attention. "We have intel that crime in the city is at an all-time high. Riots, looting, violence. It's as if the angels have completely pulled their influence, and have invited in destruction."

"What does that mean?" I frown.

When Adriel turns to smile at me, I resist the urge to spit my wine in her face. "The analogy of humans having an angel and a devil on each shoulder. There are ambassadors of good and evil—light and darkness—that help to influence a person's decisions. Angels and demons cannot take away their free will, but they can sway them. The human's intentions are purely theirs though. If they seek to do harm, then they will. If they want to go in the way of goodness, the righteous one is victorious."

"And if the Seraph has decided to withdraw angelic guidance, Chicago and its people will burn to the ground," Crysis adds, his expression grim.

"An act to draw us out," Lilith chimes in, pursing her pink, glossy lips in disgust. "Petty, even for them."

"But smart," Phenex countered. His honey eyes fall to the floor. "I'm afraid we don't have much time. If we don't stop this—if they don't get what they want—they'll sentence millions of innocent people to death."

"Ok..." My gaze falls on each of the Se7en. "What is it that they want?"

"Me." Adriel releases a sigh. "They want me."

I can't stop my inner asshole, and the words fly out of my mouth. "Then what's the problem?"

"It's too dangerous," Legion remarked, defending his precious Adriel. Angry tears burn the backs of my eyes. "Uriel is unhinged. There's no telling what he'd do to her."

"And there's the little matter of your mom and the Redeemer," Toyol adds.

"Hold up. Eden might be on to something," Cain surprisingly muses. He lifts his palms in faux defense when the others turn to glare at him. "Hear me out. What if we used Adriel as bait? Promise a trade, set a trap, grab our shit, and get out."

Legion shakes his head. "Too dangerous."

"Seriously...how ancient are these fuckers? We have technology on our side."

Legion's jaw tenses, his tell for when he's contemplating a risky plan. "Their strength, their abilities...they're unparalleled. How would we know they wouldn't be luring *us* into a trap?"

Cain releases an exasperated huff. "I get that, but—"

"I'll do it," Adriel announces, her chin raised.

"What?" The shock on Legion's face, the flash of bewilderment...it hurts.

"I'll do it," Adriel repeats. "If it means ensuring the safety of everyone here, I'll do it."

"I can't let you do that." Legion shakes his head. "They'll

never go for it. Besides, there's no way we'd make it out of there alive when we don't even know who we're up against."

"So maybe we find out," I suggest, rolling my eyes. The back and forth exasperating as fuck, but I try to stow the underlying annoyance in my tone and be constructive. "What if we bring them to us? Scope out what we're up against. At least after that, we can formulate a plan based on what we know."

"You can't be serious," Crysis scoffs.

"Listen." I turn to Irin, who looks amused by the whole conversation. "This is sacred ground, right? No blood can be shed here."

"Not out of contempt, it can't." She smiles suggestively, and I don't even want to know what that's about.

"Which is why this is considered a haven for creatures of both good and evil, seeking a reprieve from inherent obligations. What if we invited them? What if Irin threw a party? They wouldn't suspect we were behind it. No doubt, they'd show, if only to try to sniff us out."

Legion crosses his arms over his chest, stretching that black tee almost beyond its limits. "And they'd know we were here the moment they stepped foot on the property. Then what?"

"Not necessarily," Niko pipes up beside me. "The cloaking spell used on Eden…I think I know who helped Uriel wield it." Dramatic pause. "My father."

"Stavros?" I question, remembering the suave, dark-haired man whose crystal blue stare made me uneasy, and not in a good way. He was Lucifer's bitch in Hell, but I could tell he was power hungry. He reeked of desperation.

"Yes," Niko answers. "I could manipulate that magic, use it to veil you all. Because of our numbers, I'll need some time to prepare, but I'm sure I can pull it off."

Legion pinches the space between his brows, contemplating the plan, yet he doesn't speak.

"This could work," Toyol co-signs, nodding his head. I can see the wheels already turning for the Se7en's resident tech guru. "I may even be able to get a tracking device on one of them, which would hopefully lead us right to where ever they're posting up." He looks to Irin. "Surveillance?"

The ancient beauty gives him a sly grin. "I have my own. I guess a bit more wouldn't hurt. And when are we hoping to throw this little soiree?"

It's Phenex who replies. "The sooner, the better, with your permission, of course."

"Permission granted. As long as it's alright with your leader, that is."

Legion still hasn't authorized the plan, but I can tell he's considering it. If he weren't, it would have been a hard, definitive *No*. No further discussion required.

"And you're sure you can do a spell to veil us all?" he asks Niko, his silver gaze shaded in skepticism.

"I am," Niko nods. "It will only last for a few hours, but I can do it. I'll need to prepare, but it'll be fairly simple."

"Whatever you need," Legion states. "We appreciate your help."

Niko shrugs. "Thank your brother. Besides, it's been a while since I got to show off." He turns to me and gives me a flirtatious wink. We both know Legion is tracking his every move. What game is he playing at?

"If that's settled," Legion grumbles. "Lilith and Andras, you'll be point for all party arrangements. Toyol on tech. Phenex and Jinn will be my eyes and ears on the ground. Cain…I want you to sit this one out."

"What the fuck for?" the scarred demon roars.

"Because I want you with Eden's sister. Do not leave her side. She's human—vulnerable and still recovering. If something happens, you need to be able to get her out of there."

"I assure you," Irin pipes up, "the precaution is not necessary."

"That's final." Legion's tone is the proverbial period on the edict.

Cain stiffly nods his obedience. I'm sure it's hard for him to be benched, but he knows it's for the best.

"In the meantime, I'd like you to work with Eden when she's not training with Crysis." That gets our attention, and both Cain and I frown at Legion. "You're the best arms man I've got. She should know how to wield a weapon."

"Would I even need to? Given my abilities?"

"The Seraph are the oldest, strongest immortals in history. They're indestructible, their power immeasurable. You're a newborn Nephilim—no more than a flea to them. You'll need all the help you can get."

I know he speaks the truth, but it still stings a bit, especially coming from him. I've always known I was weak in comparison to all the supernatural creatures in my life, but damn…a flea?

"Is that it?" Crysis questions, climbing to his feet before Legion answers.

"Yes. I'm sending my scouts out tonight. Hopefully, we'll

have more information in the morning."

Crysis gives a stiff nod then strides out the room as if he can't wait to get away from the rest of us. He seems extra prickly, especially in comparison to how he was earlier. I can't help but wonder if it's because of me.

"You eat?" Niko asks as we all rise to disperse. I look across the room to Legion. To my surprise, he meets my gaze and doesn't look away.

"Um, not yet. Wanna meet for dinner? I have to do something real quick."

Niko follows my line of vision and shoots me a naughty smile. "Something or *someone* you have to do real quick?"

I shake my head and chuckle before placing a soft peck on his cheek. "Give me five minutes."

I know I should be furious with him, but I can't help it. I need to hear him say it—I need to know if he still has feelings for Adriel. I know where her heart is, but what about his? And is he even capable of love now?

"Can I talk to you?" I ask quietly. The rest of the Se7en cease their chatter and look to their leader. So much for not feeling like a total outsider.

Legion steps to the side and nods. "Of course."

"I just want to…" Shit. What do I want to talk about? There's so much to say, but this is neither the time nor the place. Especially with Adriel standing just feet away, pretending to be engaged in a conversation with Irin. "I was hoping you…if you had time…that we could talk. Like, talk-talk. Things have…changed. And I just want to know exactly how much they've changed, ya know?" I sound like an insecure fool, but that's exactly how I feel. I'm like a puppy at his feet, just hoping—praying—he'll drop a scrap of food every now and then.

Legion is quiet for longer than I anticipate. Fuck. This was a mistake.

"This was a mistake," I say aloud. I try to turn away to salvage what's left of my wounded pride, but he grips my arm at the elbow. His skin is hot…hotter than I remember. He's burning up.

"Don't…" There's an urgency in his tone that I haven't heard in so long. I look up to see his silver eyes swirl with unnamed emotion. He still feels. I know he does. "Don't go. Please. Yes, I want to talk. Can I come to you? Tonight?"

The way he says the words, it's like he's uncertain that I'd agree… I don't understand it. Little does he know that I would say anything—do anything—just to have him back with me. Just to hold him close under the glow of moonlight and let the hum of his heartbeat lull me to sleep. I miss him, more than I've let myself admit. The revelations about my father, my birthright, and Legion's own transformation have been a welcome distraction. But even those truths can't soothe the constant ache in my chest.

"Yes. Tonight." My voice is merely a hoarse whisper, but he hears me—he always does—and nods.

"Well, well. Someone's got a little pep in her step," Niko comments as he sees me approach. He's waiting outside the kitchen holding a tray of dome-covered dishes."

"Shut up," I retort, but I can't help the broad smile on my face. *Tonight*. Legion is coming to me tonight. Not a half-assed *Later* like he promised Adriel.

"Everything good?"

"Yeah. I think so."

He leads me down the hall, to his living quarters, which is in the opposite direction from mine. It's decorated similarly to the one I'm in, although it's more masculine with its darker colors and heavy, wood furniture. Even the giant four-poster bed screams sexuality and strength.

"Geez, Niko. If you wanted to get me alone in your room, you didn't have to bribe me with food." I flop down at the edge of the bed and kick off my shoes.

"Well, I figured I'd feed you first. Usually, when ladies spend the night with me, they pass out from overwhelming pleasure, not hunger."

Niko sets down the tray, then with barely a flick of his hand, a bottle of red and two stemless glasses appear beside it.

"Damn. Sometimes I forget you can do the hocus pocus shit," I jibe.

"Don't let the good looks fool you, baby," he winks, uncorking the bottle. After he pours us each a glass and strolls over to the bed to hand me mine, he says, "I have to admit...I did kinda lure you here under false pretenses."

"Oh?"

"Yeah." He takes a sip. I guess even warlocks need a little liquid courage every now and then. "The preparations I need to make for the veiling spell? I need to recharge...to replenish my magic so I'm at full strength in order to pull it off."

"Ok..."

"I need to *breathe* someone."

"And by breathe you mean..."

He releases a heavy sigh. "I need to siphon the essence

from someone's body. Not enough to kill them, but enough that a human would not survive it."

I take a swig of wine. "Oh."

"Yeah. And even if I did feel comfortable going to a demon or an angel, which I absolutely do not considering it could kill me, my only other option is Crysis. And you."

"Oh." I sound like a broken record. "Well, sure. Do me. Whatever you need. When?"

"Before I attempt the spell. So the day before the party."

"Ok. Yeah, I'm down."

Niko nods, and tacks on, "I just need you to understand what the process entails. It can be extremely sensual in nature. Magic is seductive to my kind, and the ritual usually leads to sex." Before I can open my mouth to protest, he adds, "Of course, that won't be the case with us. But I want you to know that there may be lingering, unavoidable effects for me. And for you."

"So what are you saying? You'll be aroused?" I swallow thickly.

"Most likely. And you may be too."

"I see."

"Look, if this is too uncomfortable for you then—"

"No," I shake my head. "No, I'll do it. You're the closest friend I have in the house, and you're doing this to help my mother. And you're in this mess because of me. I'll do it. It'll be fine."

A long beat of silence stretches between us as we preoccupy our hands with drinking wine, pretending not to be thinking of the breathing ritual that looms ahead.

When our glasses are dry, Niko turns to me, a devilish

slash of a smile blessing his beautiful face. His crystal blue eyes shine with mischief. "So now that that's out the way, shall I take off my clothes? Or would you like to do that?"

I playfully punch him in the arm and order him to refill my glass.

T HERE'S SOMETHING ABOUT NIKOLAI.

Either he's lacing my wine with some warlock magic or being in his presence brings me a sense of peace so potent that I'm able to forget all the crazy for just a few moments. But the minute he's gone, and I'm back in my room alone, all the anxiety comes rushing back in.

Legion said he'd come to me tonight. Yet after an hour… two hours…of waiting and still no word, I finally give up and slide my freshly showered, shaved, and oiled body between cold silk sheets. He had mentioned sending his scouts out (what scouts?) so I try to force my mind to understand. Still, my heart is more than a bit fractured at being stood up.

After training with Crysis, plotting and planning with the Se7en, and polishing off a bottle of wine with Niko, sleep comes easier than I expect. And soon, I'm tumbling into darkness towards a room the color of fresh blood. Fire burns all around me, yet I cannot feel their burn on my flesh. There is no smoke that fills my lungs, no soot that dusts my skin. I'm comfortable within these walls made of a thousand dazzling rubies. Comfortable and content. But everything around me is burning…dying. Yet I stand, unscathed, unbothered by the world that's disintegrating into ash around me, for it was me who created it. It was me who birthed this inferno from my war-torn womb. And the man who stands before me, so beautiful in his cold brutality, is the king of my wicked ruin.

I walk into the fire towards him, and it cools at my feet. Tousled hair brushed with the barest kiss of sunlight; a tailored suit poured over a body that boasts of elegance and sex. He smiles slyly, but it doesn't meet his eyes. The stars in those endless twin galaxies have been extinguished.

"Is this what you wanted?"

I look around us, watch as the rubies melt and drip into puddles of blood at our feet. "No. No of course not. This is what I wanted to avoid."

Lucifer looks away, staring into the fire. When he turns to face me, his cheeks are streaked with bloody tears. "Then why did you leave me?"

I stumble back, confused. Horrified.

"He did this, Eden. Your beloved. This is what I tried to protect you from—all of you. And you unleashed him unto the Earth. Your world will not survive him a second time."

I shake my head furiously. "No. No. I don't believe you."

"Look around you." He waves a hand, leaving a trail of fire in its wake. "Your city is burning. Everyone you've ever known—ever cared for—is dying or dead."

"He's…he's…"

"With *her*. I defied our Father to protect him. I created a scandal because I knew he would never leave her on his own. I *fell* for *him*. Don't make the same mistake, Eden. There's still time to save yourself."

"What do you want me to do?"

He offers an outstretched hand. "Come with me. Say yes, and come with me."

Timidly, agonizingly slowly, I reach for him. But just before the tips of our fingers meet, the flames rise, creating a wall of fire. And he's gone.

I'm awake. And not alone.

Legion is sitting on the bed, his back to me. Startled, I sit up and pull the silk sheets up to my chin. I'm still wearing the deep purple satin nightgown I donned in anticipation of his visit. Now, I'm wishing it was a turtleneck.

"I didn't mean to wake you." His voice is hauntingly low, and he doesn't turn around.

I frown. I waited and waited. It seems like all I've done is wait for him. And with that dream still pressing into the forefront of my muddled mind, my words are doused in annoyance. "Then why are you here?"

"Because I had to be close you. Even though I know it's wrong and it's selfish of me. I just needed to feel your presence."

Dammit. That makes me go soft all over. My weakness for him is a curse that I can't seem to break. "Why?"

He finally turns to face me, those glowing silver eyes slashing through the darkness. "To remind me of what I'm fighting for. To give me just a sliver of the peace I once felt with you in my arms."

"You've barely looked at me. You've hardly even noticed I was alive."

"I have. I just couldn't let you see me. Not like this. Not as I am now. I didn't want to scare you."

"L…" He winces at the name on my tongue, so I start over. "Legion…I've always seen you for who and what you truly are. And it's never frightened me."

He shakes his head. "You don't know what you're saying. What I was…that was nothing. The beast you glimpsed during the Blood Oath was only a fraction of my darkness."

I roll my eyes. The Se7en ritual he invited me to watch was terrifying, I'll admit, but I knew it wouldn't be a cakewalk. And I got over it. I accepted who and what he is and fell for him despite my fear. Why does he keep treating me like a child? I know what I want. And I want him—all of him.

"I'm not blind. I know you've changed. We both have."

"So you understand." He heaves out a heavy breath. "What I am now—and what you are now—you could never want something like me. Could never love…*this*." He talks of himself like he's an object. An animal.

"Why do you say that?"

"I am fire. I am rage. I am Death itself. I embody everything you should stay far, far away from. And I could never—would never—allow myself to corrupt your soul."

"My soul was corrupted a long time ago," I rasp.

Sitting up on my knees, I let the sheet fall to my waist, revealing my purple satin nightie. The semi-sheer bodice is decorated with silver threading that exaggerates the deep V that falls between my breasts. I watch as his gaze coasts from my pleading eyes to my throat and down below my neckline. He drags his teeth over his bottom lip, and I imagine him dragging those teeth over my nipples.

He only lets himself look for a moment before he's turning away. And something within me deflates.

"I shouldn't have come here. I should have let you be."

He starts to push off the bed, but before he can stand, I lunge forward and grip his arm. "Don't. Don't go. Please?"

"Eden, I can't…I can't let you…"

"Just lay with me. That's all I want. I…I miss you. Please, just stay."

A thousand battles are fought and won across his features, but he reluctantly nods. "If that's what you want."

"It is. It's what I want."

He nods again, then kicks off his boots before turning his body to place a knee on the bed.

"You're not going to sleep fully dressed, are you?" I tack on a small smile to ease the tense moment. He's agreed to sleep in the same bed with me; I don't want to push it. But I also don't want to constantly be walking on eggshells either.

Legion looks down at his dark jeans and black tee. When he raises his chin, a shadow falls over his features. "You know what I look like now. You know my body has changed."

"And *you* know I don't give a damn about any of that."

With a resigning sigh, he grasps the hem of his shirt and drags it over his head, causing his dark hair to fall over his brow. I gasp at the beauty of him, stunned at the dark ink that now mars his smooth, tan skin. That cruel, jealous beast stares back at me, taunting me. Up close, I see that its silver eyes actually do shimmer with some type of dark, daunting magic.

Even the red stone held captive in its massive fangs glimmers mystically. I'm mesmerized by it, damn near entranced by its wicked splendor. I want to look away, but it calls to me, urging me closer.

Legion turns, allowing me to see that the dragon has wrapped itself around his back, completing the mural with elaborate scales and a razor-sharp tail. *Closer,* it whispers. *Touch me. I won't bite.*

With its murmured lies singing in my ear, I move in closer, my fingers outstretched. Legion catches my hand before I make contact.

"Did it hurt?" I whisper, my lips only inches from his.

He lets me go and shakes his head. "The transformation was excruciating. I broke every bone in my body. Muscle and tissue were torn to shreds. But this…" He runs a hand over the hard planes of his chest and abs. "This was nothing."

I lean back, marveling at the sheer wonder of the beast before me. I didn't think it was possible to find him more gorgeous, more alluring. But here I am, panting with the need to have him close to me. Beside me. Inside me.

Fuck my dream.

If I am to birth fire, then Legion's seed is the spark that will set the world aflame.

"Come here." My voice is so hoarse with desire that I hardly recognize it.

He doesn't crawl to me from the foot of the bed as he's done so many times before. He prowls, like a deadly animal scenting its prey, right before he pounces and tears out its throat. My mouth dries, my knees shake, and my core clenches with anticipation.

He settles next to me, facing me, yet doesn't touch me. His silver eyes dim, but just barely, as if he's trying to contain his power. Still, I feel him. He's so hot, it would be unbearable for anyone else. Even the air between us seems to sizzle.

"I don't care. I don't care if you're different," I whisper. I need him to believe it. Even if I have to say it every day for eternity.

"I do." He matches my tone, but his voice is gravelly.

"You shouldn't. You haven't changed to me. The man—the demon—you were, and how I felt for you…nothing has changed."

"How you felt…" He grimaces, as if the thought disturbs him. "You shouldn't feel for me, Eden. Not anymore. Because the way I feel for you…" He shakes his head before turning onto his back. "I don't want to hurt you."

I don't know if he means emotionally or physically, but I don't care. "Then you won't."

"It's not that simple."

Fucking hell. I don't get it. I'm here, telling him that I accept him, whether he's man or beast, yet still he pushes me away. Maybe he's telling me something else. Maybe he wants me to push back.

"Is she a threat?"

Legion turns back to me and frowns. "What?"

"Is Adriel a threat to me…to *us*? Is it she you would rather be with right now?"

A wisp of darkness snakes between us, shading his penetrating glare. "No."

I pretend to ignore what I saw—the way black smoke and shadow manifested right before my eyes—and store it away for another time when I'm not trying to persuade him that I'm not afraid. "Then you have nothing to worry about. You won't hurt me, Legion. You wouldn't do that."

To drive my point home, I move in closer, closing the small space between us to a mere few inches. A blast of stifling heat wafts over my entire body. A warning? Or an invitation?

"You don't know what you're saying. You have no idea what you're signing up for with me."

"Then show me. Show me, Legion of Lost Souls. Show me what you are."

Timidly, I reach out and brush his stomach, right where that horrid serpent beast holds the ruby in its fangs. The hard ridges of his abs tremble under my fingertips, his body temperature searing my skin. I slowly begin to slide my hand up his smooth, solid chest. When I cup his jaw, he sags into my touch, and his eyes flutter closed.

"Eden…fuck," he curses. When he opens his eyes, they're churning with tortured desire.

"Don't be afraid of this," I urge. "Because I'm not. Don't hold back."

With a growl that rings of relief and desperation, Legion swiftly flips me onto my back and gathers both my hands in one of his, pinning them over my head. No preamble. No warning. Just his body pressed against mine. My blood races with concentrated need as I look up at him through my lashes, begging without words for him to keep going. For him to strip his soul naked and show me who he truly is.

"Last chance," he grits, his jaw tight.

I nod. "I'm not going anywhere."

I don't know how he does it, but with the barest of brushes

against my side with his palm, my gown disintegrates into ash. I'm completely naked under him, and the way his eyes glow at the sight of my bare flesh, like an animal withering of famine, I know exactly what he meant by *"Last chance."* He's going to devour me. And once he starts, he won't be able to stop. And I don't want him to.

He takes my mouth and kisses me like he's drinking the very essence of my soul. His lips feel the same, yet, this is like kissing someone else. Not quite a stranger, but not L either. I kiss him deeper, searching to taste the demon I fell for before I even knew what he truly was. He nips my bottom lip in response, hard enough to make me flinch, then soothes the tiny wound with his tongue. Groaning, his hips flexing into me, Legion sucks my lip into his mouth and savors my blood.

I am…so turned on right now. I should be utterly freaked out. Maybe even a little disgusted. But this hunger in him, this seductive violence, arouses me to the point of pain. I ache for him. My nipples go tight and hard as he releases my hands above my head and lets his fingers trail down to my breasts. He gathers them in his palms and squeezes them together.

"Please," I beg, my voice a choked whimper.

A slow smile spreads Legion's lips, and when he bares his teeth, I see that they've transformed into fangs. I barely have a chance to gasp before he lowers his mouth to my nipples and sucks them both at once. The scrape of those sharpened teeth, the soft roughness of his serpent tongue…the sensation is orgasmic, and I moan loudly and grind my naked sex against his, still concealed by dark denim.

He sucks and nibbles my pebbled flesh to the point of madness before licking a slow trail to my navel. Then he kisses me from hipbone to hipbone, all the while spreading my thighs wider. Fuck. Just the anticipation has me on the verge of coming. Legion lifts his head as if he can sense that I'm close…as if he can smell it. He drags a long, thick finger from my belly button down to my slickened folds, watching intently as my flesh quivers with the first signs of orgasm. He strokes me gently from the top of my mound to my tight entrance, rubbing circles over my clit. Up and down, over and over, he primes me for his tongue. And when he lowers his head and covers me with his mouth, I explode into a billion brilliant colors, knees trembling and hands grasping his dark hair.

He sucks and fucks with tongue and teeth, unleashing an assault so deadly, I lose my breath. My head is swimming. My whole body is shaking. I feel like I'm dying a thousand little deaths, yet still am desperate to fall on his sword and suffer a cruel, delicious fate. This isn't normal. No one should be able to feel this incredible and so tortured all at once.

I'm still shivering when Legion rises to his knees. I lick my lips as he unfastens his jeans and slides them down to the middle of his thighs. His proud, heavy hardness pulses wildly with its own sinuous heartbeat. Holy shit. It looks bigger. Thicker. How the hell…? I can't even explain it. But all I want to do is wrap my lips around him, if only to see if he tastes as delectable as he looks. However, when Legion grips my thigh and flips me over onto my stomach in one swift maneuver, then perches my ass in the air, I realize he has other plans for my mouth.

"Bite the pillow." His voice is level, but there's an edge of viciousness to it.

I do as I'm told, and just in time. Because in the next breath, Legion spreads me open and he licks me from my dripping wet sex up to my tight, puckered hole. I gasp, the unfamiliar sensation so intense that I nearly collapse. That's all it takes for me to be on the cusp of another orgasm. That's all I need before I'm whimpering into the pillow, begging for him to fuck me senseless. He must have heard my pleas because, in the next moment, he rips me to shreds in one hard, soul-shattering thrust.

I cry out into my feather down silencer, a mix of pain, shock, and undeniable pleasure rippling through me, as he fucks me deep and hard and fast. My belly is on fire with his violent intrusion, and the hotter I get, the more I buck back against him, eager for him to singe my insides with his seed. But he doesn't show signs of slowing. If anything, my coaxing only encourages him. And when I feel his hand slip between our bodies to fondle my tight seam, I moan so loudly that I don't even recognize my voice. Not even the pillow can muffle my cries as he presses into that puckered place and slowly slides a thick finger inside me to the knuckle.

I feel so full, so heavy. My thighs are shaking uncontrollably and I'm afraid I'll collapse from the intense pleasure at any moment. He must feel it too, because with one arm banded around my waist, Legion lifts my torso so that we're chest to back. His strokes never falter, even as he reaches down to play with my clit, adding to the severe sensation at my backside. And as he holds me close, fully supporting my sagging body, I feel his lips on my neck, his breath hot.

"*So He drove the man out; and at the east of the garden of Eden,*" he recites gruffly, "*He stationed the cherubim and the flaming sword which turned every direction to guard the way to the tree of life."*

I don't know what to make of it. Honestly, with him so deep inside of me, I can't even comprehend the significance of the scripture. And before I can possibly begin to decipher it, I feel his teeth on my skin, in the space between my neck and my shoulder. The sharp sting of pain is enough to make me yelp, but somehow the sound translates into a moan. And with his fangs still embedded in my flesh, he groans—guttural and animalistic—and I feel him throb wildly inside of me. His strokes turn jerky as he empties fire and vengeance within my womb, and seconds later, I'm coming again, shouting words of worship and sacrilege.

He holds me until we both still. And when I'm no longer able to sit up, Legion lays me down on the bed, covering my naked frame with the silk sheets. He could leave, and I wouldn't be able to protest, too spent and sated to say a damn word. But to my surprise, he settles down beside me, pulling me to rest my head on his chest.

Not even that hideous dragon whispers a word as we catch our breath and bask in the afterglow of orgasm. And I drift off into a dreamless sleep, swathed in fire.

NINE

I WAKE UP ALONE, BUT I'M NOT SURPRISED. IF ANYTHING, I'm relieved, if only to have a few moments of peace to wrap my head around what went down just hours before.

I told Legion I wanted to talk. *Talk.* And somehow we did very little of that. Not to mention, I didn't even get to the bottom of that little rendezvous in the hallway between him and Adriel. However, if last night is any indication of where he and I stand, then I have nothing to worry about.

I think.

I hope.

I stumble out of bed, naked, sore, and shattered. My legs are weak, and I have to hold on to the bedpost to keep from falling over. Shit. What was that? Legion and I have had great sex before. Amazing sex, even. But this was something else. This was next level fucking with a side of sadism. The monster inside him—that terrifyingly beautiful dragon—demanded blood. And while I've never been into the BDSM scene, I can't deny that it was hot as fuck when Legion bit my lip. And probed my ass. And bit my neck.

Speaking of…

I stagger to the bathroom to assess the damage, and low and behold, there's an angry, purplish bite mark where his teeth claimed me. Honestly, it's not as bad as I expected it to be considering the sting it caused. I could have sworn he went all *True Blood* on me, but it looks like he barely broke the skin. Unless…

Unless he did, and I've got a bit of that supernatural healing. Still, it's noticeable as hell, and I can't very well walk around looking like a *fangbanger*.

After bathing (very carefully around my tender nether regions), I slip on a pair of workout leggings and a heather grey hoodie, hoping it hides the lust lesion. My hair goes up in a messy top knot, and I shove my feet into a pair of Nike trainers. Sore or not, I have work to do. Uriel and his rogue angels don't give a damn about my sex hangover.

As per my new routine, I stop in to visit with Sister, who is in high spirits as she watches some ridiculous court TV show with Cain over their shared breakfast of fresh fruit and croissants. Cain nods at me when I enter, yet makes no move to leave. Okaaay.

"How are you feeling today?" I ask my sister, placing a soft peck on the side of her head that isn't bandaged.

"Good!" she smiles, her big brown eyes twinkling. "I'm feeling better every day. Phenex says they'll be preparing me for a skin graft soon. However, with all the superhuman technology they have here, they may be able to accelerate the process and skip a few of the more painful steps."

"It's still risky, Mare," Cain interjects. Concern furrows his brow. "This type of stuff hasn't been tested on humans. It could be dangerous for you."

Mare? And the way he talks to her—like he's an integral part of the decision-making—it's weird. I don't know if I'll ever get used to their bond, even if it is good for her.

"I know, I know." She smiles sweetly at him, as if he's the most handsome man she's ever laid eyes on and not a disfigured demon assassin. "But I want to get out of this bed. I *need* to get out of this bed. And you need to get back to saving the world instead of babysitting me."

Cain shakes his head. "I'm not babysitting you. Buttery pastries and shit television? Are you kidding me? This is a vacation. And the best part is that I get to pass the time with some damn good company."

Under normal circumstances, this would be the part where I start with the gagging noises. But the way he looks at her, and the way she gazes back at him…I can't begrudge them that.

I take up the seat on Sister's other side and join in on the mindless court TV watching, which turns out to be just as crazy as I expect. Some guy with a mouthful of gold teeth, cornrows, *and* a receding hairline is suing a woman for $40, the cost of a date gone wrong. When the judge asks why the date was so awful, the man asks if he can perform a song he wrote about it, seeing as he's an up-and-coming rapper at the ripe old age of forty-two. I laugh and shake my head at the sheer ridiculousness and munch on the extra croissant that

Sister insisted I eat.

It's nice. It almost feels normal. I can remember all the times we sat on our old, funky sofa, eating junk food, and watching crap reality shows on our tiny TV. For that thirty minutes to an hour, our lives didn't seem so bad. Obviously, others had it much worse if they had to prance around like idiots on national television for our entertainment. And now look at us…in a mansion, with state-of-the-art everything, and yet I miss that crappy old apartment. I miss the mundaneness of our lives, and how the scariest thing that lurked in the shadows was a wanna-be gangster or a crackhead desperate enough to try to mug someone for his next fix. Don't get me wrong—I like that I've found my place in this fucked up world and have someone worth fighting for. But I miss…I don't know…being human.

After the show ends, I say my goodbyes with a promise to drop by later.

"You've got me this afternoon," Cain says before I can clear the room. "Weapons training."

Oh yeah. *That*. "Got it," I nod.

Cain looks about as excited as I feel. Fighting is one thing, but holding a gun? Using a gun? Or even a sword like Toyol uses? I can't even wrap my head around that.

I don't see Legion anywhere when I enter the gym, but the rest of the Se7en are present. Each of them is either too occupied with their training to even notice my presence, or they're still not comfortable with my Nephilim heritage. Whatever. I hop on the treadmill, remembering what Crysis said about cardio. I am out of shape. I wasn't athletic in school, although I was more tomboy than girly girl. If I could be categorized into a group, I'd say I fit in more with the Stoners. But drugs weren't really my thing. Yeah, I smoked a little here and there, but it was only to help me drown out the voices in my head and to relieve the crippling guilt. And the pain. I hated to admit it, but being abused and abandoned hurt like a motherfucker. And I had the scars—both physical and emotional—to prove it.

"You're going to pass out if you don't hydrate."

I frown at Crysis and pull my earbuds out. "Huh?" I question, although I heard him perfectly. Another symptom of my newfound pedigree.

"You need to drink water, Eden," he instructs. "Just because you're half immortal, doesn't mean you're not susceptible to human weakness."

I hit the Stop button on the treadmill and note the timer. Thirty minutes. The hell? I've never jogged that long, let alone run. And I hardly feel winded. Maybe it was Chance the Rapper in my ears or the hit of carbs from the croissant, but somehow, I've managed to do five miles while barely breaking a sweat.

Damn.

Crysis gives me a knowing grin. "Your body is adjusting. Keep pushing it. It'll adapt as long as you will it to."

"But I didn't will it to," I reply, stepping off the treadmill. It's true. Yesterday, I was actually trying, and I felt like I was the verge of passing out. Today, I just wasn't thinking about it, too consumed with other shit to notice my pace.

"Maybe not consciously, but this…" He brings a hand up to gently flick my forehead. "…is a lot more powerful than you could ever imagine. The average human uses only a small fraction of their brain. Nephilim are able to tap into a much higher percentage, allowing certain abilities to manifest. Your brain was locked by your father. Pulling Adriel out of you must have undone whatever spell he cloaked you with."

I roll my eyes. I don't care how nice Adriel seems to everyone else. I don't trust her. Just the sound of her name makes me want to hit something.

"Cool story, bro. Now can we get to work?"

Reading my mind, or maybe just seeing the need for me to work on my fighting skills, Crysis leads me to the heavy bag. He positions himself opposite of me and holds it in place.

"Do your worst, half-breed," he jibes.

I flip him off. "Um, don't I get some gloves? Or tape at least?"

"Will you have on gloves when you step outside Irin's gates and have to fight for your life?"

"No."

"Then you won't have them on now. Mind over matter, Eden. Your brain is stronger, but so is your body."

I take a deep breath and let it out through my nose. "Whatever you say, sensei." Then I punch the heavy canvas sack with all my might.

Pain blasts through my knuckles, through my wrist, and up to my elbow.

"Motherfucker!" I yelp, shaking my arm to stave off the ache.

Crysis is on the verge of a laugh, and if I weren't already hurting, I'd knock that smirk right off his handsome face. "Good. That's good. A hit like that would've shattered your hand if you were human. Look at it."

I look down and find that while my fist is a good shade of bright red, it's still intact. I could've sworn I had scraped all the skin off my knuckles.

"See? You're capable of more than you could ever imagine. Now just get a handle on your pain. Block it out, just like you blocked out the exhaustion while you were running. Don't think of hitting the heavy bag. Think of crushing an enemy's skull with your bare hands. That's not your bones you hear cracking. It's not you who is feeling that pain. Channel it—the rage, the fear, the resentment. Take it and use it to your advantage."

Unlucky for Crysis, I have enough rage, fear, and resentment for three lifetimes. Because after a few more hits with me biting down on the pain in my hands, I find my stride. And soon even he can't hold the bag steady without feeling the impact of my blows. And that skull I'm crushing? It's not one of an enemy. At least not an enemy to the rest of them. But anyone who threatens my happiness and peace of mind—anyone who thinks they can smile sweetly to my face then turn around and try to take what's mine, is certainly not my friend.

I don't even realize I've drawn a crowd until Crysis calls for a break. Everyone regards me with expressions of shock and appreciation, nodding at me with esteem, even a few approving smiles. Everyone except for Adriel, who stands in the doorway of the gym, arms crossed over her chest. Her green eyes glow with something I can only describe as steely resolve, and her perfect pout is flattened into a tight line.

Crysis follows my line of vision, then looks back to me. "We're done for the morning."

"No." I break my vengeful stare only to glare at him with

determination. "More."

He shakes his head. "Not like this, Eden. You need to get your shit on straight."

"My shit *is* straight," I snap. "I'm never going to learn if you keep handling me with kid gloves. You said so yourself—I'm stronger than I think. But none of that means jack shit if I don't know how to fight."

Crysis looks away and shakes his head again. The Se7en take it as their cue to disperse and resume their own workouts. I guess a spat amongst Nephilim is none of their concern. Honestly, they probably wouldn't mind if we ripped each other apart.

"Fine. But no more of the heavy bag. You wanna fight someone? Fight me. For real."

I nod, but I'm inwardly nervous at the thought of going toe to toe with him. Crysis is light years ahead of me in strength and technique. He was raised by the Alliance, so he's been a soldier his entire life. And now that he's almost at 100% after being tortured by his own brethren, I'm pretty sure he could kick my ass in two seconds flat. Hell, yesterday he wasn't even trying, and I saw stars a few times.

Yet, my pride won't let me back down, and I follow him into the ring. There's no way I'm punking out with Adriel watching.

Realizing I'm drenched in sweat, I strip off my hoodie so that I'm down to a sports bra and tank top, and approach the middle of the ring, my hands up to guard my face.

"What the fuck is that?" Crysis drops his fists and stands straight up from his fighter's stance.

I frown. "Huh?"

"Your neck, Eden. What the fuck…is that a bite mark?"

Shit.

I clutch my neck, my eyes darting around frantically, praying no one else noticed. "It's nothing."

But if they didn't notice, they surely heard. "Nothing, my ass!" Crysis shouts. "Are you fucking kidding me? Please tell me you're not that stupid. You cannot be that hard up for dick that you would let *him* fucking take a bite out of you."

"Will you shut the fuck up?" I whisper harshly. Hand still shielding my neck, I scurry to where I tossed my hoodie and shove it back on.

"No, I will not. You know…" He snorts, shaking his head. "I knew you were naïve as shit, but I never thought you were so blind that you'd risk your life. Maybe I was wrong about you being mentally stronger. Because all I see is you acting like a brain-dead gutter rat who would rather be beaten by her abusive boyfriend than be alone."

I nearly flinch at the sting of his words, my face burning hot. "Don't pretend to know me. You don't know shit about me, so please spare me the righteous indignation. I'm not the one who's on the run from their own brothers after being caught for being two-faced."

"No, you're just on the run from your own father after he made you then left you with a mother who didn't want you either."

And that's it. That's the finishing blow to my already fractured heart.

I knew Crysis didn't like the idea of me with Legion—I get that. But for him to go there? What drives a person to cut someone that deep over a petty grudge? I did nothing to him.

If anything, I'm the only reason why he's here and still breathing, because Niko knows what he means to me. *Meant* to me. A friend doesn't purposely try to hurt someone just for the fuck of it, just because he doesn't like what goes down between two consenting adults. What Legion and I have is none of his fucking business. Better yet, *I'm* none of his fucking business.

"Fuck. You," I spit, turning to exit the ring.

"Eden, look…"

"Shut your fucking mouth. Don't even whisper my fucking name. We're done."

I march over and snatch up my iPod and earbuds. I can feel Crysis on my heels.

"I shouldn't have said that. I'm sorry."

"Fuck your sorry, and fuck you."

I turn towards the only exit, ready to escape this gym and this day. Even through the angry tears burning my eyes, I can clearly see a trail of fiery red hair retreating from the gym.

Adriel heard and saw everything. And that hurts just as much as Crysis's betrayal.

TEN

"E? You ok? Open up or I'm breaking the door down."

Niko has been knocking on my door for the past five minutes. No doubt, he's heard about what went down between Crysis and me. Shit, I wouldn't be surprised if even Irin's staff was buzzing about the ordeal.

Fuck. Me.

High school sucked enough. I hated being the topic of gossip then, and I hate it even more now.

"Come on, open up. I have food. And booze."

"I'm not hungry," I call out, my voice hoarse from crying.

I hate that I let myself break like that. I hate that I fucking cared enough about him to allow him to hurt me. I've been called every name in the book and didn't give a damn about it, just like I didn't give a damn about the person spewing the insults. But Crysis…I thought he was my friend. And when you grow up not having many of those, losing just one feels like a knife to the heart.

"Well, I'm hungry," Niko says. "Let me in so you can watch me eat and tell me how good I look doing it."

I chuckle, even though I don't want to, but don't respond.

"Seriously, I will break this door down."

I roll my eyes and drag myself from the bed and across the room. "No, you will not," I say by way of greeting, swinging the door open. "Irin would be pissed. She probably paid a fortune for it."

"Eh," Niko shrugs. "I can afford it."

As promised, he has food and booze, and somehow, he looks gloriously handsome in a navy blue button up and slacks, all perfectly tailored to his lean yet muscular body. Meanwhile, I'm still gross in my workout clothes.

Niko enters the room and sets down the tray of food and drinks. No wine today. He's gone straight for the scotch. The good stuff too.

"What's all this?" I question. It's barely early afternoon.

"This is letting you get me drunk so you can take advantage of me." He uncovers the domed plates, revealing cheeseburgers, fries, and macaroni and cheese. Trans fats and comfort food. I could kiss him right now.

Still, I retort, "I can't eat that, and I damn sure can't drink that. I have weapons training with Cain."

"Not anymore, you don't." He plucks up a fry and stuffs it into his mouth. "Some super-secret Se7en thing. Besides, you need a day off."

"A day off? I'm not even on the job yet."

"Well, I need a day off," he shrugs.

As much as I want to pretend that Crysis's words didn't get to me and that I can dust our fight off my shoulders, I have to admit that hiding out with junk food and Niko's easy personality is more than tempting. Plus, I am starving.

I snag a couple fries of my own in resignation. "What super-secret Se7en stuff?"

"I don't know. But they all disappeared to their section of the house. Not even the staff is allowed entry to that hallway. Must be serious."

Strange. And kinda disheartening. The Se7en saw what went down and heard every word, meaning that Legion heard every word. I had expected him to check on me, not that I'm not grateful for Niko. But in a way, I'm glad Legion didn't come. I was embarrassed in that gym. I was humiliated and demeaned. I don't want to show that weakness to anyone, especially him.

As if knowing where my thoughts are headed, Niko cracks open the bottle of scotch and pours us each a few fingers worth. I take my offered glass and sip. The searing burn is soothing to the lump still caught in my throat.

"Wanna talk about it?" he asks, taking a swig of his own drink.

"Nope."

One stiff nod. "Ok."

We take our plates to the bed where we sit and eat and avoid talking about anything of substance. Niko woos me with stories of his home, Skiathos, and what it was like to grow up as the little prince of the Dark in his older brother's shadow.

"Compared to Dorian, I was a spoiled, entitled little shit."

"Noooo," I jibe. "Not you!"

"You laugh, but if you knew half the shit I'd done, you may never speak to me again."

I shrug. "We've all got skeletons. I'm no angel." I shake my head and chuckle. "Well, only *half* angel."

"You honestly don't give yourself enough credit, E. Yeah, you're a bit rough around the edges, but it's not your fault." He lays a hand on mine, his skin cool to the touch. "And it doesn't make you desperate or stupid to want to love and be loved. It makes you human. Something I only got a taste of. And let me tell you, I'd trade anything—*anything*—to have that once again, even for just a moment."

"Thanks," I reply with a solemn half smile, determined not to cry again. I take a cleansing breath. "Now pour me another glass. It's our day off."

Two burgers, a pile of fries, a heaping mound of mac and cheese, and a bottle of scotch later, we're laying on our backs, side by side, staring at the ceiling.

I made Niko tell me everything about him, from how his one and only true love was sent to change his heart so he could one day save Gabriella, to the twisted shit he did to impress Lucifer and get in his good graces.

"He told you…about Legion," I utter. "Didn't he? He knew what would happen if he was unleashed on the world a second time."

"He didn't have to."

"You think he has it in check? I mean, he doesn't seem like a murderous beast that wants to wipe out mankind. To me, nothing has changed. But then sometimes…I don't know. It's like he's not there. Like he's dead inside. I know he's different, but I just don't know *how* different."

"Does he love you?"

I turn to face him, my brow furrowed in surprise. "What?"

"Do you think Legion loves you?"

I turn back to look up at the ceiling, if only to hide my reddening face. "I don't know. I don't even know if he's capable of it. But when I'm with him, and he holds me so tight to him as if he's afraid I'll slip away, and I'm filled with an overwhelming sense of peace and safety, I think to myself, "this must be what love feels like.""

"Awww, that's beautiful as shit, E," Niko muses, a smile in his voice. I reach over and pinch his side and nearly break a nail against the hard muscle. He laughs when I jerk my hand back. "But in all seriousness…if he loves you, he'll always come back to you. Even when it feels like you've lost him. He'll find his way back to you."

I scoot closer and lay my head on his shoulder. "Old guys are so wise."

"Old? I'm an infant compared to the dinosaur you're fucking."

I can't argue with that, so I just laugh. I laugh until tears spring from my eyes. And this time, I don't mind them.

I know I drift off to sleep, but I don't remember it. All I know is that when I wake up, my head is pounding and the room is dark. Shit. I better not have slept the day away. I promised Sister I'd come back to see her. I hate not following through, plus I wanted to get more information about the skin graft.

After dragging my ass out of bed, rinsing my mouth out, and taking a much needed shower, I go in search of my first priority: water. I hate to say it, but maybe that asshole, Crysis, was right. I need to hydrate.

After gulping down a gallon from the kitchen, I roam into what I've deemed the ballroom to find Lilith and Andras sitting at the bar, a half a dozen magazines, a laptop, and a couple iPads in front of them. Andras is scribbling something on a pad of paper while Lilith holds up two fabric swatches.

"Hey," Andras calls out without looking up from his notebook. "Come here; we need your opinion on this."

I look around. There's no one else here.

Lilith and Andras both turn and face me at the same time. It's like they share a brain.

"Yes. Please tell us which one would work better for the party," Lilith chimes. "We can't decide."

I walk over tentatively. Before today, I wasn't sure if I even existed in their eyes.

"Um, sure," I say. Lilith holds up the shimmering swatches. "They both look like gold to me."

"What?" she scoffs. "Clearly this is Honeycomb, and this is Anjou Pear." She holds them up to my face so I can get a better look.

"Oh. Well…this one?" I say pointing to the more metallic of the two shades.

"That's what I said!" she exclaims.

"This isn't Vegas," Andras grumbles. "Gold doesn't have to be gaudy."

"It won't be," Lilith retorts. "I'm going for old Hollywood

glam with a touch of goth."

I scan the books and samples sprawled out on the bar top. "This is all for the party?"

"Yes!" Lilith nods enthusiastically. She sets down the fabric and begins an online search for stemware.

"You do realize that this is a party to—I don't know—trap a horde of killer archangels?"

"We're aware." Lilith looks up from the laptop and paints on a tight smile that doesn't meet her clear, blue eyes. "This might be our last chance to do something like this. I know it's silly, and our time should be invested in about a billion other things, but if our time on this planet is limited, I think we should make the most of every single second."

Her solemn expression, the sadness in her voice…she doesn't believe they'll survive this. Words escape me, so I simply nod. I hadn't even considered how scared they must be, which is saying something considering I can't imagine them being afraid of anything. And while Lilith and I have had our differences, I can't deny that she was once my friend. Even if it was all a ruse on her end. I cared for her. And if I'm being honest with myself, I don't want to see her dead.

"Besides," she perks, turning back to the laptop, "wait until you see your dress! You're going to look so stunning, no man or beast within a fifty mile radius will be able to keep their eyes off you."

"She's right, you know," Andras adds. "The dress is amazing. And with your newly unveiled Nephilim blood—" He scents the air as if he can smell the essence racing in my veins, "you'll be downright irresistible."

I shiver. I can't imagine a bunch supernatural creatures

sniffing around like I'm their dinner. I hadn't even thought about that, and now that I have, I'm kinda freaking out about it. Maybe that's why the Se7en have been so distant with me. At least I hope that's the only reason.

"It looks good," I remark, not sure how to respond. "You guys are doing a great job."

They each mumble their thanks, too absorbed with party planning to look up, so I slink away and head for the medical wing. Of course, Sister is fast asleep with Cain knocked out in his recliner beside her. I guess whatever super-secret Se7en business that had pulled him away earlier is over now. Normally, I would question them, demanding I be kept in the loop, but I just don't know if it's my place now. They felt an obligation to me, as I was cursed with the Calling with an angel taking up residence in my body. But I'm not anymore. So where does that leave me? Technically, I'm not their problem anymore.

Feeling like a total slacker after an afternoon of day drinking and burger bingeing with Niko, I decide that I should probably hit the gym. It's dark and empty, so I have the whole place to myself. I start to flip on a light so I'm not stumbling around blind, but then I wonder…what if I've got some freaky night vision? I'm not even sure if that's possible, but it doesn't hurt to try.

Deep breath. Eyes closed. When I reopen them, I try to focus on penetrating the dark, zeroing in on the blurry shadows before me.

Nothing.

I try again, channeling light and clarity. I stare into obscurity for what seems like hours, my eyes straining and burning.

Something shifts, as if the darkness flutters, but it happens so quickly that I can't be sure of what I saw.

Resigning to defeat, I rub my aching eyes and flick on the lights. I have no idea what I'm doing. But there's no way I'm relying on Crysis for help, not after what went down earlier. So from here on out, I'm on my own with Nephilim training.

Taking advantage of the privacy, I ditch the earbuds and crank up my workout playlist before hopping on the treadmill. And somehow, a quick cardio warm-up turns into 3.5 miles of full-on sprinting on the highest incline. My mind was so consumed with my spat with Crysis, uncertainty with Legion, and the upcoming party that I didn't even realize it until glanced down. I've never been an athlete, and I damn sure didn't run from anything or anyone. And to be honest, it feels kinda good to know that my body is capable of more than I could have ever dreamed. For so long, I relied on my secret ability to bend the wills of humans as a defense mechanism. But now...now I can be a force to be reckoned with both mentally and physically.

I hit the weights and am damn grateful that no one is here. I have no clue what I'm doing, and I'm sure I look like an idiot. Still, even with my muscles screaming for mercy, it seems like nothing is *too* heavy.

So...

Insane endurance, check.

Super strength, check.

Crazy mind tapping ability, check.

Now I'm a little excited about weapons training with Cain, if only to see what else I can do.

I've moved on to the speed bag, music blasting, my body

working seamlessly to a smooth rhythm, when I feel it.

The hair on the backs of my arms stands up straight. There's a tingling sensation at my nape. The air all around me feels charged with an electrical current.

I'm not alone in here.

I frantically scan the room, but it appears to still be empty. That means absolutely nothing though, not when cloaking spells and wards are a legit part of my world. Still, I can't fight what I can't see, so I gather my stuff and hurry the hell out of there.

Just before I hit the hallway, I get a whiff of something familiar that makes me freeze in my tracks. Something I had forced myself to forget.

Belladonna blooms.

Sex.

Blood.

I race to my room as quickly as I can and lock the door behind me.

ELEVEN

WEAPONS TRAINING KICKS OFF FIRST THING IN the morning, and even though I'm still a bit shaken about the night before, I'm pretty pumped to see what Cain has in store for me.

Fortunately, I don't have to wait to find out.

"We'll start with the basics. Beretta M9, the standard issue military pistol. Sleek, concealable, reliable as fuck. It's like the Toyota Corolla of firearms."

Cain picks up a loaded mag and glides it into the pistol before pulling the slide back with a daunting click, a round securely chambered. It all happens within seconds. His movements are careful, skilled. For a demon that's known for brute strength and ruggedness, his handling of the weapon is strangely meticulous, if not graceful.

"Now when you have a slightly bigger job on your hands,"

he begins, carefully setting down the M9, "you want a bit more muscle." He picks up a gun that looks as long as my forearm. "The Desert Eagle. I prefer the .50 AE."

Unload. Reload. One in the chamber.

He picks up another, and I watch with wide fascination at the sheer beauty and splendor of his expertise. Before now, Cain had only seemed frightening and brash. Now, with him explaining the intricate details of each firearm, I see that he is so much more than he allows others to see. He's smart as hell, passionate, precise. I can see why he's Legion's right.

"Now this is your boy's favorite toy, for obvious reasons," he explains, holding up a steel grey handgun and placing it in my hands.

"My boy?" I absorb the heft of the gun, careful not drop it. It's freakin' *heavy*. Especially for its compact size.

"Sig Sauer P229 Legion."

Just the sound of his name makes my cheeks go hot with the remembrance of the last time his hands were on my body, and the implication that he is *mine* in any way. I still wear his mark on my neck, lovely little scars of the teeth he sank into my body as he emptied his fire into my womb. I lick my dry lips and set the handgun down.

"Heard there was some secret Se7en emergency yesterday. What happened?" I question. This may be the only time I get Cain alone. And while he may tell me to *fuck off*, it's worth a shot.

Cain shakes his head, but answers, "L isn't as…reserved… as he used to be. The half-breed was about to get his throat ripped out after what he said to you. Took us all to calm him down."

"Wait…what?" I frown.

"Don't act so surprised. Had it not been for Irin's accord, your Nephilim buddy would have been choking on his own blood the moment he fixed his lips to insult you. You had to have known that shit wouldn't fly, especially now that he's…"

Cain shrugs, his expression grim. He doesn't have to finish his thought. I can tell even he is struggling with Legion's rebirth. They're friends…brothers. And have been for centuries. Maybe I'm not the only one Legion has been distancing himself from.

"So, is he ok now?" I run my fingers over the cool, polished steel in front of me out of nervous energy.

"As good as one can expect," Cain responds. "Let's just say it's a good thing Irin's house is fucking huge."

I nod my understanding just as Cain turns to me, a slate grey pistol nestled atop his palm.

"This pretty thing is for you. Glock 43. Sleek, compact, yet powerful." He places it in my hand, and I reluctantly grasp it. "Decent grip, so you shouldn't have any problem handling it. How does it feel?"

"Good. Comfortable." It's the truth too. Out of all the handguns he's had me hold, this one seems to fit me just right. He knows his stuff.

I nod along as Cain runs down the specs for the Glock, pretending like I understand what he's talking about. It's just surreal to me. And incredibly intimidating.

"Go ahead and give her a try," he suggests.

"Huh?"

Cain nods to the other end of the room, where a target is suspended from the ceiling. "Shoot it."

"Ummmm," I begin, my eyes darting around the room. "I doubt that's safe."

"Why not? We're underground. The walls are solid concrete. That's what this room is for."

He's right. I know I shouldn't have been, but I was more than a little shocked when Cain led me down here. I'd seen the stairwell beside the gym before, but there was no way in hell I was going to willingly explore The Watcher's dungeon. Fuck that. To my surprise, there weren't any rabid beasts or sex slaves chained and shackled, but a shooting range with a pretty extensive collection of firearms.

Cain presents two more gifts: safety goggles and protective earmuffs. "Since you're a beginner, I'll let you get away with these. Don't get used to them though."

Grateful, I slip them on then I look to the other end of the room, mentally psyching myself up for the task ahead. This shit is so far out of my comfort zone that my hand is shaking as I raise it to aim.

"Easy. Deep breaths," Cain instructs, placing his palm over my hand to help soothe the trembling. "Just aim, inhale, and squeeze the trigger on an exhale. You got this."

I close my eyes, channeling my courage. When I open them, I do just as Cain says: aim, inhale, exhale, shoot.

It's a sensation I've never felt before. A sense of release, of calm, yet an exhilarating thrill trembles through me, rattling my bones. It's like a gulp of oxygen after being held under water. I've heard of shooting being cathartic to some, but never in my wildest dreams did I ever expect this. A tingling energy simmers at my fingertips, seducing me with the need to squeeze the trigger once more. I fire off another round, then another, watching as bullets slice through the air and burn through the paper target.

"Feels good, doesn't it?" Cain grins after I've emptied the mag and slipped off the earmuffs.

"Yeah," I admit sheepishly. Honestly, it felt more than good. It was intoxicating. Empowering, even.

He looks toward the target, and to my surprise, I've actually managed to hit more than air.

"Pretty good. Next time, aim for the head. Headshots with silver are the only thing that will take a demon down."

I nod, a bit rattled by his statement. Shooting in a controlled environment is one thing, but shooting demons? He's teaching me how to kill his own kind.

"And what about angels?"

Cain busies his hands with reloading the gun, but answers, "Just like demons, there are lesser angels. We suspect that's who Uriel has managed to sway." When he looks up, a disturbed line is etched between his brows. "Until now, we've never needed a reason to kill them."

A dark torment roils within his eyes, and I look away, unable to decipher the root of his confliction. I don't relish the prospect of killing anyone, especially not an angel. But if the reports are true, this seems like a kill or be killed situation. Surely the Demon of Murder understands that. If anything, I would think he'd be delighted to cut down Uriel's zealots.

After a bit more target practice, we head back up to the gym, and all buoyant feelings of victory are quickly admonished as I come face to face with Crysis, looking more solemn and defeated than I've ever seen him.

Fuck. I was not ready for this. And, for his sake, it's a good thing we left the guns in the basement.

"Eden, please. Let me explain."

I swiftly brush by Crysis, my jaw tight with contempt. Cain steps aside, but I can feel his eyes on me. If what he said about Legion flipping his shit is true, he's probably preparing to step in before things escalate.

"Will you just hear me out? I didn't mean what I said."

"So you're a liar?" I spit back, not even bothering to turn to face him. I head straight for the heavy bag, the urge to punch something so strong that my fists are shaking at my sides.

"No. But what I said…" He stands on the other side of the bag, holding it in place. Bold move. How easy it would be for my hand to slip *accidentally*.

"What you said was fucked up," I finish, slamming my fist into the hefty sack. I'd like for it to be his face, but a few of the Se7en are here working out, and many of Irin's servants are milling about in the hallway. I don't need witnesses. "What you said was exactly what you've always thought about me. Nothing but gutter trash that's too desperate and too pathetic to know when she's getting played."

"I didn't say that." He slightly winces as he absorbs the impact of another blow.

"You didn't have to. I saw the way you looked at me." Jab. Punch. Hook. "I felt your disgust." Jab. Punch. Hook. "You really think I could ever forgive you after that shit?"

"Well, you forgave him after he took a bite out of you."

I pause, standing straight up. The heavy bag swings back and forth between us.

"Leave," I demand, my voice low and as cold as ice.

"No. Not until you—"

"I said, leave, Crysis. Or Legion's temper will be the least of your worries."

He makes a face, as if the threat amuses him. "What are you going to do, Eden? Throw me out?"

"Leave. Now!"

With all the fiery rage within me, I knot my hand into a fist and strike the bag. A burst of blinding light explodes around it, the sheer force of the blow causing Crysis to go flying back into a display of kettlebells several yards away. The heavy bag is nothing more than flecks of ash raining down around me.

What.

The.

Fuck.

Cain is at Crysis's side in an instant, hoisting him to his feet. Phenex and Andras race over from their stations to help him.

No one dares to come near me.

"What...what was that?" Lilith says from behind me. I don't have to turn around to know that she's regarding me with a mix of shock and horror. I can see it so plainly on everyone else's faces.

"I...I..." I look down at my hand and flex it, turning it over. I can't explain what happened any more than they can. "I don't know."

"Eden..." Phenex takes a tentative step toward me, his palms raised. He's using that voice again, the one that sounds like he's trying to pacify a wild, vicious animal. And that wild, vicious animal is me. "Are you ok?"

I nod. "I think so."

Another step forward. "You know I would never hurt you."

"I know. And I would never hurt you."

His eyes flick over my shoulder for just a fraction of a second, and he gives a single, sharp nod. "Good. That's good."

Phenex slowly walks until only six feet separate us. Behind him, Andras and Cain help a dazed Crysis to a bench.

"Can you tell me what you're feeling? Physically? Emotionally?"

I think I shrug. "I don't know. Confused?"

"Any pain? Nausea?"

A shake of my head. "No."

"What about when you hit the bag...when your hand was engulfed in flames of light? Did it burn you?"

"No."

"And before that? What were you feeling?"

I glance over to where Crysis is slumped over on the bench, elbows to his knees and his head down. I feel terrible for what I've done, but still, I answer truthfully.

"Rage."

And like always, I feel him before I see him. Before I hear that gravelly baritone. Before I scent the clean sweat and midnight jasmine on his skin.

"What happened?" The question is a demand, yet no one speaks. Every gaze darts around wildly, as if the answers lie somewhere within the falling ash.

I turn around and face him, the man who is the source of my carnal weakness and my greatest fears. Legion strides to me without stopping, without any consideration for his own safety, and gently grasps my shoulders. His touch is hot, but I don't feel it. I don't feel anything.

"Eden, talk to me. Are you hurt?"

"No," I answer truthfully, shaking my head.

He glares over to where Crysis is still trying to regain the wind that was blasted out of him, and a low growl escapes between his teeth.

"It wasn't his fault." I reach up and squeeze the top of a hand, holding him to me. "I was hitting the heavy bag. I must have…I must have hit it too hard."

He looks down at the hand atop his and turns it over in his palm before bringing it between us. The scratch of his callused fingers makes me shiver as he runs them over my knuckles. He doesn't say a thing, but the look on his face speaks of awe and reverence. And when he brings my hand to his lips and kisses each knuckle, a part of me is filled with relief and un-abashed joy. Whatever I managed to do in those moments of uncontained fury did not scare him. No. Just the opposite. I made him proud.

"Is everything ok?"

At just the sound of her voice, that same fury begins to trickle back in.

"Fine," Legion calls out to Adriel, still holding my hand.

"Eden is apparently a light wielder," Phenex adds. I had forgotten he was even here the very moment Legion put his hands on me.

"That's impossible." Skepticism rings loud and clear in Adriel's voice. I don't have to see her to know that her beautiful face is pinched in disbelief. "There has never been a Nephilim in history that has been able to wield holy light."

"And there has never been a Seraph-made Nephilim," Phenex counters.

At that, Adriel goes quiet. It's Cain who pipes up, leaving Crysis's side. I'm sure neither one of them were thrilled with that scenario.

"I saw it. Her entire hand was consumed by it. I doubt she even knew what she was doing."

"And it appears that her ability is tied to her emotions. Mainly anger. Rage," Phenex explains, reciting the single word I gave him when he asked what I was feeling.

"Makes me wonder just how much of himself Uriel gave to her. He doesn't seem like the type to share." Cain snorts a laugh. Legion narrows his eyes in warning but doesn't dispute his words. He knows about Uriel's unwillingness to share all too much.

Phenex steps to my side, his honey gaze first going to Legion, then to me. "I'd like to run some tests, if that's alright."

"Yeah. I guess," I shrug.

For the first time since we arrived here, something like excitement erupts in Phenex's eyes. "If you can wield His holy light, then there may be other things you can do with it."

"Let's not get ahead of ourselves, Phenex," Legion quietly admonishes.

"Of course." An apologetic bow of his head. "Please come see me at your convenience, Eden."

He swiftly walks out of the gym, a little extra pep in his step. I have no idea what he meant by "other things," but if Phenex is optimistic about my newfound ability, then it can't be all bad.

Still, it doesn't excuse what I did to Crysis. Even if he did deserve it.

I reluctantly slip from Legion's grasp, causing him to frown with confusion. As he watches me cross the room to where Crysis sits with Andras, I'm certain that frown is morphed into one of contempt.

"Crysis?"

Slowly, the handsome, green-eyed Nephilim lifts his head. A lock of wavy blonde hair falls over his sweat-beaded brow.

"Crysis, I'm sorry. I never meant for that to happen. I don't even know what *that* was."

He paints on a pained grin that makes my heart twist with regret. "Does this mean we're even?" he rasps.

"Deal," I nod, before gently placing a hand on his shoulder.

I'm helping him to his feet when Lilith appears in the doorway, her cheeks flushed. I'm not sure when she slipped out, but it must've been her who went to alert Legion.

"Irin has requested an audience."

"Tell her we'll talk later," Legion replies sharply, watching every labored breath Crysis makes as Andras and I help him limp towards the exit.

"She's requested to speak with us *now*." Her gaze goes to me, and something like worry flickers within it. "All of us."

"Shit," Legion curses. The word pretty much represents the grim expressions on everyone's face, aside from Adriel, of course. I can't tell if she's purposely trying to come off as smug or superior. Either one makes her look like an asshole.

"What's wrong?" I whisper to Andras over Crysis's drooped head.

"Irin has one rule," he answers. He turns to me, his blue eyes touched by sorrow. "And you broke it."

TWELVE

NOBODY SPEAKS AS WE WAIT FOR IRIN IN HER chambers. Not even a sarcastic remark from Nikolai, who sits rigidly beside me. Most of the usually cheerful servants have all been dismissed, and the ones who remain are pensive and quiet as they wait for their mistress at the back of the room. Even the vibrant jewel tones seem muted, drab.

I hate to admit it, but I'm scared. Not for myself, but for the people I've put in jeopardy with my unpredictable temper. My sister—what will happen to her if she's thrown out? I can't very well take her to a typical hospital. And my friends—the Se7en, Nikolai, even Crysis—they all have targets on their backs. Until we know who and what is after them, they'd be as good as dead on the streets of Chicago. We could flee the city, the state, maybe even the country, but destruction would follow. You can't outrun fate.

When the gemstone-encrusted doors swing open on a gust of perfumed wind, I'm not sure if I should stand and bow, or stay seated. I follow Legion's lead and simply dip my head, chin to chest. I've never seen him regard Irin with such formality and respect. This is serious.

"Well, well," she muses as she strolls to her place on the curved sectional. "Seems like the gang's all here. So glad you could make it."

Legion begins, "Irin, what happened—"

"I don't believe I was speaking to you," she cuts in, her tone as sharp as knives. "To my knowledge, you were not present. And considering I am omniscient, my knowledge is gospel within these walls."

Legion nods his head in resignation, but the temperature in the room rises by at least ten degrees.

"Temper, temper," Irin tsks. She then turns to me, her eyes as black as night. "My dear, Eden. I was certain I had made myself clear upon your arrival."

I look across the room and meet Phenex's gaze who inclines his head, urging me to answer. "You did, Irin. I apologize. Truly…it was an accident."

"I believe you. But still… Rules are rules." She taps a pointed red fingertip to her lips, pondering words that she already knows she will speak. "However, I do like you, Eden. Very much actually. And while your actions may have been born in rage, I don't believe you intended to hurt our lovely little Nephilim boy. Unless…unless he feels differently."

Every eye goes to Crysis, who looks much better since leaving the gym, save for a bit of swelling on his cheekbone.

With a wince, the blonde man sits up straight, the movement a bit awkward as if his ribs are sore.

"It was an accident. Eden was training. She asked me to leave several times and I didn't listen."

I've barely released a relieved breath when Irin queries, "And why would she ask you to leave?" She knows why. She knows everything: she just wants to fuck with us.

"Because she was angry. I had insulted her. She wasn't ready to forgive me and I tried to force her to."

"So she struck you in anger?"

"No," he shakes his head. "She struck the bag in anger. What happened next was completely out of her control."

Irin sighs, pondering Crysis's explanation. She's already made up her mind about what will happen to me. She just likes to see us squirm.

"Thank you for your honesty. I agree—Eden had no control over the light that she wielded in her heightened emotional state. So here is my ruling: you, Nephilim, will continue to help train her. However, Eden will need someone with first-hand knowledge of the manipulation of holy light." She looks to the redhead at her side and smiles. "Adriel, I'd like you to help Eden get control of her newfound ability. If only to avoid another mishap."

"What?" I all but shriek. "No way."

"*Way*," Irin retorts. "If you want to continue to be a guest in my home, you will need someone to help you get your powers in check."

"No, I don't. And I especially don't need any help from *her*. No. I'm not doing it."

With her next words, Irin's voice echoes with the timbre

of a billion years, rumbling the very ground beneath our feet. "You, your sister, and everyone you care for lives because I allow it, girl. Are you not grateful for the breath in your lungs right now? Because the very second you broke my rule, I could have willed you dead where you stood. I could have made it so that you were never born, wiping your existence from history entirely."

Too shocked, too afraid, and too embarrassed to respond, I simply stare in disbelief at the petite creature glaring black daggers at me. I knew Irin was old, and a being unlike any of us in this room, but I hadn't realized how far her power extended. Not even Legion, at full strength, challenges her ruling. Nikolai won't even look at her.

What *is* she?

"Now," she chirps, all darkness from her tone erased. She snaps her fingers and her perky staff files in with platters of fresh fruit and glasses of wine. "Now that's settled…Legion? What of your scouts in the city?"

Legion steps forward, head high, but I can tell that fire still simmers beneath his silver gaze. "Crime is increasing. The government has moved in, declaring a state of emergency. Military units have been dispatched."

"Any sign of Uriel?"

"No. But the lesser demons…they've become bold. They're showing themselves, even in the day. Countless reports of beasts and ghouls have been received. Toyol has been able to hack into CPD's system and erase a majority of the digital reports, but they're coming in at an alarming rate. Hospitals are overrun with psychiatric patients. They're saying a mysterious gas leak is causing the mass hysteria."

Phenex moves forward, hands steepled under his chin. "We need to make contact with Lucifer. If he can reel in the lesser demons, maybe we can alleviate the destruction in the city."

Everyone turns to Niko, Luc's former wingman. He shakes his head in response, knowing exactly what they're thinking. "Don't look at me. I was sent here on a conditional basis. I have no sway over him."

"He couldn't do anything anyway," Irin points out, plucking a grape from an offered platter. "He'd never allow his pets out of their cages in this magnitude. Someone else is letting them out."

And it hits me.

Niko's release. The reason *why* he wanted to stay in limbo and not return to Earth…

"Stavros," I whisper, my eyes wide with horrified realization. "He's linked to Niko. If Niko gets out, so can he. And if Stavros was the one to help Uriel cloak me for all those years, maybe…maybe he's still working for him, and letting out the lesser demons."

"You really think Stavros has that power?" Cain scoffs.

"He was once the most powerful warlock on Earth," Nikolai answers. "And the only thing worse than a powerful warlock is one with a taste for revenge. Trust me. I've felt the brunt of his vengeance once before."

"Shit," Cain curses. "So what? Luc is just gonna let his stray dogs run free?"

"You know how he is," Andras pipes up. "If it doesn't have shit to do with him, he doesn't care."

"But this does have something to do with him," Phenex

adds. His gaze falls on me. "He wants Eden. He wanted her when he Called her. He wanted her when he stole her away to the underworld. Who's to say that he doesn't want her still?"

"But he let me go," I explain. I look at Legion to find that he, too, is back in that bedroom when he came to find me. I thought he had to fight his way in, when in reality, Lucifer left the door open for him. "Right?"

"He's playing a game," he answers. "Lucifer is prideful. He wants you to come to him by your own volition. He could not take you against your will, so he blackmailed you. And when you still did not warm to his advances, he set you free. This could be a way for him to try to win you back."

The taste of truth is so bitter on my tongue that I have to resist the urge to spit. Because for a few moments, as Lucifer spun me around that grand ballroom in his massive home while his glittering court watched in envy, I felt something other than sheer hatred and contempt for him. I saw something in him that made me want to stay a little longer, hold on a little tighter. And in those tortured minutes when he glamoured me with his charm and power, I began to realize that the man—the monster—that had been revered as the greatest villain in existence was not a villain at all. Misunderstood? Yes. Selfish? Entirely. But there were worse creatures in the world than he. Besides, his brand of evil was one that I could comprehend. In certain lights, it looked a lot like my own.

Lucifer would never change, and I didn't need him to. That's what scares me the most—my undoubted acceptance of who and what he is. He showed me dark. He showed me demented and depraved. And I sat there and watched without flinching, without turning away. Because he had done what

Legion had failed to do. He showed me his true self, and he made no apologies. He didn't hide his ugly. He displayed it proudly without a drop of doubt or shame.

And, strangely, that made me more comfortable, more accepting of my own.

Still, it's not enough. Never enough to make me turn from Legion. No matter what was depicted in my midnight delusions.

"So what now?" Toyol inquires, breaking me from my regretful reverie.

"Andras. Lilith. Where are we on party preparations?" Legion asks.

Andras answers, "Nearly complete."

"You have two days. Irin, with your permission, we'd like to move forward with our plan immediately."

The Watcher nods. "Permission granted. I'll send invites. I'm sure everyone has been wondering why it's been so quiet here."

"Thank you," Legion says with a dip of his head before turning back to Andras and Lilith. "What can you tell me about set up?"

Lilith smiles gleefully, the same way she did when I stumbled upon their planning session. "The theme is Venetian Masquerade. Glitz, glam, with a touch of dark and sexy. It's also the perfect opportunity for us to stay concealed, giving us an extra layer of protection."

"Masquerade? But if everyone is wearing a mask, how will we know who's who?" I ask, my brow pinched in confusion.

"I'll smell them," Legion answers without looking at me. He's in leader mode. "We need surveillance up and running in

24 hours. Toyol?"

"On it. I've also been working on tracking devices that should be good to go within the day."

"Good. Jinn, Phenex, both of you will be on the floor, tracking the crowds. Blend in, listen to conversations, note any suspicious behavior. The Seraph won't be comfortable in this setting. They'll be rigid, most likely staying on the fringes of the crowd. You won't see them imbibing or engaging in lewd behavior."

"So basically they'll be a giant snoozefest," Cain jibes, rolling his eyes.

"More than that," Adriel cuts in. "The Seraph consider themselves superior beings, the Almighty the only one who exceeds their power. If they see humans as no more than ants, other, lesser creatures are the very dirt under their feet. Vampires, warlocks, and the like are abominations, according to them."

"Then why the fuck would they even bother to come?" Cain spits.

"Because as arrogant as they are, they won't let any stone go unturned," Legion answers. "They feel they are doing God's work, even now. *Vengeance is Mine, and retribution, In due time their foot will slip; For the day of their calamity is near, And the impending things are hastening upon them.* The Seraph is the hand of God. *They* are Vengeance."

I shake my head and ask, "But this is Uriel's score to settle, not God's. The rest of them must see that."

"Uriel has had a millennia to spin tales of blasphemy. Who knows what he's led the others to believe."

Great.

So not only are the Seraph out for revenge, he's most likely convinced many of their angel brethren that this is God's will. Because we needed *more* angels after us.

The Se7en continue to discuss plans for the masquerade with Irin chiming in every now and then, and Crysis completely tuning them out. Niko nudges me, noticing that my mind is elsewhere.

"And I thought the Dark and Light had issues," he comments with a half-smile. "The Seraph sound delightful."

"Seriously," I agree.

"So…you up for tomorrow night?" He raises a brow.

"Tomorrow night?"

"The breathing ritual. I'll need to garner my strength before veiling you all."

"Oh." I swallow. "Yeah. Totally."

Noting the uncertainty on my face, Niko assures, "I'll try to make it as comfortable as possible, I promise. It may be awkward at first, but I hope you trust me enough not to cross any lines."

"Of course, I trust you." Hell, he's about the only one I trust. Which is saying something.

"I'll answer any questions you may have beforehand. You may feel a little weak at first, but with your regenerative abilities, it should only last a couple hours."

I place a hand on top of Niko's. "It'll be fine. *I'll* be fine. Whatever you need, I'm your girl. You're doing a huge favor for me…for all of us."

"You sure *all* parties will see it that way?"

I don't have to look across the room to know that Legion has tracked our every movement. So it's no surprise when he cuts in with, "Nikolai, do you have everything you need for the veiling spell?"

Niko shifts to face him, the perfect picture of composure. "The spell requires a great deal of magic. I'll need to siphon it from a source of power. Eden has graciously agreed to be that source."

"Siphon?" Legion's voice is the calm before the storm.

"I'll need to breathe her. Other than Crysis, she's my best bet. The process would be too risky any other way."

"No."

And there it is. The alpha puts his proverbial foot down.

Unfortunately for him, I'm nobody's pet.

"No?" I interject. "I've already agreed. I'm doing this."

"I said no."

"Well, it's not up to you, now is it?"

The entire room braces for his blazing temper as he goes eerily still, his penetrating stare unblinking. He isn't used to being challenged, at least by his subordinates. Well, I am anything but. Maybe once upon a time, I would've listened to him, but that time has come and gone. I'm not some helpless human girl anymore. I'm not his captive. And I will not be kept.

Realizing that I refuse to wither under his simmering rage, Legion reluctantly turns away, releasing me from the intensity of his smolder. I turn back to Niko, a small victorious grin on my lips.

"You were saying?"

The meeting drones on for another half hour as the Se7en discuss strategy and security. I'm tempted to dismiss myself, seeing as Legion completely ignores me, talking about my position as if I'm not even there, but I'm determined to prove that I'm an asset and just as invested in this plan as everyone else. Hell, maybe even more so. It is *my* father who wants to kill us all.

We file out of Irin's quarters and head towards the dining room after Kairo comes in to inform us that lunch has been prepared for all of us. Surprising, considering that there haven't been any "family" meals since we arrived. But with me still on Irin's shit list, I'm not one to argue. When a peculiar chime echoes throughout the hallway, everyone stops in their tracks.

"What?" I ask, looking from face to wide-eyed face.

"My, aren't we jumpy. It's just the door," Irin sighs, brushing by us with an exaggerated sway of her hips.

Hackles raised and fists clenched, nobody breathes as we trail her to the foyer. There haven't been any outside visitors since we arrived, and while a wise person would hide until the coast is clear, curiosity and pent-up energy has us all eager to see who would be crazy enough to show up unannounced. Someone on a suicide mission, that's for damn sure.

"Get behind me," Legion orders under his breath, coming up to my side. I think to argue, but catch Phenex's eye, who then shoots me a nod.

"Listen to him, E," Niko says, gently grasping my arm. He positions himself at my back. Cain and Toyol at my sides. The rest of the Se7en fan out, positioning themselves in pockets of empty space so not even Christ Himself could make it through their line. Even Crysis is on guard.

A member of Irin's staff is already at the front door, awaiting her signal. With a flick of her hand, the door swings open.

Time stops.

Movement ceases.

And every eye is fixed in disbelief at who stands before us wearing a slash of a seductive smile. Dark suit sans tie. Buttons unfastened at his throat to reveal a flash of smooth, marble skin. His hair is sunlight and earth, and his eyes are glimmering galaxies churning with mirth and mystery.

I've never seen anything so devastating. So beautiful.

Lucifer casually leans against the doorjamb and lets out a low whistle. "Now surely you can't have a party without me."

THIRTEEN

I F I WERE HUMAN, I WOULDN'T HAVE BEEN ABLE TO TRUST my eyes. I would have chalked it up to delirium—a result of lack of sleep, lack of food, and too much alcohol. But I'm not human. Yet, what's happening before me is still unexplainable. Because shit like this doesn't happen. Shit like this doesn't even exist.

In one blink, we're all standing there, gaping at the Devil himself as he dons a lazy grin as the early afternoon sunshine brushes kisses along his proud forehead.

And in the next, all holy hell breaks loose.

Legion erupts into a plume of ink black feathers and glowing embers, completely disappearing from where he stood right in front of me. And within a fraction of a second, he rematerializes into flesh and bone out of thin air. Directly in front of Lucifer.

Legion roughly snatches him by the lapels of his dark suit jacket and literally lifts him two feet off the ground before slamming him into the marble floor with a sickening crack that makes my stomach lurch. It all happens so fast that I have to force myself to blink to ensure I'm not imagining things.

Lucifer is here. And currently pinned under Legion's deadly hold.

"What the fuck are you doing here?" he roars, just inches from Lucifer's face.

Of course, Luc appears unfazed. Not a single hair out of place. Not even a wrinkle in his pristine suit.

"Nice to see you too, brother. You're looking well. Almost like a new man. How are all those wayward souls treating you?"

He's goading him. He knows that Legion has been remade into the beast he had fled Hell to escape. And now I finally realize what I should have seen the moment I laid eyes on that horrifying pendant: Lucifer wanted him to have it.

It was a setup. It had to have been. Lucifer probably divulged the whereabouts of Legion's power to Nikolai during one of their raucous evenings, drinking and doing God only knows what, knowing that Niko was only playing a role. Lucifer knew that once he appeared to be too distracted, Niko would go for it.

Just like he knew Legion would come for me.

Just like he knew where to find us.

It's all a game. All a fucking game. And I'm just a pawn.

"You have seconds," Legion seethes. "What do you want? Speak or find yourself disemboweled."

"This all sounds strangely familiar." Lucifer feigns a yawn.

Legion is ready to rip his throat out, and he actually has the balls to sound bored. "You really should brush up on the scary demon act. I know you're out of practice and all, but you need some new material."

"Death will be a kindness when I'm fucking done with you. Not even Father will be able to identify what's left of your body."

"Tough talk, little brother. Do you kiss Eden with that mouth? Or is it Adriel these days? Maybe both?" He attempts to sit up, but Legion slams him back into the ground even harder, the sound of his skull against the marble echoing throughout the foyer. I brace for blood, but surprisingly none appears.

"Legion..." Phenex's gaze is frantic as he approaches cautiously. "Please."

Cain follows. "Come on, L. Not here. You can't..."

Then Toyol. Then Andras and Lilith. Even Jinn moves forward, silent yet pleading. They're afraid. Afraid that he will do the unspeakable on sacred ground. But Legion is too far gone to hear them, consumed with fury so great that its stifling heat clings to my skin like a wet blanket. Even with all of them coaxing him, even physically pulling him, Legion doesn't budge. It's like he doesn't even feel them.

"You better listen to your underlings, brother," Lucifer wheedles. "Would hate for them to have to scrape up what's left of their fearless leader from off the floor. How embarrassing."

An animalistic growl rumbles in Legion's chest as he bares his teeth, revealing razor sharp fangs that weren't there seconds ago. His fingers morph into claws at Lucifer's neck, piercing straight through the fabric of his jacket.

He's going to kill him. And in return, he will be killed.

Niko spoke of a weapon that was strong enough to slay Lucifer. Legion is, and always has been, that weapon. He's the only thing strong enough to end him.

I cold dread races in my veins.

"Legion," I call out, racing forward. Crysis steps into my path before I can even clear five feet. I nearly collide with his chest.

"Don't, Eden."

"Get out of my way, Crysis."

He shakes his head. "Seriously, please listen to me. You don't want to get in the middle of this."

"Why wouldn't I?"

"Because this has nothing to do with you."

"What?" I scoff. "This has *everything* to do with me."

He shakes his head once more. "This feud has raged on for centuries, long before you were even a glimmer in Uriel's eye. You were just one of several catalysts. Trust me…your presence will just add fuel to the fire."

He's right. Their problems go far beyond petty jealousy over me. If anything, they began with the red-haired, angelic beauty dressed in white, silently looking on with an expression I can't quite decipher. It all starts and ends with Adriel.

"Enough!" Irin calls out, the single word echoing through the space. She marches forward, a hand on her shapely hip. "Get up. Now."

Her words are laced with compulsion, and somehow, someway, the Se7en are able to peel Legion off Lucifer. But just barely.

"Is this what you wanted?" he roars. It takes all six demon

assassins to hold him back. "Is this what gets you off? Innocents dying in the streets? When will it be enough for you?"

Lucifer stands to his feet and casually brushes off his suit. "I don't know what you're talking about."

"You knew!" Legion rages. He pants like the very weight of the words are a burden. "You knew what Uriel was doing. You knew what Eden was, and you did nothing to stop him! You just saw another way to feed your treachery."

Lucifer simply rights his cufflinks, not even looking in Legion's direction. However, the corner of his mouth twitches a fraction. "I did what had to be done."

"Had to be done? You doomed an innocent girl to sate your own sick desires, you twisted fuck. You tortured her, left her to a life of pain and poverty. For what? To wield her as you saw fit? To keep her as your prized pet? Or maybe you're on Uriel's dick in an attempt to get into Father's good graces…"

"No."

Legion begins to break away from the Se7en's hold. They each grimace as they struggle to regain control of his massive frame. "Then what? To torture me? To take from me once again, just like you take everything else?"

"No."

Legion sneers, his eyes glowing brighter than I've seen. "You just have to make everything about you. You're so fucking miserable with your own existence that you couldn't stand it. Just admit it…admit why you *Called* her. To get back at me for leaving? To prove once and for all that you're nothing but a cold, selfish prick that will always be beyond redemption? Thinking we wouldn't see past your lies and deception, and notice you for the pathetic, lonely son of a bitch you are?"

His words seem to slice right through Lucifer's calm exterior, and his hard glare snaps to Legion. Lips tight, knuckles white, he hisses, "You know nothing."

"Then why? Tell me you coward!"

"You wanna know why—"

"I swear to fucking—"

"So you would kill her!"

Lucifer's answer is like a bucket of ice water and Legion stumbles back, yet his fists remain tight at his sides. "What did you say?"

An electric storm brews within Lucifer's eyes. He rakes a hand through his hair and spits a curse. "I *Called* Eden… so you would kill her. Just like I manipulated you into falling from grace before our brothers killed you. To protect you. To save you. Everything I've done is for you. Eden was created to be a weapon, but not in the way you think. She was made to make you weak—to distract you. And that's exactly what she's done. I hoped that if you had scented my influence on her, you would hunt her down before she could fulfill her purpose, but that never happened. You fell right into Uriel's trap, so I tried—again—to save your ass when I took her. But you knew that, didn't you? You just didn't want to believe it—that you could fall victim to a seemingly helpless girl. So I did what needed to be done."

Lucifer's gaze falls to the ground, to the fresh crack in the marble, the only evidence of centuries of wrath. When he looks back up, his expression is dark, smoldering. "Surprised? Is that so hard for you to believe, dear brother?" He spits the last word as if it's tainted with poison. "That even though you betrayed me—abandoned me—I could still find the capacity to give a damn about you?"

A heavy silence falls over the space, as if everything has been muted. Sound, color, even my emotions are stifled. I...I don't know what to feel, or even how to feel. Lucifer didn't want to use me. He didn't even want to seduce me.

He wanted to kill me.

He wanted to save the one he loved above all else—his brother.

And that's the most human thing I've ever heard.

Even as I stand here now, he doesn't acknowledge my presence, as if my life has always meant nothing to him. Maybe I'm not worthy of his attention. Or maybe I'm just a reminder of his failure.

Silence stretches like an endless sea of turmoil. Without a word, Legion turns around and stalks out of the room. The Se7en follow, staying close behind.

There's nothing left for me here.

"Let's all take a breather and reconvene..."

I'm already headed for the opposite hallway before Irin can finish her sentence. I feel Nikolai and Crysis at my heels, but I don't slow. I can't. If I see the sympathy on their faces, I won't be able to hold it together any longer. I'll shatter into a million, jagged pieces and reveal just how irrevocably broken I truly am. How damaged I've been since the day I was carved from my mother's womb. Because the cracked ones, the spoiled ones, you throw away. No matter how much you try to patch them up, they'll always be wrong underneath. They can never be repaired.

When I get to my bedroom door, I slip in, close, and lock it before either one can make it past the threshold.

And then, I fall apart, letting my marled, misshapen pieces tumble to the floor.

I was so sure…so sure he wasn't the monster the world thought he was.

And I was right.

FOURTEEN

IRIN GIVES US A COUPLE HOURS TO COOL OFF AND regroup before demanding our presence in her quarters. I'm tempted to tell her and everyone else to fuck off, but the truth of the matter is, I'm a little more than curious to know why Lucifer has dared to show his face here, of all places. And if he knew about me—if Legion knew about me— then why keep me here? Why not just hand me over to Uriel and save themselves? If I was made to merely be a distraction, so why not eliminate the problem?

None of this makes sense. It's like they're biding their time when they know it won't end well as long as I'm a liability. But what other option do I have other than sitting and waiting? My sister is here getting medical treatment that she needs. I can't leave her. And if I did, what would that mean for her survival?

Too many questions, and not enough answers, so I begrudgingly drag myself out of my room and head down the long hallway, past the enormous space where Irin likes to entertain, and hit the opposite wing where we've held all our meetings since we arrived. I swear, between Irin's lounge and the gym, I don't have much of a life.

I'm not surprised to find Lucifer lazing beside her and casually chatting, but the sight of him still gives me pause. Refusing to make eye contact, I take up residence in my usual corner of the oversized, plush sectional, which seems much smaller than it did hours before. Only Niko has arrived so far, and I note that he barely looks my way when I sit down beside him. Looks like the cold playboy act is back on, which I can't blame him for. Lucifer is his boss for all intents and purposes. Showing any sign of vulnerability or fondness for me could inevitably be used against him. And now I understand why Niko wanted to keep his family out of this.

To say the atmosphere is uncomfortable is an understatement, and it feels like I'm sitting on hot coals as we wait for the others to arrive. When Adriel flits in and settles on Irin's other side, I want to hurl. But whatever I expected to feel when Legion and the Se7en arrive pales in comparison to the sorrow and dread that coils in my gut when they step into the room.

"What the fuck is he doing here?" Legion spits, stopping at the entrance. The others follow suit.

"Lucifer is a guest," Irin answers, not at all perturbed by Legion's reaction. "I asked him to be here."

"This has *nothing* to do with him."

"Actually," Luc chimes in. "You may want to hear me out,

brother. It certainly can't hurt, considering the sorry state of your cause."

"And as this is my home, you will abide by my rules," Irin adds. "Sit. There is much to discuss."

Legion glares at Lucifer for a long, furious beat before reluctantly going to the other side of the sectional. However, he doesn't sit. One small act of rebellion.

Irin begins, although there's no sign of Crysis. "The masquerade party will proceed as planned. Legion, you and your people have full use of surveillance and security services."

It's Phenex who answers. "Thank you, Irin. We appreciate your hospitality."

"Yes, very hospitable, as always, Irin," Lucifer pipes with a mocking grin. Asshole. I guess whatever sincerity he displayed upon his arrival is long forgotten. "But one has to wonder—with the fate of the human realm hanging in the balance, why on earth would a gaudy party seem appropriate?"

The Se7en don't answer. And I damn sure don't plan on lending any information to that manipulating prick.

"They've decided that with the Redeemer still in the hands of the Seraph," Irin offers, "that a party would potentially draw them here, revealing their numbers. It was young Eden's plan."

I know he turns in my direction, because I can feel the very moment his eyes fall on me, roaming my entire frame. I keep looking straight ahead at nothing at all.

"Interesting. Noble," he notes. "But what would be the point?"

"Well, considering the Seraph want to use the Redeemer to kill us to fulfill some petty revenge fantasy," Lilith snaps at her former co-conspirator, "it's probably a good idea to know what we're up against."

"Wants to kill *you?*" Lucifer guffaws unceremoniously, causing every one of the Se7en to glare at him with contempt. "Oh dear, thank the Almighty I arrived when I did."

"And what the fuck is that supposed to mean?" Cain questions, his expression dark and his fists clenched at his sides.

"It means that you all are completely clueless, although I'm not surprised. The Seraph want you dead, but that's just the tip of the iceberg. Honestly, exacting revenge is merely a bonus."

"So what do they want?" Phenex asks.

Lucifer leans forward, elbows on his knees, his violet eyes swirling with obsidian. "To kill *everyone.* Chicago is just the beginning, and killing you," He waves a graceful hand towards the Se7en, "is merely eliminating a speed bump. And once you're no longer an obstacle, they'll move on to every major city in the world. New York. Los Angeles. Miami. London. Hong Kong. Paris. Debase and destroy—that's what they want."

"Why?" The entire room turns to me at my uttered outburst. So much for acting indifferent.

Lucifer's gaze softens a fraction. Even his tone isn't as sharp and taunting. "So they can justify the end of humanity."

"Bullshit," Legion barks. I'm grateful when Lucifer turns to face him, releasing me from his uncomfortable stare. "They don't have the power."

"But they're betting on Father seeing reason. If humanity is doomed, why not wipe the slate clean and try again? He's done it once before, in a failed attempt to undo what *we* achieved when we fell. Who's to say he won't try again?"

Legion's clenched jaw quivers with an unleashed curse. I can see it written all over his hardened features—what Lucifer says holds some merit. And it makes sense. Violence, prostitution, drugs, corruption, pedophilia. The poor get poorer, the sick get sicker, and the rich get richer. And that's just in Chicago. Even when there's a beacon of hope and light, things don't seem to ever get better. Of course, there'd be cause to want to give humanity a fresh start. But that doesn't mean I want everyone I've ever known and loved to die. Even the people who have wronged me in my lifetime. I would never wish for them to be wiped from existence.

"But you could stop it," Phenex tries to reason with Lucifer. "The lesser demons are destroying the city. People are dying; children are starving. What are you doing to alleviate the carnage and suffering?"

The accusation hangs heavy right before him, but Lucifer pretends not to notice. "I could seal Hell to keep any more from escaping, but it would have to be with me in it."

"And that's a problem because…?" Cain challenges.

"Because you need me." Before I can brace myself, Lucifer turns to look right at me, his stare terrifying in its ability to cause my insides to liquefy. "You all do."

"I'm certain many of us would be willing to argue that assessment," Phenex comments.

"Then you're all fools," Lucifer snaps, turning to him. "You think the Seraph will make this easy for you? You have one greater demon, a gaggle of heavily armed minions, a mute angel, and two Nephilim, one of which wouldn't be breathing had it not been for me sending the warlock. So yes, you do need me. You'd still be chasing your tails, trying to find out the Seraph's plan—the plan I just laid out for you. So let's see…I've been here a matter of hours, yet I've accomplished more than any of you have in a week. Pathetic."

Every hackle is raised, but no one disputes his claims. And honestly, as much as I hate to admit it, he's right. We only have one demon strong enough to fight a Seraph. One. And there's no telling how many angels they've dragged to their cause. Lucifer could be a valuable ally, but would he really be on our side? Is anything about him honorable and honest?

Other than the love and loyalty he holds for his brother, of course.

So maybe he is telling the truth. Considering that's the only person he's shown to care about, I don't think he'd do anything to jeopardize Legion's existence.

Fuck the rest of us though.

"So what do you propose?" Legion questions, his expression anything but receptive.

Lucifer shrugs. "Have your little party. But I want in. One word of advice though…bench the angel."

"Why?" Adriel frowns, showing her first sign of disapproval.

Lucifer completely ignores her and speaks directly to Legion. "Well, if the Seraph somehow detect her and take her, you've screwed yourself out of your insurance policy."

I swear, I can hear crickets from the other side of the room. Insurance policy? How? And why didn't that ever cross my mind?

"Oh. She doesn't know, does she?" Lucifer muses donning a wicked smile. "My bad."

Adriel looks at Legion; her expression crumpled with hurt. "What is he talking about?"

Legion squints his disdain for Lucifer, yet speaks to Adriel. "Uriel still wants you, meaning he'd be less inclined to strike knowing we have you."

"And let's not forget the little matter of your blood," Lucifer adds. His shit-eating grin is so wide, he looks like the fucking Joker.

Legion releases a little growl of warning, but confirms Lucifer's claim, shoving the knife embedded in Adriel's heart in a little deeper. "We have reason to believe that angel blood can be used to heal a wound from the Redeemer. Phenex has been working on a way to synthesize it, so your presence here is necessary."

"So in other words, dearie, they need it straight from the tap." Lucifer is diabolical. I know they have history, but damn. This attack seems personal.

I see the pain on Adriel's face, and I can't help but feel a little bad for her. Still hate her, but I can't imagine what she's thinking right now. She's only here to act as leverage, plus they need her blood. So maybe...maybe Legion isn't keeping her around because he still has feelings for her. Maybe her presence is merely necessary for survival.

"Now that everything is out on the table," Lucifer says, turning to take one of The Watcher's petite hands, "Irin, I want to thank you for having me. Anything you need from me is yours." He brings the hand up to his lips and brushes a kiss along her knuckles.

"You're quite welcome, Lucy. As long as you manage to behave, this should be entertaining." She snatches her hand back and snaps her fingers. Kairo appears seconds later, looking red-faced and flustered. "Kairo will show you to your room. My staff is at your disposal for *whatever* you may desire. Enjoy."

Kairo bows, then looks up at Lucifer through long, black lashes, a seductive smile gracing his lips. Now I understand why he looks so flushed. He wants Lucifer. And judging by the way Lucifer gazes back, unblinking, I'm thinking he isn't opposed to Kairo warming his bed during his stay here.

And that makes me feel…warm. Stifling hot.

I never thought about Lucifer with men, but now that the idea has been presented, I'm more than a bit curious to know what that might be like. Would he be rough with Kairo, or gentle? Would he worship his body, or demand that Kairo devote himself to please him? Shit. Just the thought of two beautiful men together, sheets twisted at their feet as their naked bodies tangle in ecstasy…I don't see how I can focus on anything else for the rest of the night.

The Se7en begin to rise and disperse, but Legion seems hesitant to leave, his eyes going to me then to Lucifer. He's worried. About what, I'm not sure. The cat's already out of the bag—I know everything. Legion knew more than he let on. *He lied to me.* And even though what Lucifer did was ten times worse, if it wasn't for him, I may not ever know the truth. He's an asshole, but at least he's somewhat of an honest asshole.

"Eden." Lucifer is suddenly in front of me, hand extended to help me to my feet.

I quickly glance over at Legion, who stares back unabashedly. I opened my heart and my body to him, and he knew things about me—things he hadn't planned to disclose.

He didn't want to believe that being with me would affect his judgment because maybe he didn't care enough or think I was significant enough. I'm not stupid enough to think that Lucifer is any better, but what Legion and I shared…I thought it was special. I thought it was real. Now, I find it was all a lie. I was literally made to be his plaything, something for him to fuck and fondle instead of focusing on the real threat—my father. It's sick and degrading, yet I let it happen. More than that, I craved that sickness. I dropped to my knees and begged to be degraded over and over again.

I take Lucifer's hand, ignoring the pang of guilt and shame in my chest. His touch is just as I remembered, and a dozen memories of my time with him flood back to the forefront of my mind. The way he watched me over his wineglass at his many elaborate dinners. How I woke to find him watching me while I slept. How he wasn't afraid to show his sense of humor when we had breakfast in his suite. And the way I felt in his arms as he twirled me around his ballroom…

I don't think I've ever felt so beautiful in my entire life. The dress and the shoes were gorgeous, yes, but the way he looked at me in them is what had me coasting on a cloud of contentment.

"You're looking beautiful, as always. Angel blood agrees with you," he drawls.

"What do you want, Lucifer?" I huff, hating the way his touch makes me feel. Hating the way my body instantly remembers what it was like to have him deep inside of me in Irin's bathroom.

"Just wanted to extend my congrats. As you know, Nephilim are rare. Seraph Nephilim even more rare. You should consider this an esteemed honor."

"And should I consider you trying to get me killed an honor too?" I bite back, snatching my hand from his grasp. "Or how about threatening to hurt my sister so you could kidnap me when that plan didn't work?"

He raises his hands and shrugs. "All's fair in love and war. And in war, there are casualties, even those that you love. You'll understand that sooner than you think." He spies my neck, where a fading bite mark still lingers, and his brows raise. "I see you may already know what I'm talking about."

I shake my head and look away. Angry tears sting the backs of my eyes, but I refuse to let him see that he hurt me.

Lucifer hurt me.

I wanted to believe there was something redeemable within him, and there was. Just not where it pertained to me. Silly, stupid girl. What made me think I could change the Devil's heart? And why did I want to?

"Look, you're here, and I can't change that. But do me a favor? Stay the fuck out of my way."

With that, I turn on my heel and march out of Irin's quarters without a single glance in Legion's direction. I don't stop until I'm in my bedroom, panting, my back pressed to the door. When a knock sounds from the other side, I yelp with a curse.

"Holy shit," I gasp when I swing open the door to find Niko standing there. He hurriedly enters and shuts it behind him.

"Seriously, if you don't want to get him worked up, maybe you shouldn't speak his love language."

"What?"

"Lucifer," he answers. "He practically had an instant hard-on after you told him to fuck off. You're playing right into his sick, twisted game. The best reaction is no reaction, E. He literally thrives off your resistance."

"So what? I'm so supposed to fawn over him like Kairo? No thanks." I cringe at the thought of looking like a lovestruck puppy for Lucifer. I'd rather pull a Jinn and cut out my own tongue.

"No. You're supposed to make him believe that no matter what he does or says to you, he can't affect you. I told you this before when we were Hell. Same rules apply."

He's right. Shit. I should have followed Niko's lead and remained quiet and cold.

"I know," I say, shaking my head. "It's just…I hate him. I hate him so fucking much."

"Well, that won't do either." He goes over to the bed and settles down at the foot.

"Why not?" I frown, sidling up beside him.

"Love. Hate. They're the two strongest emotions one can covet. And to him, they're both essentially the same. If he can make you feel one, he can make you feel the other just as passionately."

I flop back on the bed and release a frustrated breath. Niko does the same, resting his head beside mine.

Shit.

I'm so fucked.

THE LAST THING I WANT TO DO IS WORK ON MY LIGHT
wielding abilities with Adriel, so I put all my energy
into weapons training with Cain, who is a little more
than surprised at my improved skill at target practice.

"I'm a quick study," I remark, slipping off my headphones
and safety goggles. I set down the Glock. It's starting to feel
good in my hands. Natural.

Cain glances over at the paper target and nods. Headshots,
just like he taught me, although I landed a few in the chest.
"Can't argue with that."

"You think it's the Nephilim thing? The reason I'm able to
pick things up a bit faster than the average person?"

"You say it like it's a bad thing. It's an advantage. Use it."

"Yeah, but I'm not thrilled at who gave me these abilities.
All my life, I've wanted a father. And then I find out he's a

crazed maniac angel who wants to wipe out mankind?"

Cain shrugs. "Be careful what you wish for."

After putting away the weapons, we head up to the gym for the rest of my training. Crysis is still on the mend, apparently. Being blasted with holy light, even indirectly, took a lot out of him, and I feel like shit for it. Cain mentioned that a blast like that at close range would have instantly killed a human. I wonder what it would do to a demon. Or even an angel. A tiny, jealous part is tempted to find out when I spy Adriel sitting on a wooden bench alongside the boxing ring. I dismiss the thought the moment it enters my head. I'm not that kind of girl. I don't set out to hurt females just because they pose a threat to my relationship. Especially when there is no defined relationship. Plus, Legion had no issue being affectionate with me in front of her after my mishap with holy light. And if what Lucifer said is true, Legion's attachment to her is not romantic. At least on his part, it isn't. And now that she knows the truth, I doubt she'll be arranging any more hallway rendezvous.

Still…

I don't trust her. I know learning from her is necessary to avoid anyone else getting hurt, but we're not going to be planning any sleepovers or mani/pedi dates anytime soon.

"Good luck. Don't kill anyone," Cain snickers with a menacing smirk that highlights his scar. In many ways, the disfigurement is terrifying, but it suits him. It's actually grown on me. With the muscles, tattoos, and beard he's started growing out, an unblemished face just wouldn't fit the whole bad-ass-demon narrative. Plus, I've discovered that he has a bit of red in his hair, which totally makes him look even more sinister.

I flip him the bird as he saunters over to the weights, laughing the entire way.

Actually, everyone is here. The Se7en, including Legion. Nikolai, who hasn't felt the need to set foot in the gym since we arrived because apparently *"you can't perfect perfection."* And Lucifer and Irin. Of course, Niko, Luc, and Irin aren't donning any activewear nor are they using the equipment. They're simply watching. Waiting.

They came to see the show.

Sweat beads all over my body. My mouth goes bone dry. I feel sick to my stomach.

Shit, I did not bet on an audience. Not for this.

"Eden." Adriel stands at my approach.

"Adriel," I nod and look around, noting all the prying eyes. "They're all here."

She tips her head to one side. "They've never seen a Nephilim light wielder before. Some have not even seen a full blood light wielder since not all angels are equipped with the gift."

"And you are."

She nods. "Yes. As was Legion and Lucifer. They no longer possess light…for obvious reasons."

"I don't think I can do it again," I mutter, feeling self-conscious. "I don't even know how I did it in the first place."

"Well, like all gifts, it comes from within." She touches a hand to her chest. "Imagine it as an intense emotion that's just too great for your heart to contain."

I resist the urge to roll my eyes. "I seriously doubt whatever made me do that came from my heart."

"So what was it that you were feeling at the time?"

I go back to that incident. Hard to believe it was only yesterday that I was pummeling the heavy bag, simmering with rage and pain at what Crysis had said about me. And it wasn't just his words that cut me to my core. It was the fact that part of me knew he was right. I had become stupid and blind when it came to Legion. I accepted any little crumbs that he would offer me because it was better to have a small part of him than nothing at all. And when Crysis threw that in my face to hurt me then tried to make me relive it, I lashed out because I was humiliated and ashamed.

Reading the memories playing across my face, Adriel comments, "He broke your heart."

I shake my head. "Crysis and I just had a stupid fight. It was nothing."

"I'm not talking about Crysis."

Simultaneously, we turn to Legion. His gaze goes wide as if having us both staring at him has stripped him bare. The two women who love him: the mate of his enemy and the daughter of his enemy. I wonder which one of us he considers the bigger mistake.

"Come on," Adriel says, breaking her stare first. "Let's get to work."

We step into the ring, and a quiet hush falls over the room. Fucking vultures. It's like they're begging for a fight. Adriel positions me across from her, but not into a fighting stance.

"Hold out your hands, palm side up." I do as she says. "Take a deep breath. And when you suck in oxygen, let it fill your chest until you feel it may burst. As if your heart is a balloon encased in blood and bone. When you exhale, release the heartache, the pain, the joy. Whatever you're feeling, channel it, give it life, and let it take flight from your fingertips."

I lift a brow, feeling utterly silly. Ain't no damn way white fire is spurting from my fingertips.

Adriel huffs out her irritation. "Fine. Watch me."

She closes her eyes, sucking in a deep lungful of air. As she slowly releases it, her eyes open, and within them lay pale flames, reflections of the ball of white fire suspended above her palm. It's glorious, mesmerizing. And if I considered myself religious, I would say it was the light of God. Just a fleck, but there was definitely something divine within that fire.

Our audience looks on with varying shades of amusement and awe. For all her daintiness and grace, Adriel is still one of the most powerful creatures to have ever walked the earth. The white gowns, her long auburn waves, her pale skin…it's easy to forget that as an angel, she's a formidable opponent. I just have to wonder, when all is said and done, whose side will she fight for?

"Ok. Your turn," she says, closing her palm and extinguishing the light.

I look around me, feeling every eye on my back. "I can't."

"You can. You have been given a gift, Eden. God does not make mistakes."

Mistakes. That's what I'd been told my entire life—that I was a mistake. But for some strange reason, I was created for a purpose. Abuse, starvation, neglect, poverty, abandonment, assault…I had survived them all. And this is why. Nights so cold I should have frozen to death as I curled up in a ball on a dirty mattress in a roach-infested shack without heat or electricity. I still woke up each morning—weak, hungry, and shivering, but alive. As if something inside me would not let me give up, would not let me perish. Something I could not see or touch or taste or hear, but I knew it was there.

Adriel.

Even with the knowledge that Uriel had created me to hurt her beloved, she did not allow me to die. Her presence sustained me just enough to keep my heart beating.

I owe it to her to try. I owe it to myself to prove them all wrong. I was not a mistake.

I lift my hands, palm side up, and close my eyes. I think of what it felt like the first time I woke up in Legion's arms. I felt a sense of safety and comfort I never knew existed before then. And when he touched me, running the callused pads of his fingers over my ribs, I finally knew what it meant to be cherished.

But it was when he was deep inside of me, filling me to the point of bursting, that I tasted euphoria on my tongue. Every stroke was a prayer, every moan was a testimony. I saw God in those moments of complete and utter bliss.

"Um, Eden?"

I open my eyes at the sound of Adriel's soft voice and gasp. My hands—both hands—are engulfed in white flames. Not a sphere of light like Adriel's, but something wild, passionate. Something born of an emotion so pure and deep that my knees tremble from the gravity of it.

"Now, try to reshape it. Mold it into something more obtainable."

"How?"

"Will it so, Eden," Adriel commands, taking a step forward. "You are in control. It does what you tell it to."

Deep breath. I plunge back into that memory, conjuring those feelings of pure ecstasy. And I remember what it felt like to have it all snatched away from me. Fear and rage flood my veins like ice water, dousing the fiery passion and replacing it with blazing contempt. They took from me. Stole from me. They stripped me bare and raped me of the tiny kernel of happiness I had managed to retain despite all the ugliness in my life. And now…now I would take it back.

I look down at my hands and find two glowing spheres of fire raging in my palms. This time I don't gasp in surprise. I don't flinch or shy away from the power in my grasp. I *am* the power.

"Good," Adriel notes, taking several steps back until she nearly touches the ring's corded rope. "Now what can you do with them?"

"What?" I know she is asking me what I think she's asking me.

"You have to learn how to fight."

"I know," I retort. "But how will I do that here?"

Adriel lifts her chin, hands in loose fists at her sides. "Hit me."

"What? No." I shake my head.

"Hit me, Eden. Fling your light out and try to hit me with it."

I grit my teeth. "I don't want to."

"Why not? You want to learn. You *need* to learn. This is how you do that."

"But…"

"But what?" She raises a slender auburn brow, challenging me.

"I don't want to hurt you," I admit, my eyes shifting around the gym. Everyone is watching…waiting. Waiting for me to slip up and show them that I'm a monster, ruled by her insecurities and petty jealousy. And if I hurt Adriel—or worse—I will be screwing them out of their leverage against the Seraph.

Adriel smiles, and while it may appear sweet to others, I see it for what it is: a dare. She either doesn't believe I'm strong enough to hurt her, or she's hoping I will to gain sympathy. Either situation is a lose-lose for me.

"You know you want to," she says, goading me. "I can see it in your eyes, Eden. You've been dying to strike me for days, haven't you? Ever since you saw Legion and me in the hallway."

She knew. *She knew.* She knew I was there the entire time, and she still came on to him. After feeding me all that bullshit about how Legion chose me and how she wouldn't interfere. Lying, conniving bitch.

"You think you know him, and maybe you do to an extent. But you could never know him like I do. We have hundreds of years of history together. Have you ever asked yourself *why* he wanted to gain God's favor? Why he was fighting for redemption? He wanted to get back into Heaven. He wanted to get back to *me.*"

It happens so quickly that I couldn't stop it even if I tried. But with a guttural grunt, I fling those orbs of white light from my fingertips, sending them straight towards the angel responsible for all of this. Because if it weren't for Adriel, Legion never would've fallen. If it weren't for her, Uriel wouldn't have come to Earth seeking revenge. And if it weren't for her, I would have never been born.

The balls of blinding light meet their target within a millisecond of them leaving my fingertips and stop just an inch from Adriel's face, halted by a single raised palm. Her expression is calm, almost cold. She didn't even blink.

She knew I would take the bait. That all she had to do was ignite the jealous rage simmering underneath, and I would attack. And now I see it. Legion isn't just the one who inspires my power. He's also my weakness. I care too much. And that makes me a liability.

A loud clap sounds from yards away, and I look over to where Lucifer stands with Irin.

"Bravo! Bravo!" he derides. He strides forward, and his movements are as fluid as water. "My, my, how our young Eden has grown. From minimum wage cashier to light wielding Nephilim."

If I could control the trembling in my hands, I would flip him off.

Adriel turns to Irin and gives her a conspiratorial nod. Then she looks back to me. "You did well. We'll pick back up tomorrow."

"No." My hands may be shaking, but my voice is steady. "Now."

"You should rest."

"I don't need to rest. I want to keep going."

Adriel glances back to Irin who merely shrugs.

"You wanted me to find the source of my power," I continue. "Now, I've found it. Let's go again."

Adriel looks uncertain, and I'm not sure why. Isn't this what she wanted?

"You want an opponent? Try me."

I turn in time to see Lucifer gracefully swing his leg over the ropes. He comes to stand before me, a slash of a crooked smile on his lips. I merely look up at him through my lashes, too unnerved by his proximity to stare into his eyes. I'm still angry—at him, at Legion, at everyone who lied to me. But that doesn't erase the fact that I'm grateful for his candor. I would have never known the truth had it not been for him. And I guess I can't fault him for being loyal to his family. I would have done the same for Sister.

"What do you say, Eden?" he coaxes, his voice low and sultry. "Want to give me your best shot?"

"I can't promise I wouldn't enjoy it."

"Mmmm." The sound rumbling his chest is damn near erotic. "I can't promise I wouldn't enjoy it either."

We stand in a stare-off, and for just a few heartbeats, I forget that we're in a gym full of supernatural creatures. How easy it is to fall victim to his stare—a peculiar blend of violet and obsidian with flecks of silver—and the temptation of his touch. He knows what he does to my body, even when my heart and mind revolt against the very thought of him.

"E?" Nikolai steps into view, and the sight of him breaks me from whatever spell Lucifer had cast over me. "We should get started."

I step back, putting a foot of space between Lucifer and me. And finally, I can breathe.

I nod to Niko. "Yeah, you're right."

"Get started? On what?" Lucifer inquires. His gaze goes over my head, and I don't have to turn around to know why. I can already feel him.

Legion at my back. Lucifer at my front. And Niko standing

at my side. To most girls, this would be every dark, depraved fantasy rolled into one. But all I feel is the overwhelming need to scratch my skin off until I hit bone.

"The breathing ritual," Niko answers smoothly. "In order for me to do the veiling spell, I'll need magic."

"And let me guess…you need Eden's magic." Lucifer raises a skeptical brow. "And you've allowed this, brother?"

"He doesn't allow me to do *anything*," I reply before Legion has the chance. "Unlike you, he doesn't see people as property. Or pawns." I don't know if that's entirely true, but I'll be damned if I give Lucifer the satisfaction of knowing he may have been right about Legion.

"Eden can make her own decisions," Legion mutters behind me. "Nikolai has proven to be helpful to our cause. She trusts him."

"Does she?" Lucifer glances down at me; his eyes narrowed in mischief. "And you, brother? Knowing what the process entails? Knowing she'll be physically and emotionally bonded to him? She will desire him…fantasize about him. You do realize that the ritual is just a prelude to sex, don't you?"

I turn to Nikolai, whose pale blue eyes burn brighter than I've ever seen them, his stare boring into Luc. His teeth are clenched so tight that I can see the muscles along his jawline flutter with disdain. "You know that isn't true."

Lucifer ignores him, only speaking to Legion. He takes a step forward, closing whatever distance I had put between us. Him, Legion, Niko…I feel like I'm suffocating.

"Can you handle a little extra competition for Eden's affections?" Lucifer's gaze dips down, and he runs a single finger up my bare arm, causing sensation to snake from my fingertips to my neck. "I'm not sure I would be able to if I were you."

I snatch my arm away and stumble back into Legion's rock solid chest. Reflexively, he grasps my shoulders, steadying me and wrapping me in his overwhelming heat. I inhale, desperate to soak in the feel of his touch. I don't know when I'll be this close to him again, and this distance—this chasm that's ripping us apart—it's killing me.

I only allow myself a moment to revel in his comfort before conjuring what's left of my resolve and step to the side, towards Niko. Leaving Lucifer and Legion to come face to face with their biggest weakness: each other.

The irony is just too glaringly obvious. I am what's between them. And no matter how much I love or loathe either one of them, they will always look at me and see the other, pulling on my strings. I can't help what I feel for Legion—or even Lucifer. But I can help how I let them affect me. I can stop them from controlling me. I won't be owned like property, and it's time they realize that.

"I'm leaving," I announce. *With or without your permission*, I'm tempted to tack on. Reluctantly they turn to me, not wanting to be the first one to break eye contact.

"And you're sure about this?" Legion questions, his eyes hardening as they fall on the Dark warlock beside me.

I slip my hand into Niko's, intertwining our fingers. Enough of the games. I shouldn't have to hide my friendship with him just to make them more comfortable.

"I'm sure."

"I don't think he was asking you, love," Lucifer remarks with a sneer.

Feeling protective of my friend, although he's more than

capable of holding his own, I squeeze Niko's hand tighter. He feels colder, as if there's pure ice in his veins.

"I trust him, and you trust me. So yeah…it'll be fine."

Before they can utter another skeptical word, I turn, somehow managing to take Nikolai with me. I release his hand so we can hop off the raised platform, and we stride towards the gym doors. Neither one of us speaks, despite the whispers swirling around our dramatic exit.

"Holy. Fuck," Niko hisses once we hit the open corridor. "Do you realize what was about to happen?"

I roll my eyes. "Apparently even immortal boys are immature assholes."

"No, E," Niko shakes his head. "Legion marked you as his. It's something only other supernatural creatures can sense— like a sign of ownership. Even warlocks do it. If he felt even the slightest offense from me or anyone else when it comes to you, he would be within his rights to annihilate the threat."

"And what would be considered an offense?" I think I already know the answer.

"If I hurt you. Angered you." He runs a hand over his jet-black hair, disturbing his deliberately disheveled 'do in the most delicious way. "Fucked you."

I swallow. "Well…that's good to know."

"Yeah. Of course, the fucking would be considered offensive if I took you against your will. And rape fantasies aren't my thing." He shrugs a shoulder.

"Also good to know."

"All things considered, you can imagine that Legion is not my biggest fan right now. But he needs me to do the spell, which is the only reason why he hasn't tied my guts into a bow.

It's also the reason why Crysis is laying low. It was an act of the Divine for Legion to not slaughter him for what he said to you. And after what happened afterward… Well, let's just say Crysis will be keeping a safe distance."

"Too bad the whole marking thing doesn't seem to work on *everyone*." I purse my lips in distaste.

"Luc plays by no one's rules. But he's not suicidal."

I nod my understanding. If there's one being that will gladly test Legion's boundaries, it's Lucifer.

"Alright, E," Niko begins, dipping forward to leave a peck on my forehead. "Go get cleaned up and meet me in my bedroom in an hour. I need to prepare."

"Prepare?" I literally have no idea what I'm about to walk into. I have about a million reservations, and all of them have to do with me being sexually and emotionally linked to Niko. I mean, I'm attracted to him, sure. Anything with a pulse would be attracted to him. But to want him…to crave him…I don't think I could handle that. And judging by the looks on both Legion and Lucifer's faces, I don't think they can either.

But we need him. And he needs me. So whatever he asks of me, I'll suck it up and do it.

Even if it destroys our friendship.

Even if it destroys me.

SIXTEEN

I BATHE IN THE FRAGRANT OILS AND BATH SALTS DISPLAYED beside the clawfoot tub. My skin feels like silk and smells like sweet pea and lavender. I was going for soothing, but if I'm being honest, I wanted to make the breathing ritual as pleasing to Niko as possible. And since I've been training all day that definitely called for a bath.

I let my hair dry in silver ringlets below my shoulder blades while I search for something to wear. Gym clothes don't seem appropriate, and neither do combat boots or a hoodie, so I settle on one of Irin's sarongs and bra top ensembles. I opt for all black, although the high slit that hits the top of my right thigh is a bit obscene paired with the strappy bralette adorned with glittering black gems along the bust. My first instinct is to go for comfort and slip on the flats I wore before, but it just doesn't go. Pumps it is, which sexes the entire outfit up about ten notches. For someone who doesn't want a sexual attachment to her best guy friend, I'm pretty much a walking contradiction in four-inch heels.

Makeup is minimal, mostly because I don't want to make it look like I'm trying too hard. And once my hair is dry, I tie it up in a top knot. Then it's just a couple doors and a hallway that separates me from Niko and the breathing ritual.

I don't understand why I'm so nervous as I walk to his room. Hell, even the thought of being in the confined space where he sleeps and bathes and God knows what else is freaking me out. I'm not some naïve maiden who hasn't ever been alone with a guy before, and it's not like I was raised with strong, conservative values. But this is Niko—everything about him is sex and seduction. I just never imagined being on the receiving end of his charms.

Deep breath and I knock.

Nikolai swings open the door, and the air in my lungs tumbles out of me unceremoniously.

He stands there, hair a muss of onyx waves and blue eyes sparkling. He's wearing dark slacks and a slim-fit shirt with the top few buttons unfastened. The room is dim, illuminated by at least a dozen candles from what I can see, and there's music playing.

"Come in," Niko drawls, stepping to the side to usher me in.

I nod my thanks as I pass, and take in the room. I've been here before, but for some reason, it seems different—more intimate. Not like the first time we hung out here, chatting like old friends. Even his four-poster bed looks like it's primed and ready for seduction.

"Can I get you anything?" he asks, heading to the small bar stationed in the corner closest to the bathroom. I hate that I feel like all we do is drink and talk shit, but if there was ever a time to self-medicate with booze, it's now.

"Sure. Whatever you're having."

He brings me a few fingers of scotch, which I gladly accept, taking a long swig. Another sip and I feel less awkward about being alone with him in his room. One more and this almost feels like one of our normal evenings.

"What are you doing?" I question when he sits down at the small, two-seater table and pulls out a rectangular tin.

"I thought this might help us both loosen up," he replies. He opens the tin and takes out rolling papers and a tiny Ziploc bag.

I watch Niko expertly roll the most beautiful joint I've ever seen, while we make small talk about everything from Crysis to my sister's recovery. When he's done just a few minutes later, he holds it out for me.

"Want to do the honors?"

I shake my head. "Nah. Go ahead."

He sparks it. Inhales. Takes another hit then passes it to me. I take a couple puffs while Niko refills our glasses of scotch. And within that cloud of potent smoke, I forget why I was ever so nervous to be here.

"Come." Niko stands, his eyes seductively low and glazed. He drags his teeth over his bottom lip before wetting it with his tongue.

"Where?"

"Just over to the bed. More comfortable."

I put out what's left of the joint and take his outstretched hand, letting him lead me to the bed. He promised we wouldn't do anything I wasn't comfortable with, and I believe him. I'm just not sure what I'm not comfortable with at this point.

We sit side by side like we've done a dozen times, and I kick off my ridiculous heels. Niko notices the way my sarong parts and exposes my entire thigh.

"You look beautiful tonight," he notes. "But you didn't have to dress up for me."

"I didn't," I half-lie. "Didn't know what to expect, so I felt loose and flowy was best."

"Yeah." His eyes go to my exposed throat. "You like the music?"

"I do. Who is it?" I sway lazily to the hypnotic bassline.

"*dvsn*. I thought you'd enjoy it."

I smile and playfully smack him on the arm. He's still so gorgeous even through my hazy eyes. "Don't tell me you dusted off your coveted bedroom playlist for me."

Niko laughs, and I swear it sounds like a slow-motion melody. "Unfortunately, mine would be incredibly outdated…by almost twenty-five years."

I faux gasp, clutching my chest. "You haven't had sex in twenty-five years?"

He shakes his head. "I didn't say that. I just haven't found it necessary to woo anyone in recent decades."

I lean back on the bed, resting on my elbows. Head tipped back, eyes barely open. "So that means you're not wooing me?"

Niko leans back as well. "Should I be?"

I don't respond. Not because I'm speechless, but because there just isn't an appropriate response. We've always been flirtatious, but this feels different. More intimate, more crucial.

As if it was always meant to happen, and slowing down would be trying to stop a runaway train.

He leans forward. I hold my breath. His fingers trace the jeweled bodice of my bra top, his cold skin brushing my cleavage. He slides his hand to my back, steadying me as he pulls me towards him. A tiny sound escapes my lips when he brings his face to my chest—to the space between my breasts—and slowly drags his nose up to my throat, inhaling deep.

Each draw on my magic takes me higher, and I grip the back of his head, fisting his hair, desperate to stay tethered to him. He groans as he rolls his body over mine, placing a knee between my thighs. His hands grip my back as he buries his face in my neck. I feel his lips on my throat—cool and unbelievably soft—but he doesn't kiss me, no matter how my body craves it. No matter how I whimper as he grazes my skin in maddening, feather-light strokes.

The weed and scotch are twin weights on my frame. I feel so heavy in his grasp, but he handles me as if I weigh nothing at all, manipulating my body like I'm a precious porcelain doll. I'm dizzy, but so present in this moment…so fucking aware of his every inhale, his every groan, his every rapid heartbeat.

I don't know how Niko pulls away, but he does, panting heavily. My breaths are just as labored. It was just a couple minutes—if that—but it felt like being fucked for hours. The kind of fucked that you still feel days later whenever you squeeze your thighs together, remembering the slickness, the fullness.

"Please…" I beg. I'm so wet that I can feel dampness seeping through my panties and onto the sarong. And my nipples are so hard that it physically hurts as they press against the restricting bra top.

"You should go," he manages to say, his voice strained. He still lies on the bed, propped up by his elbows, but his hands are tight fists at his sides. Sweat beads on his brow. And his entire body is tight and tense. His *entire* body.

I don't mean to gawk at the pronounced bulge in his pants, but I'm way past the point of trying to appear decent and moral. Mouth dry, I lick my lips, imagining how he would taste—how he would feel—against my tongue.

I tingle. I ache. I need.

This isn't sexual attraction. That doesn't even begin to describe the intense feeling of hunger simmering in my soul. And now that I've gotten just a taste…I don't know how we can ever go back to how things were before.

"Go, Eden," he grits, his jaw locked tight. "You need to go. Because if you don't, I'm going to ask you to stay."

I force my eyes away—from his sexy mussed hair, from his tortured expression, from the erection throbbing painfully in his slacks—and slowly push my heavy body from the bed. I can't do this to us. I won't. My life is complicated enough. I won't risk his life or his friendship. He means too much to me.

"I'm…I'm sorry," I stammer, picking up my shoes. I don't even bother to put them on before stumbling to the door to let myself out.

Niko stays on the bed, fisting the duvet and working to catch his breath. His eyes are radiant when he looks to me. "You did well, E."

I nod, not believing a word of it, and open the door before I beg him to let me stay.

I don't realize how high I am until I try to make my way

back to my room. But this doesn't feel like a normal high. This is like being on a combination of the most potent strains of X and Molly, with a champagne chaser. However, I know exactly what I'm doing. I'm in control of my actions and my feelings, yet all I want to do is turn back, slip into Niko's room, and slip out of my clothes. I'm so beyond horny that I'm imagining sex noises…moaning, the slap of skin, grunts of pleasure.

No. Not imagining it.

I stumble past a door that's partially open. Just cracked, yet it's enough for me to bear witness to what's going down on the other side.

Lucifer.

Naked.

And fucking.

A woman is sprawled out before him on the bed, her long legs straight against his shoulders. He holds her by her hips as he strokes her deep and mercilessly, each thrust more violent than the next. Yet, the harder he fucks her, the louder she moans and begs for more. And in my hazy stupor, I no longer see the woman. It's me with my ankles resting on his shoulders as Lucifer takes me fast and deep and hard. I can still remember what he feels like as he punishes my womb. And when his hands trail up her body to clutch her breasts, I can still remember how I cried out when those elegant fingers pinched and rolled my nipples while I slid up and down on his cock.

And that's a problem.

I try to force myself to walk away and leave Lucifer to his depravity, but the sight of a third party traipsing into view freezes me where I stand.

Kairo, naked and hard as steel, climbs onto the bed and sidles up beside Lucifer. With a look of worship in his eyes, he begins to kiss and stroke Lucifer's neck, his chest, his taut abs. Lucifer rests a hand on Kairo's lower back and slides it down to palm his pert ass, his other hand still fondling one of the woman's breasts.

I thought I was turned on before, but this…I wasn't prepared for this. And I definitely wasn't ready for what happens next.

Lucifer pulls out, his massive hardness glistening with the woman's arousal. As she shifts onto her knees and turns around, Kairo kisses a trail down Lucifer's torso, going lower…lower…lower. Until both he and the unknown woman are licking and sucking Lucifer together, eagerly feasting on his stiff, throbbing flesh.

I cover my mouth with a trembling hand, biting back a gasp. Or a moan. I can't be sure. But I know I shouldn't be here. Still, my legs are immersed in cement, my limbs leaden with my own unquenched desire. That's not why I stay though. The erotic scene playing out before me isn't the reason I can't look away.

His face.

Lucifer's beautiful, cold face. His features aren't contorted in ecstasy. His dazzling eyes aren't narrowed in concentration as he fights to hold on to his orgasm. His sensual, full mouth isn't parted as he releases a rousing hiss. His strong, angled jaw isn't tight as he prepares to release himself onto their willing, snaking tongues.

He looks…bored. Detached. As if he can't force himself to feel. As if he is far, far away from that bed, this room, maybe even this realm. As if all this—the sex, the indulgence, the debauchery—is just a distraction. From what, I don't know. And I don't think I want to find out.

But still…I can't look away. It feels like turning from him now would be an act of abandonment, and somehow, in this moment, we share a secret that no one else will ever know. I know what it feels like to be left behind by those who had sworn to love and care for me, and so does he. Maybe that's our biggest secret of all.

I hear voices approaching from down the hall, so before I'm caught, I step away from the door and go the opposite direction. Whatever high I was feeling from the joint and the breathing ritual has been replaced with something different entirely. Sadness. I feel sad for Lucifer. To be so powerful, so feared, yet so melancholy…

I wasn't supposed to see that. Not from him. And as irrational as it is, I resent him for it. I wanted to detest him despite my body's draw to him, but now…now I pity him. I *feel* for him. And that makes me want to hate him even more. Because he doesn't get to make me feel. He hasn't earned that privilege. After all he's done to me, to my sister, to Legion, he doesn't deserve a fucking ounce of sympathy from me, kindred spirits or not.

I've barely made it inside my room when there's a knock at the door. I expect it to be Niko, checking to see how I'm feeling after things got way awkward, so I swing open the door without asking whom it is.

Legion stands in the doorframe, his massive build absorbing the light around him. His silver eyes are pinched into a slight frown and he shifts his gaze from my head to the tops of my pushed up breasts to the flat expanse of my exposed belly to my bare thigh. After he's finished taking inventory of my body, he flicks his glare up to my face, still flushed with longing.

"I had to see…" he begins, his voice raw. "I had to know that you were still—"

Mine.

He doesn't even get the word out before his mouth his mouth covers mine and he sweeps my body into his arms. But his desperate, fervent kiss feels like *Mine.* He traces those four letters with his tongue as he tastes the yearning building deep within me. And when he walks us to the bed to lay me down on my back, the word is reflected in his starlit stare as he stands over me, watching me writhe with need.

Mine.

"Yes," I answer, without needing to hear the question.

And when he rips off that ridiculous sarong and jeweled top, he carves the edict on my womb, claiming me. Staining me.

Yet, even as my back arches and I come so hard that I see stars behind my eyelids and my limbs go limp with exhaustion, I can't deny a niggling feeling at the back of my head, telling me that I'm wrong. He's wrong. Something feels…wrong.

Mine.

Am I?

SEVENTEEN

I 'M SURPRISED WHEN I WAKE UP WITH LEGION STILL wrapped around me, my cheek to his chest, his deep breaths stirring the tousled hair atop my head. I've missed this so much, so much that I want to cry. I've never felt more secure than when I'm in his arms. I've never felt more beautiful than when I'm splayed out before him, naked and achy. I didn't think I'd ever get this feeling back, and now that I have, I'm afraid of letting go. I'm afraid that he'll wake up and realize that too much has changed, and what we were before cannot be salvaged.

But that fear is spawned from something else too.

Last night, as Legion loomed over me, those eyes flecked with stardust roaming my body, I saw a man possessed. Not by lust or passion, but possessed with a ravenous hunger that made me shiver under his stare. He touched me as if it was the first time, with awe and wonder and excitement. Or maybe he was committing each dip and curve to memory in anticipation of what was to come. Our days could very well be numbered. What if last night was our last time?

I don't know. But while he felt good—better than good—as he stroked me to the brink of death, he felt like a stranger. His body was the same, his heat as smoldering as ever, his scent still masculine and intoxicating. He even tasted just as I remembered. But he wasn't *him*. And as hard as I closed my eyes and pretended we were back in his room, drowning in a sea of dove grey linens, our naked limbs tangled together, I felt it in my gut, twisting my insides with the truth.

Legion was different. He *is* different. And I don't know what that means for either of us.

Nature takes its hold on my body, and even in my commiserating, I can no longer ignore my desperate need for the bathroom. I slowly wriggle out from under his arm that's draped over my shoulders, careful not to wake him. Luckily, he only stirs and rolls onto his side, allowing me to release the breath I was holding and get to the bathroom to release my bladder. I finish up, slip on the silk robe behind the door, and return to the bed just as Legion begins to wake.

"Hey sleepyhead," I whisper, settling onto the bed beside him and slide under the covers.

Legion blinks rapidly, looking around. His sleep-weary eyes fall on me, and a dimple forms between his brows. "Eden?"

I smile, despite the uneasy feeling in the pit of my stomach. "Who else were you expecting?"

He blinks again and looks down his body, covered only by a silk sheet. Confusion is etched deep in his features.

"Something wrong?" I ask, running a hand through his

tousled hair in hopes of soothing him.

Legion clears his throat and shakes his head. "No. Just… tired."

"Go back to sleep. It's still early."

He shakes his head again and my heart plummets. "I need to get going. A lot to do for tonight."

Right. Tonight.

The big masquerade party that Lilith and Andras have been tirelessly working on to draw out Uriel and his zealots.

Legion gently shrugs away from my touch and sits up, swinging his legs over the side of the bed. With his broad, chiseled back to me, I get a glimpse of the horrid dragon's spiny vertebrae and vicious tail, all elaborate scales and talons. Even without facing me, it taunts me.

His elbows on his knees and his hands tugging at his hair, Legion heaves out a wistful breath then stands. It's hard not to stare at his beautiful frame and feel a little sad as he tugs his jeans back on. I want to ask him what he's thinking, but I'm not sure I'm ready for the answer.

"I'll see you soon," he mutters. Then he leans over and brushes his lips over mine. I don't know why, but the gesture causes tears to sting my eyes and a hard knot to form in my throat, making it impossible for me to respond.

I'm still watching the door long after he leaves, wondering if he'll ever come back.

Deep down, I know he was never really here.

I meet up with Adriel in the gym for a bit more light wielding training. She instructs me to generate those glowing orbs of concentrated sunshine over and over again until my head is throbbing and my eyes feel as if they're being torn from their sockets.

"Again."

I grit my teeth to keep from snapping and close my palms, extinguishing the perfectly round spheres already in them. Deep breath. Two more appear within seconds, and it takes minimal focus on my part.

"You're getting faster. Good. In battle, you'll need to be able to conjure the holy light without thinking."

"Then shouldn't I be learning how to use it?" I counter, annoyance ringing clear in my voice.

"Soon. Now, again."

I ignore the order and look around the empty gym, needing to give my brain a break. "Where is everyone?"

"Preparing."

I guess the masquerade has everyone on edge. Even Cain was absent during my visit with Sister this morning, which I didn't complain about. It was nice to have her all to myself for a little while. I have to admit, she looks amazing for someone who survived a bomb blast and suffered serious burns all over her body. She mentioned a skin graft, and while I'm no physician, I'm pretty sure the recovery for that would still be pretty extensive. But Sister's wounds seem to be healing at an expedited rate. Not just healing—disappearing. She's starting to look and sound like her happy-go-lucky self again. When she smiles, it isn't pinched with pain. She has almost full function of her limbs and her skin coloring is evening out. It even looks like some of her hair is growing back. The transformation is incredible.

I glance back at Adriel, my chin lifted. "Are you planning to attend tonight?"

"I am, despite Lucifer's suggestion," she answers coolly. "It's been a while since I've attended a party."

I close my hands and when I flex my fingers, two new balls of light rest atop my palms. "Do angels even have parties? Isn't that a sin?"

Adriel laughs, the sound like tinkling wind chimes. "Not at all. Lasciviousness, drunkenness, fornication...those are sins. A simple jovial gathering of friends is not."

"But aren't we committing sin just by having a party under false pretenses? Isn't that sorta like lying?"

Adriel shrugs. "No one's perfect. Not even angels."

I lift a brow, dropping my hands to my sides. My muscles are stiff with exertion. "Isn't that the whole point of angels? The whole "perfect being" thing?"

"We strive to be, if only to be closer to Christ. We often fall short." She bites her rosy-hued bottom lip in contemplation. "My own history has proven that to be true."

We stare each other down, neither one of us willing to address the big ass elephant in the room. Luckily, we don't have to avoid the subject for too long.

Both our heads flick to the entrance of the gym just as Legion comes stalking in, his expression unreadable.

"Eden." He looks from me, his current lover, to his former lover. Awkward. "Adriel."

"What's going on?" I question, jumping off the raised platform of the ring. Adriel does the same, although a little more gracefully.

"We have a problem." His eyes go all shifty again, as if he's uncertain who he should look at. "Irin's quarters. Now."

He doesn't even wait for us to catch up with his long, hurried strides as we trail him to The Watcher's lounge. He hardly grumbles a greeting when we enter, the rest of the Se7en, Lucifer, Niko, and Irin are already seated and waiting for us.

"What's wrong?" I ask as I take my usual spot.

Kairo immediately comes to offer me a glass of cold water. Blushing, I accept. I literally just saw him in the most compromising position ever, and now he's back to being poised and polished. My gaze flicks to Lucifer reflexively. I'm startled to find that his eyes are already on me, an amused smile gracing his sensual lips.

"Crysis has disappeared," Legion announces, pulling my attention away from Luc's uncomfortable stare.

"What?" I nearly choke on my water.

"My staff checked his quarters," Irin confirms. "There's no sign of him, and no one knows when he disappeared."

"Surveillance?" Toyol questions.

Irin shakes her head. "Whether he was taken or left of his own accord, he went undetected. Camera signals were scrambled. There's no trace of him."

Shit. Crysis must've used his nifty Nephilim trick of evasion to sneak out. But why? He isn't a prisoner here.

"I knew we shouldn't have trusted that half-breed fuck," Cain spits. "He probably went straight to the Alliance and told them everything."

"I don't think he would do that," I blurt out, drawing every eye. I swallow, feeling self-conscious. "It's just that...I don't think he'd go back to them after what they did to him."

"Yeah right." Cain rolls his eyes. "He was probably just biding his time, waiting on a piece of info that would put him back in bed with them. Once a rat, always a rat."

I shake my head. "I felt his mind. I saw it. There was no sense of betrayal in it. There was warmth…sincerity. But no malice." I leave out the part where he touched his mind to mine, a gentle stroke along the side of my consciousness.

"But that still doesn't prove that he's not spilling our secrets right now. After what happened in the gym…"

Cain doesn't have to finish the accusation before I know where's he's going with this.

After what I did to Crysis, he may now be feeling more inclined to betray us. And if that's true, then I did this. I'm to blame for Crysis's shifting loyalty. I swear, if my temper somehow put us all in danger, I will never forgive myself. So I have to believe in him—I have to believe that Crysis would never turn on us in an act of petty resentment. He was my friend. Even after our fight, I looked into his green eyes and saw goodness and kindness in him. *That's* the Crysis I grew to know and care for. And if he's in trouble, we have to find him.

"Plans still stand," Legion states, climbing to his feet. "The party is still on."

"And risk an ambush?" Cain challenges. This new piece of knowledge has him more rattled than usual.

"We'll be veiled." A glance to Niko who nods in response. "And even if they are planning something, house rules still stand. No bloodshed on sacred ground. Violence in the city is growing at an alarming rate. People are literally dying in the streets, their numbers so abundant that emergency services can't remove them fast enough. My scouts have reported near-ly 300 citizens have been murdered or seriously injured in the last twenty-four hours."

"What scouts?" I've heard him mention them before, but I had never questioned him about them. If crime in the city is rapidly growing and we're the Seraph's #1 target, I don't see how he could—or would—send people out into this chaos.

"His little birds. Rats, raccoons, and other vermin. Maybe even a few puppies and stray cats," Lucifer answers, drawing a growl from Legion who gives him a narrow glare. Lucifer, as always, is nonplussed and seems more interested in flick-ing an imaginary dust speck from his sleeve than addressing Legion's warning. "My dear brother is a regular Dr. Doolittle."

"Enough, Lucy," Irin gently chides, patting Lucifer's hand. She also climbs to her feet, and everyone else follows her lead. "There is much to do in preparation for this evening's festivi-ties. Rest up. It's going to be a long night."

The Se7en file out one by one, each of them wearing vary-ing looks of unease. Crysis's disappearance doesn't sit well with them, but Legion's edict will not be challenged. Niko, looking more radiant and dashing than ever, turns to me.

"How are you feeling?" he asks, his pale blue eyes bright. I fight back a blush, remembering the night before.

"Good. A little tired."

His gaze flicks downward as if he's recalling the way he brushed his lips up and down my throat, coming dangerously close to my breasts. "It'll pass." He runs a hand through his black, meticulously styled mane. "I want to apologize for tell-ing you to leave so abruptly. It's just…"

I shake my head. "I totally understand. We're good. No

apology necessary."

Niko lifts a hand to brush a wisp of hair behind my ear, his fingers grazing my jaw. I turn into the touch, inhaling his scent of ocean mist, salt air, and fresh rain, and release a euphoric sigh. My blood is singing with pleasure. My skin tingles with sparkling specks of ice. Reflexively, I take a step forward, nearly drawing us chest to chest, wanting more. Needing more.

"Careful. Or you'll take it back," he says quietly.

"Sorry," I whisper, my face flushing furiously with embarrassment. I stumble back a foot.

"It'll wear off…the connection," he explains with a soft smile. "If you're worried."

"I'm not," I say, returning his shy grin.

"Good. I, uh…" He runs another hand through his hair, almost like he's nervous. Odd. I've only known Niko to be recklessly confident. "I need to get ready for the spell. I'll see you tonight."

He leans forward to touch his lips to my forehead, leaving a shivering chill on my skin. I guess the distant, nonchalant act is dead. Or maybe he's just as affected by what went down between us as I am.

I watch him as he exits, wondering if we'll ever get over this and go back to how things were…Wondering if that's what I truly want.

I could fall in love with someone like Niko. Hell, that part would be seamless. But that's just the thing…his time here on Earth is not promised. And even if it was, his heart will always belong to another, and he'll forever be tortured by thoughts of the love he once had and lost in the most tragic way. Just like me.

"How is he doing with fighting them?"

I spin around; my features first contorted in shock, then confusion. Lucifer reads my expression and clarifies.

"Legion. How is he dealing with the voices? You know, for all his strength and tenacity, his biggest challenge has always been his own demons. No pun intended."

"What are you talking about?" I snap out of embarrassment and shame. I have no idea how long he's been standing there watching the tense exchange between Niko and me. And now he brings up Legion? I already feel like an ass for practically begging my friend to fuck me, only to spread my legs for my supposed boyfriend. And the fact that I can still feel the ghost of Legion inside me, yet still desire Niko? I'm all types of fucked up and conflicted.

Lucifer soldiers on, ignoring my terse tone. "The Legion of Lost Souls is tormented for eternity by the cries of the wayward, the wicked, the depraved. They call to him, taunting him with their malice. They do not rest; therefore, he does not rest. Not if he wants to resist them."

"And what would he be resisting?" I ask with faux cynicism. Truth is, I know what Lucifer is saying is true. What I saw in Legion last night, and then again this morning…it was as if he had checked out.

Lucifer smiles slyly, and casually sets a hand in his pocket. "Many of those souls have unfinished business. And they'd love nothing more than to persuade Legion to carry out their plans."

I frown at the thought of Legion being used as a conduit for evil. He's a demon, yeah, but he doesn't believe in hurting innocent people for sport. Even Lucifer only gets off on punishing those who deserve it.

"But doesn't *he* rule *them?* Not the other way around?"

"One can only take so much before he succumbs to the darkest parts of himself," Lucifer says. He takes a step forward, his gaze serious. "And sometimes a lost soul is simply bored with being ignored."

I don't want to give him the satisfaction of seeing me rattled, so I simply nod and turn to walk out. Lucifer isn't done with me though.

"Be careful, Eden," he calls to my back. "You know what they say about idle minds. They're the Devil's playground."

Fuck.

A bored, lost soul could be manipulating Legion's mind.

I've seen Lucifer's playground. It's not nearly as fun as it sounds.

EIGHTEEN

ILITH AND ANDRAS HAVE ALREADY SHOWN THAT THEY can throw together one helluva costume. And as I slip on the dress and heels they've left in my room for the masquerade, I'm sure they've proven themselves once again. However, when I step into Irin's lounge, I find that my assessment is a little off.

They haven't just proven themselves. They've completely knocked it out of the park.

A resounding gasp echoes throughout the space as I step through the jeweled double doors on sparkling silver stilettos. Every eye travels up to my bare legs, showcased by the shimmering black high-low gown that's ruched at the waist and falls seamlessly over my hips to kiss the middle of my thighs. The back flows down to the marble floor in a waterfall of lace and satin adorned with silver beading to match my shoes. The neckline is modest yet intricately designed with scalloped lace and more beads that cover my cleavage. Coupled with the off-the-shoulder style that shows a tempting amount of skin, the entire ensemble is the perfect fusion of elegance and sensuality.

Light makeup with bold, red lips and long, full lashes. Glittering diamonds in each ear and dotted in my black lace choker. My hair in an updo that leaves a few loose curls to brush my bare shoulders. I honestly can't say that I've ever felt so dangerously seductive.

Lucifer is the first to let out a low whistle. "I must say, Eden. You look absolutely edible tonight."

I nod my thanks and hurriedly take my seat to hide my blush. I'd never admit it, but he's looking especially dashing in a black tux that looks like it was poured over him in the most delicious way. There's a certain gleam to the fabric, as if it's infused with metallic thread. Not too tight, but fitted to highlight broad shoulders, sculpted arms, and muscular thighs. And while Lucifer is definitely wet dream-worthy this evening, nothing compares to the exquisiteness of Legion as he steps to the center of the room.

His massive build is swathed in a black-on-black suit, no tie, with the top two buttons of his shirt undone, displaying just a peek of the dragon that's masked underneath. He's shaved, his dark hair slicked back in a way that makes him look refined, yet roguish. The very first time I saw Legion, I thought he was the sexiest man alive in jeans, a wool coat and a charcoal grey beanie over his mussed locks. But seeing him now, looking every bit like the fallen angel who had ruled and ruined me into sweet submission, I have to bite my red-painted bottom lip to keep from whimpering with need.

Everyone is dressed to the nines, yet I only see him. Even the way he moves seems more feral, but there's a gracefulness to it, like the way a panther would stalk in the shadows undetected as it sizes up its prey. His starlit gaze touches mine, and my mouth parts reflexively, a heated breath escaping. Whatever distance I felt earlier has been erased. I see him. I can feel his heat from yards away. I can even smell his scent of midnight jasmine and scorched earth. And the way he looks at me, like a man dying of thirst at a well, tells me that I'm not imagining this. Legion has come back to me.

For how long, I don't know.

He manages to force his gaze away to address the crowd, looking every bit like the bold leader that he is, simmering with power so great that it smothers me.

"I know some of you have reservations about tonight. But step out on faith with this in mind: this is our city. And it's time we take it back. And while some of you are merely here to placate selfish desires in a desperate attempt to feed your narcissism,"—A pointed scowl at Lucifer—"I appreciate your aid in protecting our home here on Earth. And protecting Eden."

"Don't mention it, brother," Lucifer mocks.

Legion continues, refusing to take the bait. "Guests will be arriving soon. Toyol, what's the status on surveillance?"

"Cameras throughout the ballroom are installed. Vacant rooms are also equipped, as well as communal bathrooms, so don't use any of them." A shrug. "Breaking some laws, but I'm pretty sure CPD has their hands full."

At the mention of bathrooms, my eyes go right to Lucifer,

who wears a sickening grin. I've learned my lesson about restrooms at Irin's parties.

"Good," Legion continues, fortunately too occupied with plans to notice Lucifer's leering. "Jinn, I want you stationed at the entrance. Phenex, you're at the terrace exit. Note who doesn't order alcohol or scoffs at those who do. Lilith and Andras, circulate the room. Listen to conversations, watch for any odd, overly conservative behaviors. Eyes and ears open at all times. Toyol, I need you behind the scenes, monitoring the cameras for anything that seems the slightest bit off. Someone strays from the party, I want to know about it. Cain is with Mary. And Eden…" His gaze is on me now, his tone softer. "I want you close to me at all times. I need to see you."

I simply nod, unable to respond to the touch of vulnerability in his voice and the earnestness of his words.

"And me? Where would you like me?" Lucifer derides. He clearly has no intention of doing anything Legion says.

"I'd like you back in Hell where you belong. But for now, out of our damn way."

Lucifer shrugs, obviously amused. He lives to piss Legion off.

"And what of our warlock?" Irin interjects. She's swathed in head to toe gold, complete with a radiant headdress and black and gold winged liner on her eyes. She looks like a petite Cleopatra, and I'm curious if she'll enter the party lazing on a matching palanquin held up by her dutiful servants.

Right on cue, Nikolai enters, looking absolutely flawless. Royal blue tux, hair intentionally messy, and eyes glowing so bright, they're nearly fluorescent. A mystical current seems to roll off him in glittering, iridescent waves. The magic literally shines through him. He comes to stand in the middle of the room, his gaze touching us one by one. When his eyes fall on me, his lips twitch.

"Good evening," he greets with a graceful dip of his head. "The spell is complete. The moment you leave this room, your identity will be cloaked from all that wish to do you harm. Although, I must warn you—you have only a matter of hours before the veil begins to slip."

"Those that wish to do us harm? But what about everyone else?" Adriel questions, her usually serene features touched with alarm. She's wearing her signature white, although the floor-length gown is swathed in glittering jewels. She exudes innocence and grace. "You don't know the extent of Uriel's influence."

"And that's why we have these," Lilith cuts in, moving to the front of the room.

As if the moment was choreographed, Kairo, along with three other members of Irin's staff, join her, their arms full of plumes of colorful feathers, lace, and ribbon.

"Irin was kind enough to have these specially designed for each of us," Lilith continues, plucking up one of the intricately designed masks from Kairo's arms. It's fashioned with fiery red, orange, and gold feathers. "This one is for Phenex."

Lilith distributes each mask, handling them with care. I can tell they're handmade, and probably extremely expensive. I can also tell that they've been designed with each of us in mind. Phenex's is pretty self-explanatory, and keeping with the literal sense of his name. Toyol's is decorated with streaks of green, black, and red, almost resembling the mask of a samurai. Andras's white and light teal mask is constructed as the face of an owl, majestic and cunning. Sparkling blood red jewels over black lace for Lilith. And burnt orange, red, and black plumes for Jinn, striking against his beautiful bronze skin.

Nikolai is the next recipient of Irin's gift, and of course, it's the perfect depiction of him. A stylish black mask studded with blue jewels, ranging from sapphire to aquamarine, making his eyes look even more remarkable.

Adriel's mask is exactly as I pictured it would be: virginal white with lustrous flecks of silver, accented with white flowers and feathers. It's pretty, but it's typical. It's also a lie. Adriel is far from innocent. But it also could be a representation of what she wants the world to see—the real mask she wears to hide the darkness underneath.

When Legion steps forward to receive his, I bite back a gasp. Jet black feathers over metallic purple and green fabric made to look like scales. And right in the center, above the space reserved for his eyes, is a large, brilliant ruby. The dragon. It's stunning, terrible, horrifying. It's the embodiment of Legion in all his frightening glory.

It's no surprise that Lucifer seems more than a little entertained at the irony of his mask. Black, twisted horns fixed upon a deep red mask, its design reminiscent of Phantom of the Opera. He places it against his face and turns to me, and somehow, it makes him look even more alluring.

"How do I look?"

"Hideous." I roll my eyes just to keep from gawking.

"You're a terrible liar."

When Lilith steps towards me cradling a gorgeous arrangement of pale roses, silver-sprayed baby's breath, and small, gold faux apples affixed upon a white, silver, and gold mask, the breath in my lungs is stolen by awe. I stand, impatient to get a closer look at its splendor. I've never seen anything like it, and compared to the others', it's a work of art.

"Let me," Legion says, striding towards us and gingerly plucking the delicate mask from Lilith's hands. His intoxicating scent seems especially potent tonight, and I inhale, eager to overdose on the overwhelming essence of him.

I hold my breath as Legion brings the mask up to my face, reveling in the feel of his warm fingertips brushing my cheeks. He steps around me to tie the ribbon, his movements deft and careful not to snag my hair. When he's done, he lets his touch linger, trailing his fingers down the back of my neck and to my shoulders.

"So…beautiful," he whispers, his warm breath skating across my skin.

And I feel like sobbing right there in his arms. I don't know what it is—this flood of emotion. I just know that I want him, and I need him. And with Lucifer's warning still ringing loud and clear in my head, I'm afraid that at any moment now, I'll lose him.

Stay with me, I inwardly beg, urging him with any mystical influence I may possess. *Don't leave me.*

But as with all my prayers, the request goes unanswered, and he steps away.

"If we're all ready…" Irin holds out a hand, allowing Lucifer to help her to her feet. She's slipped on her own mask, a gold and black number that matches the rest of her ensemble perfectly. "We have a party to get to."

Toyol, Phenex, and Jinn have already dashed to their positions to intercept any early arriving guests. Irin, Lucifer, and the rest of the Se7en join them shortly after, leaving only Adriel and Nikolai. Per Legion's request, I hang back with him in Irin's quarters. It seems like forever, and I'm anxious to get out there, if only to appreciate Andras and Lilith's hard work. The grand ballroom was blocked off earlier, so I have no idea what's in store for us. Plus, it's flippin' awkward standing here.

"Shouldn't we be out there?"

Legion lifts his chin as if he senses something. Or maybe he's listening. "Soon."

"I don't feel them," Adriel remarks. I know it's directed at Legion, as if she knows what he's thinking.

"I don't either. Not yet," he replies to the white-clad angel who looks even more radiant dripping with diamonds. The two lock eyes, communicating through some unspoken bond, and I feel like I may vomit.

"Well, I'm bored," I whine. "Niko?"

Before Legion can protest, I brush past him and sidle up to the dashing warlock and take his hand. I don't even wait to glimpse Legion's reaction before I turn and lead us to the double doors. The second we pass them, a cold, tingling sensation snakes up my back as the veil settles over us. It's like the most intense case of heebie-jeebies I've ever felt.

"Holy shit," I squeak out as we make our way down the hallway. I can already hear music and exuberant voices.

"Yeah, magic can have jarring physical effects. At least mine does."

"Are you nervous?" I'm asking more for myself than him.

"No. Why should I be?"

"Irin's parties can get pretty outrageous."

"I know. I've been to one."

When I whip my head to face him, my eyes wide with shock, Niko merely shrugs. "I'm old."

"Does Irin know you've been here before?"

"Of course she does. But it's not that big of a deal. Every supernatural crosses her path one way or another."

I know he speaks the truth. There's something unsettling about The Watcher that goes far beyond her ancientness. Considering she's all-seeing, she has the power to put an end to all of the destruction, yet she doesn't. Why? What's in it for her?

"What is she?" I whisper.

Niko looks around as if the very paint on the walls has ears. "Something very old and very powerful that wasn't created to be on Earth."

There are partygoers just yards away, so I deem it best to file the information away for later, just in case. Irin isn't a threat to us—not yet anyway. And she's been more than helpful by taking us in and helping us to prepare for whatever battle awaits us.

The glitz, the glamour, the overwhelming beauty…it's all a feast for the eyes. Lilith and Andras have outdone themselves in every way. The ballroom is the visual embodiment of decadence and excess, from the sparkling gold candelabras to the crystal teardrop chandeliers. Even the bubbling drinks in crystal-encrusted champagne flutes look like they're flecked with gold.

"Don't drink that," Niko notes when he catches me staring after the effervescent liquid.

I nod, heeding his warning. "Let me guess…the punch." I know about that all too well. Hell, I still can't bring myself to use any bathroom other than the one in my room.

"We're on the job, and one of those will have you dancing on tables."

"Trust me. I'm not touching the stuff."

On that note, we sidle up to the bar, manned by three shirtless, damn near pantsless, beautiful men. Their bare torsos are all streaked with gold body paint, and they're wearing simple black masks to match their tiny trunks. Niko holds up two fingers.

"Champagne."

One of the bartenders nods and within seconds, brings us our drinks.

"Cheers," Niko says, tapping his glass against mine.

"To what?"

"To living forever." He smiles, but there's a certain sadness to it, like he doesn't quite believe it.

I sip my champagne and look out into the rapidly growing crowd. The DJ is spinning radio hits for now, but I wouldn't be surprised if a chart-topping band takes the stage later on tonight. Irin has major pull, plus most entertainers are supernatural in some way or another.

"Well, E, this is where I leave you. Time to work." Niko downs his champagne before coming in to gently kiss my hair. "Try to stay out of trouble."

"But what fun would that be?" A smooth baritone answers.

I don't even notice that he's beside me, leaning against the bar.

"What do you want?" I snap at Lucifer, who somehow looks good even in the horned mask. Dammit.

"Just enjoying the festivities."

A member of Irin's staff sashays by, a tray of hors d'oeu-vres hoisted on her hand. Lucifer snags two of something ba-con-wrapped. It looks and smells delectable, but I shake my head when he offers the bite from his fingertips.

"Suit yourself," he says, popping them into his mouth and devouring every morsel. "You know, you really should eat more, especially with all your training. You're starting to look a bit thin for my tastes."

"I honestly don't give a shit about your tastes," I retort.

"And you honestly aren't being honest," he bites right back. "And if I recall, we were in this very home when you cared very much about my tastes. Shall we revisit that fated powder room?"

"Fuck you."

"I'll take that as a yes."

Not able to stomach his vulgar banter and his mocking smile for one second longer, I quickly down what's left in my flute and set it on the bar. Now I'm regretting not waiting for Legion. Despite the raging violence in the city, the place is getting packed with gyrating dancers and heavy-lidded lovers, and I'm not sure if I'll be able to find him. Still, I start to walk away.

"Wait," Lucifer calls out before I can make it more than two feet. "Stay put."

"Why?" I snap, spinning around with a hand on my hip.

"Because our guests of honor have just arrived."

Horror drains the color from my face. The bubbles from the champagne riot in my belly. I feel spiders crawling all over my skin.

The Seraph are here. Uriel is here.

Oh, shit. Shit, shit, shit.

"Calm down," Lucifer instructs, his voice low. "Walk towards me."

I do what he says, trying desperately to school my features and act casual. I doubt it works.

"You're all right," he assures, his voice oddly comforting. "He isn't here. He sent his cronies."

"Who?"

"Three lesser angels. One Seraph: Raphael."

"You can sense them?"

Lucifer nods, those celestial eyes scanning the crowd. Even with him on high alert, he seems so cool, so nonchalant. "If I leave you here, will you stay?"

"What? Where are you going?" I don't even try to hide the panic in my voice. Whatever courage I thought I had before is obviously nonexistent

Lucifer winks, apparently amused at my discomfort. "Do you want me to stay?"

I shake my head. Of course, I want him to stay, but there's no way I'd tell him that.

Lucifer takes a step closer, until we're almost touching. The heady scent of deadly belladonna and sex fill my nostrils. "You can say it," he whispers. "Tell me you want me to stay. Go ahead."

I muster what's left of my waning resolve and turn to look him in the eye. "No."

"Say it."

"No," I stubbornly repeat, biting back the quiver in my voice.

Lucifer snorts out a laugh, and takes a step back. "Enjoy the party, Eden."

Then he dissolves into the crowd, leaving me to the wolves lying in wait. However, this time, it's not the wolves I'm terrified of. It's the sheep.

NINETEEN

I'M NOT SURE HOW LONG I STOOD AT THE BAR, BUT I KNOW there was champagne.

Lots of it.

I was so nervous, and after a while, the anticipation became harder to bear than the actual anxiety. So I drank.

I drank until I stopped feeling like I wanted to crawl under a barstool and hide. I drank until I stopped thinking about Lucifer getting under my skin. I drank until I stopped scanning the crowd for Legion, who I hadn't seen since we parted ways in Irin's quarters.

And when Imagine Dragons takes the stage, I decide to dance, despite the niggling feeling that I should stay put.

But we're here to blend in, right?

Well, I'm blending in.

Everyone is so friendly, overly so. You know how drunk

girls at clubs become best friends in the bathroom? It's like that, but on the dance floor, and soon I'm pretty much pulled into a circle of beautifully buoyant young women wearing colorful masks and gorgeous gowns. We laugh at absolutely nothing, our hips swaying to the beat and singing along. I don't know what they are—demon, vampire, witch, werewolf—and I don't really care either. They look normal and they're nice, which is a welcome reprieve from walking on eggshells all the damn time. Plus it's a great way for me to gauge if something is amiss. At least that's what I tell myself.

A smiling server stops by our group with a tray of sparkling flutes. The girls cheerfully begin to distribute them; however, I'm smart enough to turn down the offer.

"No, thanks," I say with a polite grin. "I'm only drinking champagne."

"Well, then," one of them replies, a curvy, mocha-skinned beauty wearing a shocking yellow gown with a matching feathered mask. It reminds me of a canary, and the color is stunning against her smooth complexion. "Let's get the girl a glass of champagne then!"

It only takes what seems like a minute before we're obnoxiously toasting to getting laid, having great hair, or whatever else giggling sorority types toast to after several drinks. One thing's for sure—these girls are definitely not human. Not with the way they're guzzling the gold-flecked punch. But who am I to judge? I'm not exactly human either.

"Oh, shit! Did you see that guy looking over here?" one of them exclaims. She's swathed in all red, her mask also matching her dress. Funny. This one reminds me of a cardinal.

I follow her line of vision, wondering if she spotted

Legion, but I can't decipher more than a couple hundred grinding, twisting bodies. I shrug and go back to dancing.

"There he is again!" Cardinal crows.

The blonde beside her beams, nearly giddy. "I see him! He is *soooo* freakin' hot!" She's wearing a frilly, floor-length frock shaded in blue from head to toe, like a...bluebird?

"Me too!" Canary chimes in.

Meanwhile, I don't see anyone looking in our direction. At least I think I don't. Maybe they have a keener sense of sight than I do. You know...like hawk-eye vision. And if that's the case, and they can see what I can't, I probably shouldn't be smack dab in the middle of a group of girls in bright colored dresses, singing at the top of my lungs.

I try to formulate a believable yet polite exit strategy. "Hey, I think I'm going to..."

"Here he comes!" Cardinal trills, grasping my arm. "He's looking right at you!"

I shrug out of her grip, suddenly feeling sober. And terrified. Because the man who maneuvers through the crowd, expression unreadable, is, in fact, looking right at me. And he isn't Legion, as I had hoped.

"I have to go," I insist with a tight smile. I try to back up without making a scene, stepping on toes and colliding with more than a few partygoers.

The girls try to coax me back, confusion pinching their perfectly arched brows.

"What's wrong? Need another drink?"

"Come back! This is a great song."

"Ooooh, I bet he wants to dance with you."

No, you squawking sycophant, I want to yell. *He does not want to fucking dance with me.*

"I have to go," I repeat, taking another step back, my eyes still locked on the male swiftly cutting his way through the sea of partyers.

Why is he looking at me as if he knows who—and what—I am? I'm wearing a mask and I'm veiled. There's no way he knows, unless...

Unless he's stronger than warlock magic. And there are few creatures on Earth that could be.

A Seraph.

I stumble back a few more steps; my feet weighted in fear. I have to get out of here. I have to run. But where would I go? And fleeing would be a clear sign that I'm the exact person he's looking for—and hoping to kill. The bar is several yards away—shit, how did I stray so far? And I don't spy any of the Se7en or Nikolai. Hell, at this point, I'd settle for Adriel.

Think, Eden. What do I do?

I brush by two guys dancing and kissing passionately, their movements nearly pornographic, and use their gyrating bodies as shields. Then I shimmy through a wall of scantily clad dancers with glittering red eyes. Vampires. Luckily, their attention is on their glasses full of thick crimson liquid, too preoccupied with bloodlust to be bothered by my intrusion. I cut right, then left, trying to put as many bodies between me and the ancient archangel as possible. But it seems like the farther I flee, the closer he gets.

I make it to the bar, only to realize that there's nowhere else to run. I'm trapped between sweat-slickened bodies on either side, as if some mystical magnetism draws them towards me, locking me in place. I don't have time to ponder the cause of it; I just need to get the hell out of here.

And it hits me.

I shouldn't. I know it's a total suicide mission. But desperate times call for desperate measures. And if the veil has somehow slipped, revealing my identity, I'm already dead anyway.

Eyes narrowed in concentration, jaw clenched, and fists tight at my sides, I fling my consciousness out towards the approaching angel. Even though he's too close for comfort, he's still a good distance away. I've never tried to infiltrate a mind from this far before, and it takes every bit of my will to stretch that invisible arm towards him, snaking through the writhing bodies separating me from my impending fate. I can feel my mind straining with effort, causing little beads of sweat to dot my forehead and the back of my neck. But I push forward, forming that invisible hand into an arrow spearing straight for the ethereal man. I have no idea what will happen once I pierce through flesh and bone and penetrate his frontal lobe, or even if I'll be able to get in, but I have to try. Anything to get him away from me.

I'm so engrossed by the task before me that I don't even see him in my peripheral vision, moving towards me like a serpent. But the moment his hands cup my face and his mouth covers mine, my mind's connection stutters and dissipates onto the dance floor. And I can focus on nothing other than his warm lips moving against my own, coaxing them to open and welcome his tongue. He tastes of the way the sun feels on my skin in July. I remember rare and treasured summer trips to Navy Pier in his kiss, the sweet taste of cotton candy while laughing at the very top of the Ferris wheel. I see fireworks behind my shuttered eyelids—sparkling reds and greens and blue streaking across the sky. And I feel a sense of safety and familiarity that makes my lips quiver as they dance with his, so desperate to wrap myself in the comfort of him for just a little longer.

My gaze is hazy when Lucifer pulls away, but I notice that his eyes crackle and glow just like those fireworks in the memory he gave me. Breath stolen and cheeks hot, I touch my fingertips to my lips and merely stare in awe at the dazzling creature in front of me.

How? And better yet, *why?* The questions are sizzling on my tongue, but I can't speak. I'm afraid if I open my mouth, the drumbeat of my heart will drown out the music that already seems to be muted in this little cocoon for two.

Lucifer kissed me. And in his kiss, I felt both human and immortal. I felt good and evil. And I felt his...his and his alone.

I begin to shake my head, dispelling the thought, when I see him, frozen amidst a sea of swaying bodies, his quicksilver stare as bright and blinding as diamonds.

Legion.

I look back at Lucifer, who oddly enough, isn't donning his usual cocky grin. If anything, he looks just as shocked and affected as I feel. And if his surprise is so blatantly obvious, how must my expression read to the man I love?

Shit. This wasn't supposed to happen. He wasn't supposed to see this.

I have to get to Legion. I have to make him understand that I have no idea why Lucifer would kiss me. I have to tell him that I didn't want it. And I have to make him believe that I didn't like it.

Because I did.

And even as I stand here, swathed in guilt and shame, I still feel the burn of Lucifer's kiss, marking itself deep within my skin. Because in those carved memories, I remembered a time when I was just a girl. Hopeless, yet so unremarkably human. And I remembered what it felt like to want. What it felt like to dream.

And isn't that just the saddest fucking thing of all?

I try to step around Lucifer, but he swiftly grasps my arm, halting my retreat.

"Let me go," I grit through my teeth.

He shakes his head. "Not yet. Raphael is still here, but he can't see you behind my veil."

"What?"

"Yours was slipping. I realized it and moved in as fast as I could."

"And you had to *kiss* me in order to shield me?"

Lucifer shrugs, a tiny smile pulling at the corners of his luscious mouth. "I had to make it believable."

I roll my eyes and look back to Legion, hoping to convey my irritation at being in Lucifer's proximity. But I only get a glimpse of his retreating back, stalking through the crowd.

"Shit," I spit out.

Lucifer follows my line a vision, and although Legion is long gone, he successfully guesses the source of my unease. "He'll understand."

"You don't know that." There's panic in my voice.

"I know that he would do anything to protect you. I was just closer. He should be thanking me."

I narrow my glare on Lucifer's smug face. "You're enjoying

this, aren't you?"

"If you're referring to upsetting my brother, actually, no. No, I do not take pleasure in his fury. There are enough catalysts that could potentially set him off. I don't need him flying off the handle over a kiss."

"Then why even do it? If not to get under his skin?"

Lucifer leans in, his head dipping down towards mine. When he speaks, his gaze flares with violent passion. "Because I wanted to."

I don't know how to respond to his confession, or even if I should, so I just look away. The crowd is still as vibrant as ever, but there are no signs of Raphael. I guess Lucifer's little trick worked, although I could have done without his particular methods. He's anything but hard-pressed for intimacy with both women and men flocking at his feet every ten minutes. So what gives? He set me up to be killed by Legion before I was even born. Kissing me was just a game to him, just a way to further prove that he's a self-absorbed prick who doesn't care who he hurts.

"I need to go find Legion," I say, shrugging out of his touch.

"I'll go with you."

"Why?" I snap. "To gloat? You already know he saw everything."

I sift through the crowd, desperate to put some distance between us, but somehow Lucifer keeps up right beside me, as if the horde of dancers part just for him. Of course, they do.

"I know, Eden," he says quietly. I hear him loud and clear, even over the music. "That isn't what I wanted."

I roll my eyes and keep pushing forward. "Whatever."

After damn near fighting my way through the half naked, half fucking throng, I hit Irin's quarters, only to find her lazing on the sectional while watching a full out orgy in the middle of the floor.

"Stay," she insists, heavy-lidded eyes glassy.

I look to Lucifer who appears to consider her offer at first. "We would…" he begins, "but we're looking for someone."

Irin turns to me, stacking up the pieces. "He isn't here. Shouldn't you all be keeping an eye on our guests?"

I try to focus on her and not the naked woman just feet away from where I stand, crying out her pleasure and pain as she takes double penetration like a pro. Yikes.

"We were, but…"

"There was a…hiccup," Lucifer interjects. Something must flare in his eyes because Irin nods with understanding.

"I see." She turns her head and one of her dutiful servants rushes to her side. "Party's over."

The young man nods once, before rushing through the double doors. Irin claps twice, and the sinuous scene before us comes to a screeching halt. "That goes for you all as well."

Without a word, the foursome stands and gathers their strewn clothing, not an ounce of shame or shyness etched in their faces. I just witnessed a woman get pile-driven by two guys with her face buried in another woman's snatch, yet *my* cheeks are red with embarrassment.

"Apologies, Irin," Lucifer drawls, taking an empty seat on the sectional.

Irin shrugs. "I was bored anyway. Drinks?"

Right on cue, a server approaches with glasses of gold-speckled bubbly. I look to Lucifer who wears a devious smirk. He'd love it if I succumbed to my irrational, basal desires after indulging in Irin's elixir.

"No, thank you," I say, shaking my head.

"Something else then?" Irin inquires. She raises her brows, almost as if challenging me to refuse.

"Champagne?"

Before Irin can even respond, the server is scurrying off to fetch me a fresh, full glass.

We don't lower our masks until the raucous sex crew is gone. Then simply sip our drinks in silence. The moment after Irin dismisses her staff, Lucifer jumps right into it.

"Raphael was here. He saw Eden."

"Even through the veil?" If it weren't for the slight frown between Irin's slender black brows, I'd think she'd found that tidbit amusing.

"He must have been able to shatter it. Unless they're working with Dark magic, which is more than a bit surprising, if not disturbing."

"Did they make anyone else?"

Lucifer shakes his head. "The Se7en apparently cut off the rest of their lot. I had eyes on Raph, but he eluded me, as if he knew we'd be expecting him. Meaning, he knew we were here. Raph has always been a spineless follower, so I'm not surprised at his involvement. I am curious to see who else has joined Uriel's cause once intel comes in."

So no wonder I didn't spot the Se7en all evening. Still, that doesn't make me feel any better about Legion being practically absent after making such a big stink about me staying close to him. Maybe whatever he had going on with Adriel was more important.

Over the next hour, the members of the Se7en—minus Legion, of course—filter into Irin's quarters, varied shades of determination on their faces. Even Adriel looks a little less superior as she wafts in, her winter white still pristine. When Niko makes it in, he rushes straight to my side.

"E, what happened?" He cups my cheeks, looking for any and all signs of distress.

"I'm fine. Honestly."

"The spell...it should have—"

Before he can get the explanation out, he's ripped from in front of me, and damn near thrown across the room. Nikolai lands on his feet, but Legion is already right in front of him, his hulking frame heaving with fury. I swear, he's about to burn through his suit as heated as he seems.

"You said it would work!" he roars.

Even in the face of violence personified, Niko stands tall. "And it did. *You* should have disclosed the fact that a Seraph could strip spells."

"A Seraph can't do that." Legion takes a step back and roughly rakes his hand through his hair in frustration. "It also doesn't help that she made friends with a flock of Harpies and was practically untraceable. What the hell were you thinking, Eden?"

Suddenly, every eye is fixed on me. Harpies? I guess that explains the bird theme. Still, it doesn't explain why Legion couldn't trace me.

"What?" I scoff. "I didn't know what they were or what they were doing to me."

"Harpies are conniving little shits," Lilith comments. "Most times, they're harmless, but they're not to be trusted,

Eden. Ever."

"Like I said, I didn't know they were Harpies. And they seemed nice enough," I shrug. I mean, I knew they were *something*, but when you're quite literally surrounded by the supernatural, there's no way to take inventory of every non-human. And they looked nothing like the Harpies depicted in books and Wikipedia.

"That must've been how Raphael could sense you," Lucifer muses.

Legion thankfully abandons his standoff with Niko and comes to where I sit on the sectional, kneeling down to meet my eyes. "Were you hurt? Did he say anything to you?"

I shake my head. "No. I don't even think he knew who I was. He just seemed…interested. Like something was pulling him towards me."

Those silver eyes scan my face, still not convinced. But it only lasts a second and then he's pulling away from me. I can see it etched in his features—all is not forgotten and forgiven. The kiss he witnessed between Lucifer and me is still heavy on his brain.

"Good news is," Toyol begins, cutting through the tension, "we were able to get a tracker on one of the lesser angels. Now all we have to do is wait and let him lead us back to their lair."

"And then what?" Lucifer questions. He casually leans back into the sofa as if he doesn't even notice Legion's ire-filled glare staring silver daggers into his skull. "You all storm the castle and hope they let you leave with your heads? Remember, even with a couple of original fallen Seraph, an angel, a warlock prince, and a handful of demons, you're still outnumbered. Uriel has Raph, meaning there's a good chance he's lured others to his cause."

"And what about me?" I pipe up. "Adriel can wield light, and so can I. I can be an asset. Use me."

Legion shakes his head. "It's too dangerous, and you're still untrained. When I found you at the church, I detected three Seraph. Add in lesser angels, and that's more than any of us can handle."

"He's right," Lucifer tacks on. "Three Seraph would be impossible to kill. But I don't agree with benching our rookie." He turns his focus on me, then Legion. "No one knows what she can do. Don't let your petty emotions blind your judgment. If it were anyone else, would you be so quick to keep her out of this fight?"

"She isn't anyone else," Legion answers darkly, a hint of a warning in his tone.

"Then use her. At this point, the ball is in our court. We have the element of surprise on our side, and we have Uriel's mate."

"And they have The Redeemer and Eden's mom," Legion retorts. His tense jaw works with irritation. "Fine. If Eden wants to fight, then I won't stop her. You just make sure you remember your place."

"Oh, and what would that be?" Lucifer goads.

"Out of my fucking way."

With that, Legion stalks out of the room, those double doors slamming shut at his back. I guess the meeting is adjourned.

I gather the skirts of my dress and my elaborate mask and stroll over to where Niko stands, anxious to find out where he was all evening.

"I'm so sorry," he says at my approach.

I shake my head. "You have nothing to be sorry about."

"That remains to be seen."

We both spin around to find Lucifer just feet away. His expression is as smug and disinterested as always, but there's a glimmer of purple fire churning in his glare.

"You heard Lilith," I say. "The Harpies could have had something to do with it."

"Maybe," he shrugs. "Maybe not. But let me remind our little warlock friend of the conditions of his freedom. You fail—you're mine for the rest of eternity. And I'm not known to play nice with others."

"I've got it."

Niko starts to brush by him, but Lucifer stops him with a hand to his chest, his eyes shining even brighter, even wilder, with vicious delight.

"No. I don't think you do, mate."

I try to step between them, but their frames are like marble over steel. "Just leave him alone."

"You see, if anything happens to Eden, I will hold you personally responsible. And then maybe I'll pay your brother a little visit…see how that gorgeous sister-in-law is doing, and that precious baby boy of theirs. Where might they be, anyway? Surely, they'd want to know of your recent resurrection…"

Eyes nearly opaque, Niko grits out, "You leave them out of this."

The temperature drops twenty degrees and my breath escapes in a frosty cloud of condensation. I shiver as the air crackles between us, charged with icy violence.

Lucifer is nonplussed. "No. I don't think I will."

"Then maybe I'll have a talk with Irin. You know, I didn't see the familial resemblance until you sent me back. Her short stature, the black eyes, even her hair is the same. And then I thought…it's funny how Saskia looks like a younger Irin. You remember Saskia, right? The impish girl you're keeping prisoner? The same girl you instructed to wait on Eden during her time in Hell? You're getting sloppy, Luc."

My gaze goes wide with realization. Saskia. The quiet, dark-haired girl that sounded like she was being choked from the inside out. She saved my life, probably more than a couple times. I've been so preoccupied with my own shit that I didn't put two and two together. Saskia could be Irin's younger sister. Or…her daughter.

Even with Niko dangling leverage over Lucifer's head—leverage that could have him struck down by Irin's wrath within seconds—Lucifer simply…laughs.

"You stupid, stupid boy." Lucifer moves in to meet Niko's glare, so close that their faces are only inches apart. "Who do you think sent her to me?"

"Bullshit."

"Is it? Maybe we should ask Irin."

Niko doesn't respond, but I can see that this revelation rattles him. Even if he doesn't want to believe it, fiction is less likely than fact. Why else would he instruct Saskia to attend me? If he wanted to conceal her existence, he could have had her stashed in a dungeon somewhere, writhing in hellfire. Instead, he basically dangled her in front of us, like he wanted us to know the truth.

"Let's just go."

I grasp Niko's forearm and try to pry him away from Lucifer's unrelenting stare. He resists at first but then turns to me, his expression softening just a fraction.

"Leave my family out of this," he hisses, bumping Lucifer's shoulder as he passes.

"You can't hide them forever," Lucifer calls after him. "I'm not the only one anxious to find them."

Simmering rage ripples off Niko's frame as we exit the room and head down the hallway. I don't dare say a word. When we turn the corner, he kisses me on the forehead, his lips like ice, before turning to stalk the opposite direction. Lucifer's threat to his family has not only shaken him to his core, but it also aroused his venomous demons that had lain dormant for decades. I'd only seen a mere fraction of the Dark's power. There's no doubt in my mind that Niko is capable of much more than he's let on.

I'm so preoccupied with my own inner musings that I don't even pick up the scent as I approach my bedroom door. And by the time my Nephilim instincts kick in, it's already too late.

Because within the stutter of a heartbeat, I'm face down, the salty taste of tears on my tongue as I cry out while my body writhes in agony.

And he's already taking exactly what he came for.

Me.

TWENTY

EGION FUCKS ME LIKE A MAN POSSESSED. LIKE A MAN who's shed his skin and let his inner beast claw its way out and take the reins of his body and soul.

My moans are muffled by the bedspread to the point of being suffocating. But every time I lift my head to gulp in air or even turn to get a glimpse of him, he pushes my face back down. As if he doesn't want me to see him. As if he's so far gone that he's afraid I won't recognize him.

He gathers my wrists in his hands and secures them behind me, using his hold to ride me harder and deeper with every stroke. With his fire branding my insides and his touch searing my skin, I'm lost to him. Utterly lost and helpless under his control. Part of me is afraid at the rough way he fucks me, without an ounce of tenderness, but the carnal part of me is so turned on that our wet slaps of drenched flesh can be heard echoing even over my tortured mewls and moans.

I come so powerfully and tragically that my knees buckle beneath me. But even with me calling out his name, begging for him to ease his assault on my sagging body, he doesn't stop. If anything, he gives it to me harder and grips my wrists even tighter, ensuring that I can't get away. I try to keep steady, but as pleasure merges into pain, my sex-clouded brain begins to sober. He's not going to stop. Even as I beg him to, even as I cry out for him to let me go, he doesn't even seem to register that I exist.

His hands are bands of molten steel around my wrists as his cock spears me faster and deeper, slicing me open with every thrust. I understand being caught up in the moment, but something about this is wrong. He feels wrong. And the fact that he won't stop, no matter that my tears are no longer tears of ecstasy, is just so fucking wrong.

"Oh God. Please," I rasp, my voice hoarse from screaming. I have no more strength within me to fight him off. I'm completely powerless to him. "Please let me go."

Then as if he's been blasted by an unseen energy, his body is ripped away from mine, and he's thrown across the room with enough force to shatter one of the wardrobes into splinters. I spin around, pulling the comforter around my naked, sore body, just as he stands. Legion's eyes are wide with terror, and the color has drained from his face. He opens his pale, dry lips to speak, but his wild gaze says it all.

That wasn't him.

"Eden," he manages to croak. "Eden, I'm sorry. I…"

I shake my head. There's nothing he can possibly say that can make this okay. There's nothing he can do to make *us* okay. We both know it. This isn't just another crack in our already fractured relationship. It's a crater as wide and deep as the darkest pits of Hell.

With tear-filled eyes, I watch as Legion rights his clothing and exits the bedroom, closing the door behind him. As soon as he's out of sight, I release all the fear, pain, and humiliation that had been strangling me since he had lost control. In chest heaving sobs, I cry into the satin comforter, hating him for hurting me. Hating myself for lying there helpless, too caught up in his violent frenzy to fight him off. I don't know what any of this means, but I know, undoubtedly, that he could have done much worse. He could have killed me tonight, and if he hadn't come back to me, he would have.

Now the question is, who's to blame? Legion? Or the twisted fuck within that possessed his soul and stole him away?

I don't know how long I lay there and cry, my naked body covered in the scent of his sweat and sex. But when I finally look up, I see that I have an audience. Reeling back, I gasp audibly and clutch the covers against my chest tighter, hoping that I haven't exposed any more skin than has already been on display. I don't know how long he's been sitting there casually reclining, one leg bent with his ankle resting on his knee. But he knows what happened. I can see the pity dimming his star-flecked violet eyes.

"How…how did you get in here?" There's no way he came through the door. I would have heard it, even over my sobs.

"I tried to warn you," Lucifer mutters, ignoring my question. "I thought we had more time—at least until the threat had passed. I should have been here."

"You knew this would happen?" My voice cracks, still raw

with emotion.

Lucifer shakes his head. "The wayward souls are full of malice and resentment. They feed off the anguish and misery of others. It fuels them. And Legion's resistance only entices them to torture him more."

"But you knew he would get like this. You knew he would turn into a monster." And he let it happen anyway. Not only that, he set it up. He wanted Legion to become what he once was.

"Eden, I don't think you understand. What happened to-night…what you saw… That was nothing."

"Nothing? *Nothing?*" I scoff. "He…he…" I don't even know what he did. And even if I could describe it, I certainly wouldn't be able to say it out loud. Not to Lucifer.

"He is what he is. What you pretend not to see. A savage. A killer. A demon. I'll admit, I relied on shock value during your short stay in my realm. But Legion…this isn't for show. This isn't a game to see how far he can push your boundaries. It's who he is."

He climbs to his feet, his movements lithe, yet there's an unexpected tension that's set in his shoulders and along his defined, chiseled jawline. He strides to the bed and sits before me, close enough that the scent of deadly belladonna near-ly eclipses the remnants of sex lingering on my skin. With him here—in my bedroom, on my bed, with only a rumpled comforter shielding my naked body—I feel uneasy. Nervous. Scared, but not frightened of him per se. Just anxious of his mere presence.

"Eden," he begins, those twin glimmering galaxies search-ing my face before finally settling on my mouth. "I never wanted this for you."

"I know. You wanted me dead."

He nods solemnly. "I did at first, but only because I knew what Uriel was capable of. I didn't know you. And once I did… Well, the damage had already been done. Adriel had already found you. It would only be a matter of time before the Se7en found you too."

"And they would do your dirty work."

He shrugs. "Better them than me. Uriel is a prick, but he's a resourceful prick. If he had a plan for you, I wasn't about to be the one to foil it. But I would not have allowed you to be hurt. That I can promise you."

But he did. He stood by and watched me suffer at the hands of my mother. Hungry, dirty, and forgotten, I was left to perish before I'd even learned how to tie my shoes. And when I failed to die from my mother's neglect, she took things into her own hands.

And Lucifer did nothing.

So many nights I lay awake, silently praying for someone to take me away from the cruel reality of my life. So many nights I had hoped for someone to care—to just give a damn— enough about me to check in with us. They would have seen that she was sick, her mind corroded by drug use and hysteria, just as Uriel had wanted. And I could have known something other than the rot and ruin, dread and destruction that I had believed was my birthright.

And still, Lucifer did nothing.

"Is that supposed to make me feel better?"

Lucifer works his sensual mouth, searching for the right words, and I'm hit with the memory of his lips on mine just hours ago. But when he speaks, his tone is sharp. "It's supposed to make you understand. Yes, your life was shitty, but you survived, just as I knew you would. Just as it was prophesized."

Prophesized? Why would my existence be worth prophesizing?

Before I can ask him to clarify, he pushes off from the bed. I notice shadows around his eyes as he looks down at me.

"This will not kill you. It will hurt you, yes, but it won't destroy you. He doesn't have that power."

I don't have the heart to ask him if he's referring to Uriel. Or Legion.

I cast my gaze down to my knotted fingers clutching the comforter around my naked breasts. But when I look up, Lucifer is gone, stealthily leaving the way he came. I'm left wondering if he was ever truly here. Or maybe his presence was merely a figment of my imagination, a conjured comfort in the midst of my desperate sorrow. Either way, I can't deny the truth that's staring me down: I was glad he was here. And I was glad Legion was not.

I fall into a fitful sleep soon after, my dreams just fragments of color and flashes of light. When I wake, still exhausted, I drag my weary body past the wreckage of my wardrobe to the bath to soak and scrub the night before off my skin. My face is still streaked with melted makeup and salted tear trails, my eyes bloodshot and puffy. I don't know what happened last night. I don't even know who it was that was holding me down and fucking me. And now that I've slept on it, I feel an overwhelming sense of disgust—at the violation and for finding a semblance of pleasure in the violence. I trusted Legion with my body, and even though he had no control, he betrayed that trust. I don't know how we come back from that. And until he deals with the demons wreaking havoc from within, I don't know if we should.

I don't bother with makeup, and barely have enough energy to pull my hair into a messy bun before dressing down in the first casual garments I can find. My appearance truly matches the darkness in my soul. I look drab. Tired. But after what happened the night before at the masquerade party, I can't afford the luxury of hiding out in my room and crying into my pillow like some heartbroken teenager. Now more than ever, it's evident that I have to be trained and ready. So if that means shelving my current crisis and slapping on some manufactured confidence, that's what I'll do.

But all of that steely resolve vanishes the moment I step into the gym and every soul—demon, angel, or otherwise—stops and turns to stare, ceasing all prior activity.

I'm used to getting funny looks—that's never bothered me before. But this is different. And they're not gazing at me with expressions of curiosity or even disdain. I read pity in their eyes. Confusion. Shock. As if they lived that moment with me in my bedroom as Legion relinquished control to the darkest, most devious parts of himself. As if they felt that same pain that pierced straight into my heart when I realized that I wasn't strong enough to help him fight those demons. That I wasn't enough to make him fight for us. They know. They must all know. And how pathetic I must be for feeling grateful that he isn't here right now, bearing witness to their judgment. Even now, I want to save him, when last night was a clear indication that I can't.

"Eden?" Lilith's voice is soft, and it almost startles me as she slowly approaches. "How are you?"

I try to manage a casual shrug, but I can't fake it. "Ok."

"Have…have you heard anything?"

I frown. "From who?"

Lilith mimics my expression. "No one's told you?"

"Told me what?"

"Legion…he's…gone."

I can feel the blood drain from my face as I read the hurt etched in hers. "What?"

"He left…sometime late last night. We don't know where he is. We can't track him. We can't even…feel…him. He's gone." She looks around the gym, her gaze landing on the remaining members of the Se7en. "We're going out to find him. He would never leave us without at least discussing it. Something must be wrong."

Something is wrong, I want to say, but the words catch in my rapidly tightening throat.

I should have known something was up when Cain wasn't dutifully sitting at my sister's side this morning. Instead, he's here, with his brothers and sister, regarding me with a glimmer of skepticism in his black eyes. Maybe they don't know what went down between Legion and me last night, but I'm sure at least Cain suspects something. Especially if they know what happened with Lucifer at the party. Maybe they think I'm to blame. Maybe they think that kiss sparked a raging darkness inside Legion. And honestly, I wouldn't be able to dispute that, not when I experienced that darkness for myself.

"We're training one last time before we leave. We don't know what we'll come up against," Lilith says.

"I'm coming with you."

She hesitates before she nods in response. "Adriel, Nikolai, and Lucifer have agreed to join us. Are you sure you're ready?"

Truth be told, I'll never be ready for what's to come. There's no way you can prepare for what's meant to be your execution.

But still, I lie. To her, and to myself. Because the truth is just too painful to admit, even within the prison of my own mind.

"Yes."

TWENTY-ONE

I SPEND MY LAST COUPLE HOURS WITH SISTER, STRUGGLING to keep the crippling fear from dimming my features. Irin agreed to let her stay until she is completely healed, and after that, she will be free to stay or return to her old life, whatever is left of it. As much as I would hate to imagine my sister in a skimpy outfit, serving drinks to supernatural creatures during lavish parties, I truly hope she decides to stay. Safety is a novelty that only Irin can provide for the time being. If Toyol's reports are accurate, the city is a war zone. There is no place for her there.

"So are you just going to let me ramble on about these rich chicks' botched boob jobs, or are you finally ready to tell me what's bothering you?"

I turn from the Housewives show I'm spacing out on, and plaster on a tight smile. "Nothing is bothering me."

"Bull." She clicks off the television, giving me her undivided attention. "I know you, Eden. You can lie to everyone else and pretend like you're not scared out of your wits, but you can't pretend with me. Come on…talk to me. Between you and Cain, I'm starting to freak out here."

That piques my interest. "What did Cain say?"

"Nothing. That's the point. He tells me nothing, as if he's afraid that any hint of bad news will break me. I'm not that fragile. I know something is going on and I deserve to know what it is. Being in the dark nearly killed me, remember? I don't think I'll cheat death a second time."

A pang of guilt pierces my chest at the mention of the explosion that nearly took her from me. The explosion that was a message for me. She's lying in that hospital bed because of *me*. I may as well have pushed the button on the detonator myself.

"Well?" she says impatiently. Determination narrows her glare. "I'm waiting. Spill it."

I take a deep breath. Then another, just to stall. "L…he's gone."

"Gone? Like, stepped out for a smoke-gone? Or went to the store for a gallon of milk and been gone for twelve years-gone?"

"I don't know. I guess the second one?" I shrug. "He just left. Didn't tell anyone."

"Damn. Like that other guy, right? Crysis?"

Shit. She's right. Like Crysis, Legion left without a trace, without telling a soul he was leaving. And the only thing I can think about is how I had a part in both of their disappearances. Crysis ghosted shortly after he and I had that tiff, resulting

in me blasting him with holy light. And last night, after....
whatever...happened between Legion and me, I can see why
he dipped out too. Although, I didn't blast him...I think. I just
assumed he had gotten ahold of himself and threw himself
back into that wardrobe, leaving it in a pile of splinters and
strewn clothing...

Fuck. What if that was me? I didn't mean to. I didn't want
to hurt him, despite the fact that he was hurting me. But what
if some inner angel, flight or fight instinct kicked in before I
even realized what I was doing? It's certainly possible. I didn't
see any light, but I was also being held facedown into a tear-
stained comforter.

"Are you ok?" Sister asks, her voice full of sympathy.

"I don't know. I'm worried." And terrified. And angry.

"I know." She rests a partially gauzed hand atop mine.
"Did something happen?"

I look away and shake my head. There's no way I can tell
her about last night. She wouldn't understand. Hell, I don't
even understand. But I know he left because of me. He abandoned his family—the ones who have fought alongside him
for centuries—because of me. There's no way I can stomach
that fact without choking on my own guilt.

"I wanted to see you tonight because we're leaving," I finally admit.

"Leaving? When? Where are we going?"

"Not we, Sister," I explain, turning back to face her. Her
big, brown eyes fill with concern and confusion. "Me. I'm going with the Se7en to find L."

"But I thought it wasn't safe."

"It's not. Not for you, at least." I try to smile through the pain, but I can't force the act. "I'll be fine, I promise. I've been training every day. Cain says I'm pretty lethal with a gun."

Her mouth twitches as if she wants to appear optimistic, but I know just the mention of her newfound companion pains her. She's not at risk of just losing me. She could very well lose him too. And even if we somehow make it out alive, there's no telling how long we'll be gone. Or in what state we'll return.

"Don't go," she whispers, her voice cracking under the strain of emotion. "Stay here with me. Please? I can't lose you too."

I blink back tears, refusing to let them fall. It wasn't that long ago that she lost Ben, the man she had been planning a life with. She loved him. And it's a miracle that she's opened her heart enough to heal and find solace in Cain. Her life was stolen from her. Her job, her home. Yet, she never let it ruin her. Somehow, it only made her more determined to survive.

But I fear that losing me and losing Cain will destroy her.

Still, I believe that I have to do this for her. *We* have to do this for her. Even if we don't survive, she deserves another shot at happiness.

"I wish I could," I reply to her pleas. "I do. But I can't let others fight on my behalf anymore. All this…it's because of me. Uriel is still out there, and he has my mother, plus a weapon that could kill the Se7en permanently. I won't be a coward. If everyone else is willing to risk their lives, I need to do the same."

She nods, knowing that my words are as true as they are earnest. But I know they do nothing to soothe her aching heart.

"When?"

"Tonight," I answer. When her gaze goes wide with terror, I continue. "The sooner we leave, the easier it may be to track Legion. Before he gets too far. He could very well be in danger."

"I understand," she replies, casting her gaze downward.

I don't want to cause her any more undue pain, so I climb to my feet and lean over to leave a kiss on her forehead.

"I'll be back as soon as I can. I promise."

"You better." Her beautiful, brown eyes well with tears. "I love you, little sis."

"I love you, too."

I turn away before the first of my tears have a chance to fall. The sniffles at my back have me swallowing my own sobs as I open the door that leads to the hallway. I'm not surprised to find Cain standing there, propped against the opposite wall.

"You told her."

I nod. "I don't want to lie to her."

"So she knows there's a good possibility that none of us will make it back?"

"She knows there's a chance that will happen, yes."

A frown dimples the space between his dark, bushy brows and he strokes his beard. I've grown to learn that it's his tell when he's contemplative or troubled. "If things go awry, I want you to make it back here. If it looks like we'll lose, leave us. Come back to her. She'll need you more than ever if we're not successful."

"Successful. In finding Legion? Or in stopping Uriel?"

"Either. Both. If we fail at either one, it won't matter anyway. If Uriel doesn't destroy your world, Legion will finish off the job."

My stare goes sharp and narrow. "How can you say that?"

"Because it's the truth." He pushes off the wall and comes to stand in front of me. Even with his proximity, I'm not afraid of him anymore. Actually, I've grown fond of Cain. And with his newly grown beard covering most of his scar, I might even find him handsome. "There was a reason he surrendered his power to Lucifer. He could've resisted, but he didn't. He didn't want this."

"So what do we do now?" I ask, my voice barely above a whisper.

"We find him. Then we go after Uriel."

"In that order?"

He nods. "L is a sitting duck out there. Uriel knows that if he presses the right buttons and provokes him, Legion will do the very thing he desires. He will wipe out mankind."

"And if it's too late? If somehow Uriel finds him first?"

Cain looks away. Even his tone is distant. "We stop him."

I hear the words, but know they mean something different—something more. We won't just stop Legion. Cain is prepared to kill him.

"We meet in twenty. Suit up."

He steps to Sister's door but doesn't turn the knob to go inside. Instead, he gently presses his forehead against the polished wood, a move that is so vulnerable, it almost makes him human. He's in pain. Maybe even a little afraid.

I wish I had some words of comfort to offer him, but there's no way I could offer fake confidence and optimism, not when my insides were twisted with anxiety. So I turn and slowly make my way down the hall, letting my tears leave a salty trail from Sister's door.

When I make it to my room, I find that someone has taken the liberty of laying out clothes for me. Black leather pants, a long sleeve thermal, combat boots. Fighting clothes. There's even a matching leather jacket with half a dozen inside pockets and straps built in, for weapons, I assume.

Holy shit. This is happening.

I mean, I knew it was happening, but it didn't really sink in until now. I'd grown spoiled during our stay here. Too comfortable with the safety and security that Irin's home provided. Now we are deliberately stepping into a war zone. And to be honest, I'm scared shitless.

I dress quickly just to give my shaking hands something to do and then slick my hair back into one long, silver braid. Whoever left the clothes also thought to include wool socks and leather gloves. It's sweltering with all my layers, but I know it's necessary to combat the Chicago chill. It'd be downright tragic to make it this far only to fall victim to hypothermia.

When enough time has passed, I make my way to Irin's sitting room for the last time. The mood is somber. Even her staff have stowed their usual cheery demeanor. The Se7en are stationed at their designated space on the opposite side of the sectional, but Legion's absence makes them seem even farther away. His presence filled the room. I could feel him in every cell, vibrating with the hum of his unnatural heartbeat. And now, he's left a gaping hole—in my chest and within the Se7en. None of us are complete without him.

Irin is dressed in one of her many sarong and bra top ensembles, but this set seems less flashy. It's black, just like everyone else's clothing, and I have to wonder if we're subconsciously having a funeral. Even Adriel has swapped out her flowing winter white for darker layers.

I've only just sat down when Lucifer comes striding in, Nikolai right behind him. The dazzling warlock comes to sit beside me, his expression unreadable. He isn't in his usual dark suit, having traded the designer threads for slacks and a leather jacket similar to mine. I release a relieved breath.

"You're coming?"

Niko nods. "Luc told me how he found you last night. I'm not letting you out of my sight."

He stares straight ahead, his jaw tight. I can't imagine what he must think of me right now.

"He didn't mean it… It wasn't him."

Niko's head turns towards me so unnaturally quick that I nearly yelp. His eyes are pale and speckled with azure fire. "Wasn't it though?"

He holds me with his glittering glare for nearly a minute before Lucifer clears his throat from his place beside Irin. When I look to him, he gives me a tight smile, so unlike the cocky grin that usually curves his sensual mouth.

Cain steps to the center of the room to address us all, his expression serious. He's trimmed his short beard, revealing more of the scar that mars his face from lip to ear.

"If any of you are even the slightest bit uncertain, this is the time to speak up. Because the moment we leave this house, there is no turning back. There is no mercy beyond these walls—no safety from the terrors that await us. There is only violence. Only death. If you survive, you will live out your days with blood on your hands. Blood that may never wash off. So if you're not one hundred percent sure that you can handle that, do us all a favor and stay behind. The training wheels are off from this point forward. This is war."

I know he's talking to me, but he gives me the courtesy of diverting his beady, black eyes. I wouldn't back down now, even if I were uncertain. There is no option other than fighting. For Legion. For my sister. For every innocent human life. All I have left in me is the will to fight.

"Well, that's one hell of a pep talk. Is this the part where we feel a rousing sense of inspiration?" Lucifer jibes, rolling his eyes. Cain flips him the bird and stalks back to the Se7en.

The polar opposite of his demon brother, Phenex angles his body to the right and bows his head gracefully. "Irin, we appreciate your hospitality. It will not be forgotten."

The Watcher nods in response. "Of course. My doors are always open."

The next moments feel like sleepwalking. Both Cain and Toyol approach me with a small arsenal and a few gadgets that look to cost more than most homes. I swallow down my trepidation and stand with my head held high, not willing to show the barest inkling of insecurity.

"This is an earpiece," Toyol says, holding up a tiny black dot. "Once activated, you'll be able to communicate with each of us through it."

I nod and dip my head forward to let him secure it to my ear. When he's done, he holds out the small sensor I wore the first time I visited Irin's home. The one Legion gingerly placed on the inside of my dress, right against my heart. I still remember the way his warm fingers felt brushing against my breast. I can still smell the masculine scent of his skin— scorched earth and midnight jasmine. And the way his eyes swirled with molten silver as they roamed my body.

That was the Legion I had grown to know and care for. That was the Legion I had laid beside in the darkest hours of night, relishing the heat that emanated from his frame. And when I surrendered my body to him, along with my heart, it was that Legion who took me in his arms and made me feel like the most desired woman on Earth.

And I lost him.

I wanted to prove that my feelings hadn't changed so badly that I ignored the fact that he was slipping away. He was disappearing, bit by bit, right before my eyes, and I did nothing to stop it. Like a naïve little girl, I just kept hoping he would come back to me.

"Eden? You with me?" Toyol lifts a brow.

"Uh, yeah," I stammer, carefully taking the censor from his fingertips and securing it against the skin between my breasts. The time for modesty has come and gone.

Toyol gives me a few more items—compact night vision goggles, a high-voltage taser, flares—and sure enough, there's a pocket for each item as if the jacket was specially made for me. When Cain steps up with the weapons, a dark, nervous energy quakes in my bones.

"These are for you," he says, handing me a holster outfitted with twin Glock 43s.

He shows me how to secure the firearms, giving me a quick rundown on the specs, and then offers me two other gifts—knives longer than the length of my hand. The hilts are studded with red jewels, much like the ones embedded in The Redeemer. The slightly curved blades are sheathed in thick leather and slide right into two pockets inside my coat.

They're positioned perfectly, and I find I can retrieve them in a hurry without managing to slice off a finger in the process.

"Are you ready for this?" Cain asks me while Toyol outfits Niko with an earpiece. I guess the other gadgets aren't necessary for the warlock.

"I am," I reply, mustering what's left of my confidence.

He nods to himself, busying his hands with the task of securing his own weapons. "The bullets are tipped in angelsbane, a weaponized form of demon blood. It won't take down a Seraph, but it should subdue them. It'll work on both lesser angels and demons too. Something Phenex and Jinn have been working on. The blades were forged in Hellfire. They will send lesser demons back to Hell."

"And is that what we want? To send Legion back to Hell."

He weighs the words in his mouth before answering. "If it comes to that, that would be the best case scenario."

"And the worst?"

He shakes his head, and I don't need to infiltrate his mind to know exactly what he's thinking. The worst-case scenario is killing him—permanently. I'm not sure how, considering Uriel has The Redeemer, and I'm not even sure I want to know. Uriel made me to be used as a weapon against Legion before the sacred demon blade was even in play, so there must be another way. We just have to make sure we find Legion before the Seraph do.

"You know, if it were up to me, you'd be sitting this one out. You're untrained," he remarks. There isn't criticism or annoyance tainting his tone, but real, genuine concern. And when he looks down at me, it's not malice that I see narrowing his gaze, but what looks oddly like fear and desperation. "But it's not up to me, and I understand your choice to go out there. I just… I need you to survive this. I need you to come back to your sister. I don't think you understand just how much I mean this."

"I understand."

"No. You don't. Because if you did, you'd be with her right now, watching whatever stupid show is on Bravo or Food Network, flipping through trashy magazines, and discussing the latest gossip. She's not like us, Eden. She hasn't been beaten and broken more times than she can count. She hasn't been stitched together like an ugly, mangled rag doll that no one wants to play with. Her pieces still fit. She's still foolish enough to hope, to dream, to want."

I never realized Cain saw us as two sides of the same coin, and although the analogy stings, he's right. Sister hasn't let life ruin her. She isn't jaded by pain and strife. And while she had been orphaned at a young age, it wasn't because her parents didn't love her. They didn't abandon her because they chose their own selfish needs over their daughter. They died in a car accident.

I never told her, but I remember envying her for their deaths. I feel terrible, even now, for thinking it. But to know that you were once truly loved the way a parent should love a child was a gift that no one could ever take from her. It was why she could still find it in her heart to hope, to dream, to want. Because she had never forgotten what that felt like. And I had never known what it was to have it in the first place.

"I will," I tell Cain, meaning it. "I'll come back to her."

"Thank you," he replies. And I realize that my survival isn't just for my sister. It's for him as well.

Lilith and Andras approach, and I recognize whom I have to thank for my new clothes, not that I'm surprised. The leather pants fit like a glove, yet provide ample movement and breathability. The thermal is also fitted, and the boots are stylish yet comfortable. This outfit has the blonde duo stamped all over it.

"You look good, girl," Andras remarks, letting out a low whistle.

"You do," Lilith adds. "How are you feeling?"

I shrug. "Anxious."

"You'll ride with us, Nikolai, and Lucifer. Cain, Toyol, Jinn, and Phenex will be with Adriel in the other car."

I look to my left, my right, then whisper, "Is that a good idea?"

Lilith steps in close, so we're nearly chest to chest. "While Luc may be a conniving prick, I trust her even less."

I follow her line of vision as she turns and glances at Adriel. Jeans, a heavy down jacket, flat boots. Not a weapon in sight.

"You think she'll betray us?" I ask, turning back to Lilith. Ironic, considering it was Lilith who sold us out to Lucifer, even if it was to protect me, in his own convoluted way.

"I don't know. She still loves Legion. I…get that." She offers a pained grin, remembering her own deceit in the name of unrequited love. "I don't think she would do anything to jeopardize his life."

I simply nod. If there's one thing that bonds the three of us, it's our love for Legion. And if I have to be constantly reminded of their feelings in order to secure his safety, then so be it.

Once everyone is outfitted with their chosen weapons, we bid our goodbyes to Irin and her staff. I don't even flinch when Kairo wraps his arms around me and leaves a peck on my cheek. He's been good to me during my stay here. And I have to admit, after seeing him in action with Lucifer—an image that will forever be burned into my skull—I wish I had taken the time to chat with him more.

"May our Lord be with you, my little doves," Irin trills as we take the basement stairs that lead to the weapons room where Cain and I had target practice. Apparently, there's a hidden door that leads to an underground garage. It's where the Se7en hid the vehicles they escaped the city in.

My nerves spike when I spy the matching black SUVs, and a pang of nostalgia strikes my chest. I haven't been beyond these four walls in what feels like months. And as I slide into the backseat, I can't help but picture Legion in the driver's seat instead of Andras, smiling slyly at my song choices. I can still hear the sound of his bellowing laughter, the way its richness would warm the enclosed space like a heated blanket as I tortured him with my singing. I can still picture the way his throat would flex and bob when he threw his head back and succumbed to those rare, jovial moments.

I can still feel him, so all cannot be lost. He has to be out there somewhere. Waiting for me to bring him back.

And I will. Even if it takes every bit of power within me.

Even if I have to surrender my humanity and become the weapon I was created to be.

TWENTY-TWO

THE RIDE TO THE CITY SEEMS LONGER AND DARKER than I remember. I sit in silence, imagining every possible scenario we may face, and how they could go disastrously wrong.

What if we meet the Seraph first? We won't beat them without Legion.

And what if they've already captured him? We could always trade Adriel for him.

What if we never find him? Do we turn around and abandon the city crumbling at our feet? The Se7en have vowed to protect mankind from the rot of evil. However, the greatest perceived evil is sitting in the passenger seat, merely a foot away from me.

So how do we kill a being that's virtually indestructible? Whose power is only second to God?

Short answer: You don't.

We're bringing a proverbial knife to a gunfight. No, not even a knife. A slingshot. Uriel has at least two Seraph standing with him, plus a posse of lesser angels. The only one of us that could potentially beat him is Lucifer. We need Legion. It still won't be an even match, but at least with two former Seraph, we could have a fighting chance.

But then I have to wonder... Will Legion stand with us? And is he even Legion anymore?

If he were himself, he would have never left without saying a word. He wouldn't abandon his brothers and sister. He wouldn't abandon *me*.

"Hey. We'll find him," Niko murmurs beside me, giving my tightly clenched fist a squeeze. Lilith sits on the other side of me.

"Do you really believe that?" I whisper back, turning to find his crystal blue eyes glowing under the cover of night.

"I do. I just hope he wants to be found."

I suck in a breath and exhale through my nose, desperately trying to release my crippling fear. That's what worries me the most—Legion won't want our help.

"Are you ready for that?" Niko asks, reading the tension on my face that not even the shadows can conceal.

"Ready for what?"

"Facing that reality. If Legion doesn't want our help, or if he reacts with violence, are you ready to do whatever it takes to subdue him? Or can you let him go?"

Let him go.

That's the one conclusion I hadn't pictured. Every scenario I had imagined ended with us bringing him back, whether it was from self-destruction or death. But I never doubted that we would pull him back from the brink of whatever horror awaited us. But to let him go…that's not something I was prepared to do. Because when I look at the rest of my life—however short or long—he's right there beside me. Loving Legion is the future I had let myself long for. Before him, I never wanted anything more than to belong. And with him and the Se7en, I finally felt that I did.

I didn't even realize it until now, but I had channeled my sister. I had allowed myself to hope, to dream, to want. I had dropped my guard, despite every reason not to, and let myself find happiness in the rarest of predicaments.

I'm jolted from my musings the moment we cross into the city limits. The breath is snatched from my body, and I'm left looking on in horror, bottom lip trembling, and hands shaking. Niko squeezes me a little harder, his cold fingers doing nothing to still the quaking.

Everything is fire and destruction. Cars engulfed in flames. Armed soldiers strapped with AK-47s patrolling the streets. Police barricades blocking off entrances to storefronts that have evidently been vandalized. Broken glass, loose garbage, and dried blood sully the pavement. My city is in ruin.

"It's worse than we thought," Andras mutters from the driver's seat as he carefully maneuvers around the wreckage.

A group of armed, fatigue-clad men waves us down. Cain and the others are just yards ahead of us, and also get stopped.

"Stay completely silent," Niko whispers just as Andras rolls down the window.

"What's your business here?" one of them questions Andras, while his colleagues surround the SUV, shining flashlights into the vehicle. The bright lights flare over our statue-still bodies, yet the men back up in retreat. As if they don't even see us.

"Just passing through. Is there a problem?"

"City-wide curfew. Where are you traveling from?"

"Minneapolis. Headed East."

"And your friend?" He nods to Cain's SUV ahead.

"Same. Traveling salesmen."

"You don't look like salesmen. Let me see some ID."

Fuck. This was not what I expected. How the hell will we get out of this without resorting to violence?

I could make him drop his weapon and turn around. Hell, I could make them all bend to my will leaving them in a hazy stupor. But before I can fling my influence out towards the unsuspecting soldier, Andras leans forward, casually resting his forearm against the window frame.

"What's your name?" he asks, his voice as smooth as butter.

I brace for chaos, but the man answers, "Bishop. Drew Bishop."

"Drew…come closer. Lower your weapon."

To my surprise, the soldier does as he's told and steps forward, close enough for me to glimpse his slackened jaw and unblinking stare. He doesn't even seem to notice Lucifer sitting in the passenger seat.

"Drew, are you married?" Andras coos, his words wrapped in silk.

"Yes, sir."

"Does your wife make you happy?"

"Yes, sir."

"But you still yearn for more, don't you?"

"Yes, sir."

"That's what I thought." Andras reaches out a hand and cups the man's cheek, drawing him further into his web. "I can give you what you yearn for, Drew. You would like that, wouldn't you?"

"Yes, sir."

"Because you want me?"

"Yes, sir."

"Call your friends off and let us pass, and you shall have me. You shall have whatever you desire."

Andras releases him from his touch, and Drew stumbles back, blinking frantically. He looks to the car ahead of us, and shouts to his cohorts, "Everything checks out. Let them pass."

"But, sir…" one of them begins to retort.

"I said, let them pass, Jones."

Jones nods to the other troops, and they step back, giving Cain's vehicle a wide berth. Drew looks back to Andras, a glimmer of lust and longing in his eyes.

"Good boy. Now, you will do what you have to in order to keep your friends from trailing us. Do you understand?"

"Yes, sir."

"For this, you will be rewarded. Come here."

Like a puppet on a string, Drew steps closer, allowing Andras to once again cradle his stubble-dusted cheek. But this time, the alluring blonde demon draws him closer still and presses his lips against his. The other troops watch on in confused horror as Drew groans into Andras's mouth, his entire body trembling with overwhelming ecstasy. When Andras releases him, an audible whimper slips from Drew's lips.

"That is only a taste of the pleasures I can give you. Do as I say, and you shall have my body."

Drew nods furiously, his breathing labored and his eyes glossy. Andras dips his head in response and eases his foot on the gas.

"Well, well," Lucifer clucks as we pull away. "Seems you haven't lost your touch, pretty boy."

"Shut up," Andras mumbles.

Lucifer chuckles darkly before turning his torso toward the backseat. "Good work, Nikolai."

Nikolai merely nods once, his jaw tight with ire. He still isn't over their heated exchange after the masquerade party.

"Get ready," Andras orders, flipping a few buttons on the dash. "We're going into stealth mode."

I watch with awe as the vehicle in front of us all but disappears before our eyes. If it weren't for a shimmery, almost oily outline, it would be completely invisible.

Then we're off, zipping down the debris-covered streets and maneuvering around roadblocks with seamless precision. If I could close my eyes, I would swear we were riding in a high-powered sports car instead of a six-ton SUV. I clamp down on my rising anxiety, only heightened by the pitch-blackness that surrounds us. Where are all the streetlights? Even the homes and businesses are darkened. If it weren't for the people brave enough to loiter in the shadows, I would think Chicago had turned into a ghost town.

"You smell that?" Lilith asks, scenting the air.

Lucifer nods from the front seat. "Sulfur."

"How many lessers do you think have intruded the city?"

He shrugs. "Hundreds. Thousands."

I take a whiff and grimace. I just thought I smelled traces of death and extreme poverty. Not the telltale signs of elevated demon activity.

We follow Cain's car into an extended-stay parking garage, which to my surprise, is fairly empty, aside from the stripped and vandalized cars parked on the lower floor.

"A lot of people were able to evacuate. Good," Lilith notes, her eyes scanning the busted up vehicles, most likely checking for any signs of lurkers.

"They evacuated the city?" I ask.

She nods. "As much as they could. But those who couldn't afford to leave were left behind."

Sister and I would have fallen under that category. She would have refused to leave, considering the hospitals are at max capacity. And there is no way I could scrape up the cash to flee, not that I could ever fathom leaving without her. We would have hunkered down in that rickety-ass apartment, Brenda the bat in hand, and prayed no one broke in. Or worse. And I would've feigned helplessness, all the while creeping into the minds of those intruders, and forcing them to turn their malice on themselves. I probably would have been strong enough to fight off the first to come for us, but then what? Who would have come to our rescue?

We park on the upper level, giving us a clear view of the city below. Once we've filed out of the cars, I go to stand on the edge, peering down at the haunting darkness stretched below us. It's nearly pitch black without the twinkling lights of bustling businesses and skyscrapers illuminating the sky, but somehow, I catch glimpses of activity below. Mostly shadows, but I can definitely see movement and make out shapes.

"Last chance. You sure you're up for this?" Niko asks, sidling up beside me.

I glance over my shoulder at the others. There's a map laid out before them on the hood of Cain's SUV. I should be over there discussing strategy, but honestly, none of that will matter once we hit the streets. They may know demons, angels, and other creatures of the night. But I know my city and its people. And there's nothing anyone can plan to prepare us for what lies ahead. Desperation makes people do desperate things. And no one knows more about that than me.

I look back to Niko and shrug. "And if I'm not?"

"Then you should stay behind. I don't want you out there if you're not one hundred percent ready for this. I know you're strong, but strength has nothing to do with it...not if we're forced to face off with Legion. I'd rather know you're safe."

"Me staying behind will only make things worse. I'll be worrying about you, about them, and about Legion. I'm not running. Not from any of you. Not from him."

Niko wraps an arm around my shoulders and squeezes me to his side, releasing a breath. "What is it with me and stubborn, beautiful girls?"

I smile, despite the leaden dread in my gut, remembering the words he spoke in my bedroom in Hell. "You definitely have a type."

"Yeah, but I think after this—if I make it out alive—it's time for me to settle down. I've been a bachelor for most of my hundred-plus years. Young for an immortal, but still old enough to know that I don't want to die alone."

I return the intensity of his hold, pressing into his side. "You won't. Not if I can help it."

"Yeah," he shrugs. "However, I am immortal. And you… well, no one knows what you are."

I swallow thickly, unable to fully digest the idea that I could possibly live forever. I'm unlike any Nephilim in existence. There's no way to truly comprehend what that means.

"And what about your lost love? Amelie?" I question. I'll unpack my mortality if and when we make it out of this city alive.

His eyes glaze over as he stares out into obscurity. "She's where she belongs. She was too good for this world."

I nod because I don't know what else to say. I guess at the end of the day, warlocks aren't much different from anyone else. We all just want to belong to someone who loves us despite our demons. Just someone to hold our hand and make us feel less alone in this big, wide universe full of unseen terrors.

I'm not surprised when we're summoned to rejoin the group. I could hear every word they were saying, just like I can hear the screams and cries below. Waiting until daybreak isn't an option. Death approaches. I can feel it.

I thought we were already armed to the teeth, but apparently not. Toyol opens the trunk of their designated ride, revealing his precious swords. Cain stalks over to seize even more guns and ammo. He presents me with four magazines, taking the liberty of clipping them to my holster.

"We think he's gone farther south," he murmurs.

I nod. "I'm not surprised."

"You're not?"

"If this area is in shambles, then the Southside must be engulfed in flames. I'd imagine he…they…would be drawn to the destruction."

"They?" Cain lifts a dark brow.

"The lost souls. He's…he's not himself. He wouldn't leave on his own accord."

"You're right. He wouldn't." A deep frown lines his forehead. "Driving into it would be too risky. He'd know we were coming. So would Uriel."

"I'm not sure which is worse," I mumble before I can stop myself.

"Me neither."

We lock eyes, both biting down on the guilt tainting our tongues. But it's true. If Legion isn't Legion, there's a good chance he will attack us. And none of us wants to fight him, even if we could. At least we could kill Uriel with a clear conscience. Well, clear-ish, in my case.

We all finish preparing in silence, each one of us burdened by the prospect of hurting someone we love, or even worse, dying trying to save him. Uriel is still very much in this fight, but Legion is the priority. There is no facing off with the Seraph without him. But I have a feeling that we'll have to go through them to get to him. It's a lose-lose situation, but there is no Door #3. There are no other options. We're staring down the barrel of a loaded gun, with no clue as to who will pull the trigger.

I'm not surprised that the parking garage elevator isn't working, considering that the electricity has been cut—whether on purpose or an act of vandalism—so we quietly take the stairs. Cain and Toyol lead, weapons drawn. Phenex and Jinn take up the rear, braced for any movement at our backs. Lilith and Andras weave through the group, moving right to left in a dance so seamless, you'd think it was choreographed.

This is the Se7en at work. This is the band of assassins that have singlehandedly executed countless would-be murders and terrorists, while also battling lesser demons doing Lucifer's bidding. I didn't fully grasp how deadly they truly are until this moment. And while that makes me feel a tiny bit better about this suicide mission, I don't relish the irony of them hunting their leader, the one who was the first to stand up for humanity. The one they followed to Earth in a search for purpose—for redemption.

When we hit the bottom level, I can feel my heart pounding out of my chest, and I'm certain the others can hear it racing like a techno beat. This is it. This is what I've been training for. This is what I was created for. To betray. To destroy. To kill.

I am the weapon to make Legion fall to his knees. And I've just been activated.

TWENTY-THREE

I<small>T'S COLDER ON THE STREETS THAN</small> I <small>IMAGINED.</small> T<small>HE</small> frost-kissed night air seeps through my leather jacket, but my blood is pumping so rapidly that I barely register the chill. It smells like snow and sulfur. Ice and fire. If those that could not leave haven't found safe shelter within the city limits are left on the streets, I fear they may freeze to death. And if they don't meet their end that way, something much more sinister is waiting for them.

We stick to the shadows, virtually silent as we maneuver through the filth and debris littering every side street and alleyway. Surprisingly, even the local vagrants have vacated their usual haunts. Or maybe something else got to them first. Whatever the reason, the eerie silence puts me on edge. We have a long trek ahead to the Southside, if we make it at all. I have a bad feeling, as if there are forces at work that hope to keep us away. And that feeling is only intensified as we turn a corner, and the sensation of frozen spiders crawling up my back sets off all my internal alarms. Something is waiting for us on the other side.

I pause and go to reach inside my jacket for one of the angelsbane-tipped blades, but it all happens too quickly.

He's draped in dingy, torn rags, his face caked with dirt, as he roars towards us with a metal pipe held over his head. Cain is the first to act, catching him with a right hook that should have at least subdued the homeless man, but it barely stuns him. He whips the metal pipe around, but luckily Cain ducks just milliseconds before it connects with his skull. Toyol strikes the man before he recovers, sending him flying back into an over-flowing dumpster with a kick to his ribs. But the vagrant jumps right back into action, barely pausing to catch the breath that was knocked out of him. He's not human. He can't be. No one made of flesh and bone would be able to walk away from a blow like that.

Weapons drawn, the Se7en brace for the man's attack, but it's Lucifer who casually steps forward from the shadows. No guns or knives, he merely raises a single palm, and the homeless man halts, sending the metal pipe to tumble from his grip to the damp concrete.

"Master," the man rasps, falling to his knees. Pitch black eclipses the white of his unnaturally wide eyes.

"Why are you here, my child?" Lucifer questions, looming over him. I inch forward, squeezing the hilt of my blade in anticipation.

"I was released."

"By whom?"

"I…I don't know." His beady black gaze shifts from right to left, and a frown forms between his brows. "You're here… with them. Traitors. You stand with the Se7en."

"Why? Why were you sent?" Lucifer asks, ignoring the claims of betrayal.

"To stop them."

"Why?"

"Because they threaten to destroy us all. They want us to cower under their tyranny. It is our time now. The fallen shall reign."

Lucifer rubs a gloved hand over his chin, pondering his subject's confession. I'm confused about it myself. *The fallen shall reign?* What fallen? This can't be anything more than a lesser demon possessing a homeless man's body.

"Eden, dear, come here please."

I'm stunned by his request, but go to step forward. Niko catches my arm before I can advance.

"Careful," he murmurs, his bright blue glare glowing with the warning.

I nod once, and it seems to placate him enough to let go. When I reach Lucifer's side, he protectively places a hand on my lower back, his heat seeping through my clothes and searing my skin.

"Do you know who she is?"

The man bares his yellowed teeth and spits at my feet. "We do not want the Nephilim girl. She will die with the rest of them."

"Then who do you want?"

"All of them. Everyone. They shall all perish one by one. This world will be made anew, and it will be ours."

Lucifer nods before turning to me, a gentle smile on his lips. "Rejoin Nikolai at his side, my dear."

I shake my head. "No. Not yet. He may know where Le—"

"Go. He knows nothing."

I frown, my jaw tight with ire. Why isn't he questioning the man about Legion's whereabouts? He may know something, yet he's treating him with kid gloves.

Seething with frustration, I turn around and stalk to my place beside Niko. He squeezes my hand but keeps his glare forward.

Lucifer raises both palms, and commands, "Come forth."

The words are wrapped in a vibrating timbre that rattles even my bones, causing my insides to thrash in anxiety, and watch in awe and horror as the man's mouth opens unnaturally wide, so wide that it looks as if his face is being ripped in two. And between his crooked, dingy teeth, a boney, red-skinned hand reaches out and sinks its claws into the man's jaw, as whatever horrid creature within in him pulls itself out.

I bite down bile as I watch the whole gut-roiling display. The demon sheds its human host as if he's nothing more than a bloody skin suit, twisting and writhing itself free. Jagged horns dot its bulbous head, only paling in comparison to its gnashing fangs and razor-sharp claws. I reflexively take a step back, running right into Phenex's hard chest. He grips my shoulders tight to still my quaking frame.

"The lessers cannot take a human form. Therefore they possess the bodies of the innocent," he whispers.

"Will he be ok?" I whisper back through quivering lips.

"He will. But I cannot say for how long."

Once the demon has shed his human host completely,

he stands before Lucifer and smiles, waiting for his master to bestow upon him a reward for his candor. But just as Lucifer returns his grin, the demon crumples to the ground, crying out in bloody agony. His whole body contorts as every bone breaks and splinters, causing jagged shards to pierce through his red skin, exposing ripped flesh and sinew. The putrid smell of his corroded insides waft over us, and I have to clamp my hand over my mouth to contain the threat of vomit. He is rotten to the core, judging by the black blood and bile that ooze from his wounds. But I stand tall, swallowing down the weakness of my humanity, unwilling to turn away from the carnage. Just as I learned to do in Hell.

After several more seconds of torture, the crying ceases, and the demon is nothing but a pile of steaming, bubbling, black sludge on the piss-stained pavement. Lucifer steps closer, peering down at the mess of torn skin and broken bone.

"Remember who it is you serve," he grits, his voice raw with uncontained rage.

Cain steps up, wincing at the sight and smell of the pulverized demon. "We've got to keep moving. Someone may have heard."

Lucifer nods and turns towards us, and I notice that his eyes are alive, shifting with sparkling shades of purple, obsidian, and dark teal. He blinks it away, but I can still see it—the wicked power simmering just beneath the surface.

We resume our trek through the shadows, but I keep peering over at Lucifer, the questions on my tongue like lead in my mouth. I know this isn't the time or place to ask, not when we're hoping to avoid further conflict, but something is really bothering me. And if there's even an inkling of doubt—a sliver of distrust—then we'll all fall. By Uriel's hands or our own.

"Spit it out," Lucifer mutters, stepping closer to my side.

I glance back at Nikolai, checking to see if he caught Luc's words on a gust of icy wind.

"Why did you let him go?" I whisper back.

"Because he knew nothing."

"How would you know that, considering you killed him before he could be interrogated? He could've known where Legion was."

"He didn't."

"But you didn't even—"

"He didn't know anything," he shoots back, loud enough for every narrowed eye to fall to us.

Seething, Lucifer keeps moving forward, taking the lead and ignoring the curious stares. Unlucky for him, I'm right on his heels, despite Cain's hushed demands for me to stay back.

"How do you know?" I ask after a few beats of strained silence.

"Because if he did, he wouldn't be worried about us. Every lesser demon in the city would be trying to kill him. Or serve him. No one knows about Legion's disappearance but us, and we need to keep it that way."

He's right. I hate it, but he's right. But surely that lesser demon could have given us *something*. He didn't know who was pulling the strings, but he may have known where to find them. He had to have received instructions from somewhere. But Lucifer's urgent execution snuffed out the possibility of learning potentially pertinent information.

"You're too emotionally invested," Lucifer throws in my face.

"And you're not?"

"Why would I be?"

"He's your brother. And he's gone missing."

Lucifer shrugs. "Not the first time. He left on his own accord before. What makes you think that isn't the case now?"

I nearly stumble on my own two feet as the blow of his words radiates in my gut. "He…He…" He wouldn't do that.

Lucifer suddenly spins around to face me. His tone is hushed yet harsh, and his eyes are glowing with violet flames. "He wouldn't do that? He wouldn't leave you? Because he loves you?" He snorts a laugh. "I thought that once, too. But you'll learn, just as I did, that Legion's true nature will always rule him. He's a demon, Eden. He can't love."

Lucifer turns back to resume his long strides, yet I'm frozen in place on the dark, damp pavement. Cain and Toyol step around me, each shooting me sympathetic glances, but surprisingly it's Lilith who stops to take my gloved hand.

"We'll find him. Come on…we have to keep moving."

She tugs gently, and I let her. We've barely been out here for more than an hour, and I'm already letting my heart override my head.

No one speaks as we trudge through the filth and head south. However, to avoid further altercations, the journey is taking longer than we anticipated. If the lesser demon was telling the truth, there's a target on our backs. And while no one relishes the thought of killing, each and every foe will have to fall if we're to make it to Legion in one piece. The only problem is, there's ten of us, and hundreds—if not thousands—of them.

"Can we just stop for a moment?" I hear from behind me.

I turn around to see Adriel; her lips dry and her skin pale. She's been so silent the entire journey; I had forgotten she was even with us.

"I need to take a breath," she explains, leaning up against a brick wall that used to belong to a popular downtown boutique. Now, it's been virtually gutted.

"Yes. You must rest," Phenex insists, pulling off his backpack. He retrieves a bottle of water and hands it to the angel, now panting with exhaustion.

I don't get it. She's immortal; one of the most revered beings in existence. How can she be winded already? It hasn't been that long, and considering we only have mere hours before dawn, we need to keep moving.

"The high volume of demons is drawing on her spirit," Andras quietly explains beside me, reading my thoughts. "The pain, the destruction, the fear…it's draining her."

I look to him and frown. "But she's been stuck in a house with demons for weeks." At least it's felt like weeks.

Andras shakes his head. "We're not like other demons. Even Lucifer…he's been dampening himself since he arrived. Probably even while he was in Hell with you."

I didn't realize it until now, but he's right. Lucifer did dampen himself around me. Until he let it slip.

Once.

I remember it all as if it just occurred yesterday. I don't think a day has gone by that I haven't thought about that night in his dining room. He had been trying to shock me for days, each nightly display more depraved than the last. It was as if he was trying to woo me with evil. And I sat there, stone-faced and cold, just as Niko instructed.

And then I made a mistake.

I challenged him.

I can still hear the sound of teeth tearing through flesh. Can still clearly see the rich crimson blood pooled at Lucifer's feet as those girls willingly, almost gleefully, ripped each other's faces to the bone. And I did nothing. I didn't cry. I didn't scream. I sat there and watched those poor women *eat* each other.

My silence was my approval. And in that moment, I realized that I'm no better than Lucifer. I might be even worse.

"Better?" I hear Phenex inquire a few feet away, crouched in front of Adriel.

She nods weakly, her breathing still a bit shallow. "Yes. Let's keep going." She pushes off the graffiti-covered brick wall.

"May I suggest you stay beside Eden?" Lucifer suggests, his voice taking on its usual enticing drawl.

Face pinched, I hastily reply, "Why?"

"Because half of you is angel," he explains. "You're stronger together. The first time you wielded light, you were with Crysis. And every time after that, you were with Adriel. The same essence that runs in your veins runs in theirs."

I nod, not able to admit that he's right...for the most part. I can't describe what happened between Legion and me on our last night together. I don't know if it was holy light that threw him against the wall, smashing my wardrobe into splinters. Or maybe it was his own consciousness fighting through the haze of deception that tried to steal him away from his body. Or maybe it was divine intervention. I. Don't. Know. But I do know that if something—or someone—hadn't stopped him, he could have very well killed me.

There was not a glimmer of Legion's former angel self in that moment. He was all demon—the full embodiment of evil. There was no saving him.

"I think you may be right," Adriel comments, coming to stand beside me.

I look to her beautiful, pale face and realize that her green eyes are sunken in and lined with purplish circles. We need her. And truth be told, I owe her. We may be in love with the same man, but I don't believe she'd ever do anything to hurt me. Not when she's protected me for most of my life.

"I agree," I acquiesce. "Let's go."

We head east to cut through Grant Park in hopes of by-passing some of the shadier areas of downtown. And as we step over mounds of broken cement and shattered glass, I audibly gasp at what's been left of it. Everything is in shambles. What was once known for being the centerpiece of Chicago is nothing more than deadened grass, chunks of rubble, and twisted metal that were once sculptures. The Art Institute appears to be condemned. The baseball diamonds at Hutchinson Field have been desecrated with spray-paint and garbage. And whatever stagnant liquid lies in the grand Buckingham Fountain is most definitely not water.

"It's going to get worse the farther we get," Toyol remarks, a note of sorrow in his tone. I don't know how long the Se7en have been here, but this is their home too. And to see it like this has got to be fucking with them as much as it's fucking with me.

I snort sardonically. "Worse than this?"

"Much worse," he nods. "Most humans on this side of town were able to evacuate. So the demons are centralizing south."

"And you think Legion would take that risk? Go *towards* the chaos and violence?"

A dozen different scenarios flood my mind. Maybe that lesser demon was lying. What if they have found him and have already begun to torture him? What if they've gotten him to give up the Se7en? Or maybe they've taken him to whomever they serve? Nikolai seems to believe that it was Stavros, his father, who is responsible for casting a cloaking spell on me. And if Stavros is still working with Uriel, maybe the lesser demons have crossed over to his side, too. I can't imagine the Seraph being desperate enough to conspire with the lowest of evil beings, but if they were just using them to further their cause…*that* I could believe.

And if there is even a shred of truth to any of my suspicions, Legion doesn't have much time.

I try to shake off the crippling doubt and keep moving forward, but the farther south we go, the harder it is to ignore the niggling feeling that something is seriously wrong. We're miles away from our destination, and we've got at least an hour and change to go before we make it, but I can't shake the feeling that we're walking right into a trap. I feel a bit queasy, and hair stands up on the back of my neck. Even the hair on my head feels electrically charged with a warning. We should turn back. We should regroup and try again when we're better prepared.

But we'd never be fully prepared, even if we trained for a month straight for eighteen hours a day. Not for what awaits us. Not for what steps out of the shadows and surrounds us, forcing us to cluster together in the center of the mob because there's nowhere to run. Nowhere to escape.

Demons.

Dozens of them. Hundreds.

And they're not here to do Lucifer's bidding.

They're here to kill.

TWENTY-FOUR

I ALMOST LOSE A BREATH WHEN LUCIFER CASUALLY strolls forward, his expression amused.

Almost.

"Lovely of you all to extend such a warm welcome," he drawls, seemingly nonplussed, "but you needn't trouble yourselves. Scurry back to where you came from, and I'll consider letting you keep your heads."

A lone brave homeless man inches forward. He's caked in dirt and dressed in filthy rags, much like the one Lucifer took out before. But it's no human that says, "You no longer have that authority. You do not rule this realm,"

"Oh? And who does?" Lucifer's mouth curls at one side, but it's all a front to conceal his rage.

The demon forces his human host to smile back, showcasing blackened, broken teeth. "He's coming. You will see him soon enough. And you and your precious mortals shall fall at his feet."

Lucifer makes a tsking sound before demanding in that rumbling timbre, "Come forth."

The soiled man, his eyes as black as coal, laughs heartily. "That will not work on us anymore. He has freed us."

"Who has freed you?" Lucifer lifts a curious brow.

A shake of his head is all we receive in response. He either knows nothing, or he's refusing to tell us. Either way, we're screwed.

I scan the crowd of people, my eyes wide with terror. Humans from all walks of life—vagrants, uniformed police officers, doctors and nurses donning scrubs, husbands, wives…these are the ones that didn't make it out in time. Chicagoans—just like Sister and me—that didn't have the time or resources to escape to safety. And now they have been reduced to nothing but skin suits for the lowest, most vile creatures in existence.

I should have noticed it all seemed too easy to breach the city. After our initial roadblock—that Andras so resourcefully diverted—it seemed as if the streets had been deserted. Maybe the demon who attacked us was acting alone. Maybe he was warning us. Or maybe he was hoping his assault would prompt us to turn east and fall right into their trap, which is exactly what we did.

The smell of sulfur is so noxious that I feel queasy. And although she's standing tall, legs planted in a defensive stance beside me, Adriel looks a little green as well. How did we not notice it was getting stronger? Or had we grown immune to the scent of death and fire?

Lucifer's jaw flutters with unshed anger as he flicks a speck of dust off his coat. "How quickly you forget the consequences for defying me. You think your realm of Hell was bad? Try me. I dare you." His eyes flare bright enough that it casts a dark violet glow across the demon's borrowed face.

"You speak as if your threats are still terrifying. Yet, you stand with those who betrayed you. Who betrayed *us*. You conspire with our angel enemies. And you protect a Nephilim girl—a girl who you have allowed yourself to fall in love with," he scoffs, the word *love* a malice-laced hiss on his putrid tongue. But that's not enough to distract me from his outrageous claim.

Love. He said Lucifer has fallen in love with me.

If this were a different time and place, and if we weren't currently facing off with a hoard of demons armed with baseball bats, metal pipes, and two-by-fours, ready to tear our heads off, I'd laugh in his dirt-smudged face. There's no way Lucifer could love me. Honestly, I don't think he even likes me. He just enjoys getting under my skin and pissing off Legion.

Lucifer must see his angle, because instead of denying the accusation, he simply lifts a palm then closes it into a fist. And with that simple movement, the demon-possessed man's body crumples into a heap of twisted flesh and broken bone. The sound of his body snapping and ripping as it contorts into a human pretzel is something out of a horror movie. He didn't even have a chance to scream. His vocal cords were shredded the moment his neck was ground into a pulpy mess on the pavement.

And while I should feel some sense of justice, I can't help but realize that it wasn't just the demon who was crushed in

Lucifer's palm. That man was innocent. His only crime was poverty and not having the resources to escape the city. All of them are. It's not these humans that want to kill us, so how can I stand here and let them die for a cause that they have no say in?

"He's going to kill them all," I whisper to Niko. He's on guard, his penetrating ice blue stare boring into the pack of demons hissing at their fallen brethren.

"What?"

"Lucifer. He's going to kill them."

"Good."

"No, it's not." I shake my head a fraction, not wanting to draw attention to our conversation. But with Adriel at my other side, Phenex and Jinn at our backs, Cain and Toyol in front of us, and Lilith and Andras at their flanks, I'm sure every word is heard. "These humans are innocent. Are you saying you'd be willing to commit mass murder?"

He looks around, taking in the scene, and, hopefully, seeing reason. There are hundreds of them. I can't have their deaths on my conscience. There has to be a different way.

"Can you get in?" he asks.

Frowning, I part my lips to ask him what the hell he could possibly mean, but then it clicks. I could breach Crysis's mind, something even he was surprised about. And now that my Nephilim gifts have been unlocked, maybe I could fling out that power and slip into the minds of all these demons. There are a lot of them, more than I've attempted. But I'm also a lot stronger than anyone anticipated.

Still, I'm apprehensive. These aren't gaudy ass Great Value gangsters in a bar. And the last time I tried to infiltrate a demon's mind, it felt like my brain was being pulverized into mush. But I can't just stand here, with my thumb stuck up my ass, because I'm too afraid to try. Even if I fail, maybe it'll serve as a needed distraction for the others to get away. Shit, maybe to set everything back to how it was before I was created by Uriel. If I'm dead, I'm no longer a weapon. He can't use me. And whatever score he has to settle with Legion will have to wait.

I suck in a lungful of cold, stale air, and on an exhale, I send my power launching towards the demon closest to the front line. From the outside, she looks like she may have been a schoolteacher, or maybe she once worked in a café as a peppy barista. But as my influence scrapes against her frontal lobe, and her dead stare flares just a fraction at the intrusion, I know that whoever she once was is now gone. I don't even know if she, or any of these people, can be saved. This could all be for naught, but I have to try. If it saves human lives, I have to do whatever I can.

I'm relieved when I'm not taken to my knees my excruciating pain, but I don't breathe. There's a roiling blackness waiting for me. A sticky, tar-like sludge that claws at my invisible hand, trying to capture it with obsidian flypaper. I merge before it can touch me, yet keep one finger of influence firmly planted in the darkness. Then I'm pushing myself out, reaching for the next demon mind to invade. Then another. And another. I don't want to linger too long. They know *something* is there, yet they can't understand what and how. And before they realize that it's *me* infecting their consciousness, I want to be far, far away from that murky pit of obscurity. Even with the touch of influence that's remained within their skulls, I can feel them, like black spiders reaching out, trying to latch on to sink their venomous fangs into me.

I extend myself until the strain echoes in my skull and burns my eyes. My jaw aches as I clench down, forcing every ounce of my concentration to the horde before us. They're restless, agitated. They won't let their friend's death go unpunished. I only have mere seconds if I want to avoid a massacre.

I'm only holding about twenty of them, maybe two-dozen tops. It's not many, but as I part my dry, trembling lips to utter the words, I pray that it's enough.

"Fall. And sleep."

Shocked horror momentarily fills their wide-eyed, black gazes before they crumple to the ground, forced into an enchanted slumber. The remaining enemy demons, stunned, look around in bewilderment, allowing Lucifer and the Se7en to spare a surprised glance in my direction.

"You can't kill them. They're humans," I bite out by way of explanation, forcing all my focus on the approaching threat.

My plan worked, thank God, but it wasn't enough. The mob seems even more agitated as they realize what's happened. Dozens upon dozens of obsidian eyes fall on me as vicious snarls ring out into the night. They all know it was me. And I've just upped the ante on their bloodlust.

Unnaturally fast, Niko pushes me behind him, shielding my body with his own. He raises his hands, and they erupt into azure flames that lick up to his elbows. With a swipe of his hands, the line of demons is pushed back, tumbling over each other like bowling pins. But within seconds, they recover and are back on their feet quickly advancing towards us. Shit, it even seems like their numbers are multiplying. Where the hell did they all come from?

Niko blasts them back again, while Lucifer turns to take on the opposite side. I grasp his arm before he can raise his palm.

"Please," I beg. "Don't hurt them. They don't deserve to die."

Lucifer's swirling, metallic-flecked eyes dim with simmering power. "I can't make any promises."

He shrugs out of my grasp and raises both hands, maneuvering them as if he's squeezing an invisible sphere. The demons begin to cry out, clutching their skulls as they wither to the ground in agony. But more quickly replace them, simply stepping over their writhing bodies.

"Get out of here! Go!" Niko shouts. He throws out another wall of blue flames, but it doesn't have the same impact as the ones before. There are too many of them. And by the time I tap into their brains, they'll already be on top of us.

"Not without you," I yell back.

The rest of us are crouched down with our weapons drawn, anticipating violence, but I don't want it to come to that. And considering we're grossly outnumbered, there's no guarantee we'll win. We didn't plan for this. Killing lesser demons or even angels, we prepared for. But not humans. They weren't supposed to be here.

"Adriel, can't you do something? Blast them with holy light?" I don't even care about the desperation in my voice. We need her. *I* need her.

She shakes her head, dashing my last bit of hope. "There's too many of them. And there's a good chance they wouldn't survive it."

"You're not even going to try?" I shriek.

"I'm sorry." Her mouth is saying the words, but I don't believe them.

"Then why the fuck are you here?" I mutter.

I grit down to keep my rage in check. We don't have time to bicker amongst ourselves. She doesn't want to help, fine. But when it comes down to trading her for my mom, I'll remember her cowardice. Uriel can keep her.

Deep breath, focus. Conjure those emotions that I've bottled up inside since I discovered Legion had left us. The fear, the pain. The unexplainable shame.

Orbs of light appear in each palm, and without even thinking, I launch them into the crowd. They explode, temporarily blinding us all and incapacitating the lesser demons long enough for Phenex to grip my arm.

"Come on. We're getting you out of here," he urges tugging my arm.

I look over at Niko and Lucifer, both still battling the growing fray. "What about them?"

"They'll catch up. If we stay any longer, we'll have no choice but to kill them."

"But I can't…" I shake my head. "I won't leave them."

"We don't have time for this shit," Cain growls out, raising his gun. "It's either them or us."

But before he can fire off the first round, there's a disturbance within the crowd. Gruff voices barking out orders. An almost electrical type of sound. And the demons are falling, their bodies seizing uncontrollably as if they've been tasered. I look around. Who is doing this? And how?

And that's when I see them.

"Fucking hell," Cain curses.

"No…it can't be," Phenex scoffs.

"Shit. This is just what we need," Andras spits.

Toyol raises his twin Katanas. Lilith pulls back the hammer of her revolver. Jinn unsheathes two curved blades.

Clad in all black tactical gear and armed with high-tech weapons, just like they had at that gas station when they tried to take me. The Alliance of the Ordained, enemy to the Se7en and all inherent evil not of this realm. And there are *a lot* more of them than there are of us.

Oh, for fuck's sake.

TWENTY-FIVE

THIS ISN'T GOOD. OUR CHANCES OF SURVIVAL WERE slim at best before, but now…we might as well surrender to whatever cruel fate we're due and get it over with. Niko is getting weaker, and with Lucifer not able to control his lesser demons, I don't see how we can save these humans and save ourselves. People are going to die, and I have a good feeling it will be us.

However, it seems like the Alliance aren't here to challenge us. They're battling *against* the rival demons as if they've come to help. They're fighting with the Se7en, ones they'd deemed their adversaries for as long as the Alliance of the Ordained has been around, instead of sitting back and allowing us to be ambushed.

I only give myself a split second to marvel at the turn of events. Then, feeling suddenly energized, I form two more orbs of light and launch them towards the demons, careful not to hit any agents. A group goes down, stunned and possibly hurt, but not dead. I can live with that.

"You're getting pretty good at that, kid," a familiar voice shouts on approach.

I spin around, and my eyes nearly fill with tears as I spy the reason for the Alliance's aide.

"Crysis," I rasp, as he jogs over to us. Even the Se7en look relieved to see him, giving him quick nods of appreciation.

"Don't look so shocked. You thought I'd skip out without a proper goodbye?"

"What...? How...?" I stammer, trying to connect the dots. I thought it was me. After our fight, I thought it had been my temper that had pushed him away...had forced him to abandon safety and security and trade it for the unknown ills of the city. And knowing that I hadn't lost him, that I hadn't completely fucked up our friendship...I could honestly kiss him right now.

He takes aim and hits a fast approaching lesser demon right between the eyes. The bullet doesn't penetrate, yet attaches to his forehead, emitting jolts of electricity that bring him down in seconds. So that's how they're doing it.

"I'll tell you all about it later." Aim. Shoot. "But I knew there were still good men out there who had no part in Uriel's plan. I had an idea of what we were up against, and I was right. I just had to get them on board. I couldn't do that holed up in a mansion with the Se7en. And I wasn't going to sit around and let you or anyone else get hurt if there was something I could do."

"Thank you," I nod, overcome with emotion. Five minutes

ago, I thought we were done for sure. Then Crysis swoops in and literally saves our asses. And as miniscule as it may seem, considering what's going on around us, I'm happy that I got my friend back.

"If you two are done squawking," Cain derides from behind us, a wicked grin on his already sinister face, "I think it's about time we get in on the fun."

His words flip some internal switch, and right on cue, the rest of the Se7en assemble to shed their cool demeanors and awaken the beasts within. I had only gotten a glimpse of the monsters that lurked underneath their human forms, and that terrified me to my core. However, seeing them now, their bodies twisting and writhing as they unleash their inner evil, ' I've never been so glad to be in the company of six of the most feared and revered demons in history.

I'd done my homework on the legends and myths of the Se7en, so I shouldn't have been surprised at how truly frightening they could be when they loosened the reins on their true nature. But even the lesser demons pause and gawk as the six assassins loom before them—bloodthirsty for carnage and pissed the fuck off.

"Stay back," Crysis says under his breath. "Once they start, they won't be able to stop."

Even the Alliance know better than to stand in their way. The mob of lesser demons has thinned considerably, thanks to their help, but we're still outnumbered ten to one. Apparently, the Se7en are fine with those odds.

It's Cain who leads the charge, a hulking mass of muscle, twisted horns that sprout from his skull, and broad, black, bat-like wings. He's still him—sorta. But he's definitely more beast than man. He launches into the fray with a terrifying roar that shakes the ground beneath us and begins to tear into the demons, tossing them around like ragdolls. The lesser demons are no match for his incredible brute strength and skill, and within seconds, they're already trying to flee to escape his wrath. But with Toyol right behind Cain, they don't get very far.

During one of our first meetings, Toyol told me that he was depicted as a grotesque baby creature with red eyes and fangs. Now I see what those legends were birthed from. He's hideous. Stringy black hair over a bulbous head, sickly green skin, and fangs that extend nearly down to his chin. His Katanas are no longer swords, but an extension of his hands, as if they've been fixed to his fingers. While he hasn't shrunk into an infant, there's something oddly child-like in his red, glowing eyes, like they've been sparked with mischief.

I'd gotten just a taste of Lilith's inner demon self when the Se7en first took me to their home, courtesy of Cain's slick mouth. But seeing her full transformation not only sends a shiver down my spine, but it also amazes me. Half serpent-like, half human form, and wholly horrifying, Lilith is a goddess of all that is unholy and malevolent. Yet even with her bones and joints contorting in the most unnatural of ways, there's something oddly sensual about her. She's a seductress; a queen cloaked in blood and fire. Now I realize that I've seen her before. Not when she pinned Cain to the marble dining room table for insulting me. The mural—the spark that created humanity. She was there.

Not to be outdone, her companion and confidant strips down to reveal his true self, and while there is definitely something grotesque about the winged man with the head of an owl, he still maintains the grace and beauty of the demon I had grown to care for. Andras is streaked with hues of brilliant gold and teal with wings more reminiscent of an angel. I'm smart enough to know that it's an illusion—a façade used to trap and kill his prey. And while he prefers to feast on the flesh of men, his hunger extends to the scattering lesser demons, scrambling for a way around the Alliance members standing guard and locking them in.

Phenex is every bit as radiant as I imagined. Where Andras's form is more owl-like, the gorgeous mahogany demon bares shimmering wings of fire. His face is that of a predatory bird yet there's a thoughtful glimmer in his honey eyes, as if the man I know still exists within. Violence is a necessity, although I get the feeling he's never reveled in it like the others. But that doesn't keep him from joining the others, trapping in his prey with his wings. He, too, was there at the beginning—the bird that lit the sky aflame. He was once an angel, and his tumble from heaven set the world on fire.

Last but certainly not least, Jinn, the deathly silent assassin, mutates into kindling black smoke and glowing, flame-lit eyes. Every step he takes towards the mob of lesser demons leaves a trail of soot behind. In movies and television, he has been depicted as what we know as a genie. But the monster slowly stalking towards our enemies is nothing out of a fairytale. He is their worst nightmare.

The Se7en leap into action, disarming the lessers with expert precision while the rest of us look on in awe. It's child's play, really. There's a reason why they've protected this realm from evil foes for centuries, and judging by the sheer terror reflected in the lesser demons' onyx eyes, the Se7en's reputation precedes them.

Lilith and Andras, side by side as always, lunge for a group headed for the Alliance officers. Before they can even take two steps, the formerly blonde duo are on them, knocking them to the pavement and rendering their human bodies useless. Phenex and Jinn take on the mob adjacent to them, the ones who just discovered that this is the perfect time to attack those of us in the center of the chaos while we're distracted. They cut them off, Phenex catapulting them back with a brush of his wings while Jinn spits flames to create a perimeter around us. Bones are broken. Skin is bruised and bloodied. But no one is dead.

We've done it. We've won. When the odds were stacked against us, we managed to make it out in one piece, while saving human lives in the process.

But before we can utter one word in relief, what sounds like a helicopter whirls around us. The ground trembles under our feet. And blinding light bursts from above as if the heavens have opened and rained holy light upon us.

A violent clap of thunder and the earth ruptures around us, sending dust and debris to spray over our faces. The Se7en rush to where we stand, abandoning their prey, and create a shield of fire and darkness around us. They shift back into their human forms and unsheathe their weapons, prompting the rest of us to do the same. There is a threat among us, and brute force and mystical powers won't help us. And, honestly, that scares me.

Our first line of defense is the Se7en, considering they are the most trained. Our second is Nikolai, Lucifer, and Crysis.

And in the center, cowering like fragile porcelain dolls is Adriel and I. We're the ones they've deemed the weakest. Or the ones that need to be protected the most.

"What's happening?" I whisper harshly.

She utters the one word that sends spider-legged shivers up my spine. "Seraph."

It sounds like a series of sonic booms that crash against the earth as each of them lands. There are five that are so loud that my teeth chatter. But then the next three… I feel their descent in my skull. My ears are ringing; my brain is throbbing like I've been pummeled with a sledgehammer. I try to sandwich my head with my hands, trying to salvage my eardrums, and I feel moisture dripping down my neck. I don't have to look to know it's blood.

When the dust settles, an eerie quiet falls upon us. That or I've been rendered deaf. But I can begin to make out their forms surrounding us from several yards away. Shockingly white wings that nearly stretch the length of a baseball diamond close us in, making it impossible to flee. This is what they had hoped for. To distract us enough with the demon body snatchers to isolate us. Each one is more beautiful than the next, with long hair that flows down their backs in waves that seem to be animated by a phantom breeze. Their eyes are captivating and bright, and I can tell their bodies are ripped with muscle even under their pristine suits. However, that's only the angels. The Seraph, on the other hand, are more gorgeous and mesmerizing than I could ever imagine. Looking at them head on literally hurts my eyes, and I don't know whether I should weep or worship at their feet.

The one to the left has unblemished ivory skin and rich

brown hair that brushes his shoulders. I remember him from the party…the one who was stalking towards me, a look of curiosity painting his beautiful face. He cocks his head to one side, as if he remembers me too, yet can't quite place where. Nikolai's magic may have been strong enough to conceal my true identity after all. Although it didn't repel the archangel completely.

The one standing to the right is magnificent, as I'd expect, but there is one detail that certainly throws me for a loop. She…is a *she*. A female Seraph. She's just as statuesque as the others and looks as if she could dominate any runway in Milan. Blonde hair styled in ringlets that fall to the tops of her pert breasts. Even the fitted white suit she dons makes her appear sultry and feminine. Her face is soft, her features perfectly aligned. She's the picture of beauty. I thought Adriel and Lilith were exquisite. They can barely hold a candle to the dazzling creature before us.

"Selaphiel," Adriel hisses with disdain. The sharpness of that name on her tongue could cut glass. I turn to her for more information, but she offers none, her focus trained on the Seraph who stands tall and proud in the middle.

Uriel.

Bronze skin and kind, brown eyes as I remembered, although he's more glorious now that he's revealed his true self. I want to be appalled by him, yet all I can do is stare. How could I have come from something so unnaturally striking? When I knew him as Rev, I could actually see myself in him. Or maybe I imagined it all, because now…now he is too great for human words. There is no term in any language to define his immense beauty.

A dark chuckle steals my attention for just a moment as a jovial Lucifer shakes his head. "Of course," he mutters. "Tuesday, Wednesday, and Thursday. Fucking sheep." Again with the arrogant heroics, he cuts through the line of the Se7en and casually strolls forward to stand before his former brothers and sister. "Well, what do we have here? Raphael, Uriel, Selaphiel. I'm shocked to see you here, little sister."

The female Seraph is stony-faced, although her voice sounds like wind chimes. "And why is that, Belial?"

Belial. Lucifer was Belial.

Just as Legion was once Samael.

"I thought you had a mind of your own. Pity I was wrong." He turns his violet gaze on Raphael. "Now Raph… Raph has always been a sycophant. His presence doesn't surprise me in the least."

Raphael snorts, although I can see a shade of annoyance darken his glare. "You've just never believed in anything or anyone but yourself."

"And why should I?" Lucifer shrugs. "Your blind faith makes you weak. It makes you stupid. Why should you whole-heartedly trust in something that you know to be a lie?"

"If memory serves, lies are more your forte, Belial." Raphael smiles, and while it is dazzling, there's something sinister in the gesture.

It's Uriel who raises a hand to put an end to their bickering. "We've come to collect my mate. No one has to get hurt. Bloodshed is not necessary," he pronounces, his voice rich and deep like warm honey.

"And if we want bloodshed?" Lucifer challenges, a smile in his words.

"Then you shall have it. But no need to sacrifice your friends over ego, Belial. This isn't their fight."

"Bullshit," Cain spits, stepping forward. "You kidnapped and tortured our brother—our leader. This is more our fight than anyone else's."

"And you took my daughter," Uriel retorts. "And he was my brother long before you were even a twinkle in your maker's eye. Besides, we all know how you treat your *brother*, Cain, Demon of Murder."

Low growls rumble the chests of every Se7en member. Even I find myself baring my teeth at his words.

"So you want your mate, yet you speak not of your own flesh and blood?" Lucifer interjects, steering the conversation. "Awfully negligent of you. Does Father know of your transgressions? *Thou shall not be a deadbeat dad* has to be one of the commandments."

I can't ignore the stab of pain his realization delivers to my chest. All this...all this for the angel he loves. He created me, abandoned me, deceived me then discarded me. For what? Why even conceive me at all?

"My daughter has chosen her side," Uriel answers as if I'm not standing here. "Although it pains me, I cannot accept her choice at the risk of my own fidelity."

"However, you accept Adriel's choice. She betrayed you. She left you. Yet and still, you pine after her like a lost puppy." Lucifer shakes his head in awed amusement. "Sounds mighty hypocritical, Uriel. Even for you."

My father's expression is blank when he declares, "The girl cannot be saved. Adriel can."

"And what if she doesn't want to be saved?"

"She has no choice in the matter."

Abusive-fucking-asshole. No wonder Adriel fled heaven. He must have tormented her for her affair with Legion. Fuck trading her for my mother. I don't want to give this prick the satisfaction.

I'm done with this conversation. I'm done with being insulted like I'm nothing more than waste that should have been collected in a condom. I'm done with Uriel thinking he has any authority as to whether we live or die. He's playing games. And now it's time for someone to call his bluff.

"She isn't coming with you," I pipe up, moving to the front of the line. Unsurprisingly, I'm not alone. They all move with me. "But you knew that, didn't you? Adriel knew what a sadistic fuck you are, so that's why she left you. Hell, that's probably why she cheated on you. So why don't you do us all a favor and tell us why you're really here. I'm getting bored."

Uriel smiles, showcasing white, gleaming teeth. "I've brought a present for you, dear daughter. For all of you."

He's still trying to goad us, yet I'm too stubborn to resist the urge to reply, "What? What could you possibly have that we'd want?" The Redeemer. My mom. His eviction from the human world. I'm doing a little bluffing myself.

As if this very moment was planned, Selaphiel produces a black satchel no bigger than a basketball. She unties it and holds it out for Uriel, who sticks his hand inside. Once he's grasped the contents, he tosses it towards us, where it lands at Lucifer's feet.

I don't want to know what it is.

I can't…I can't look.

But even as I try to persuade myself that it can't possibly

be… I still find myself stepping forward to get a closer look. However, Andras and Phenex grip my arms before I can get far.

"You don't want to see it," Phenex urges.

"What is it?"

"Eden…you don't want to—"

"Just tell me what it is!" I screech.

Lucifer bends down and picks up whatever "gift" Uriel has thrown at us. I tell myself I don't want to look, but I'm still straining to see. I just need to know if my suspicions are true.

Lucifer turns around, his hand stained with rich crimson. Within his palm is the pulpy source of the bloody mess. His gaze is somber when it connects with mine, and I know…I know…

"Eden, it's a heart."

TWENTY-SIX

I DON'T QUITE KNOW HOW IT HAPPENS.

In one second I'm standing there, being held back by Phenex and Andras. Then in the next, I'm lunging across the courtyard with glowing orbs of holy light in each palm, my vision painted in red.

I'll kill him. I'll make him wish I were never born. I'll make him regret his entire fucking existence.

Uriel remains as smug as always, not even bothering to flinch at my cries and curses. It's as if I don't even exist in his realm. I am nothing, no more than an ant crawling in the earth. Now I see…I see what Crysis meant. We are nothing to them. They come to our world, they create us, yet they feel no familial attachment. He is not my father. I've never had one. And now he's taken one of the only people I had left.

"I'll kill you!" I screech. Cain catches me around my waist

as I'm airborne, pulling me back. "I'll fucking kill you, you piece of shit!"

Just the tiniest of tics and the dip of his head to the side indicate his intrigue. "You're a light wielder," he comments. "Interesting."

"I will rip your fucking head off!" I glare back at Cain, desperately trying to struggle out of his steel-like clutches. Toyol steps in front of me for reinforcements. "Let me go! Let me go!"

"I can't," Cain grits. "I won't. He'll kill you."

"Let. Me. Go!" I demand, not giving a damn about my own mortality. Uriel is a murderer. He has to pay for what he's done.

It's Lucifer who turns and lays a firm hand on my shoulder, stilling my thrashing. He dips his head to meet my fury-filled eyes, and suddenly the red eases away. The anguish, the rage…it's easier to see through it all and just focus on his face.

"Eden, I need you to believe in me," he whispers. "You shall have your vengeance. Just trust in me, ok?"

Still panting and shaking mad, I momentarily cease my struggle. Lucifer knows Uriel better than anyone. Letting my emotions get the best of me could be the most human mistake I could make. And we still have too much to lose for me to ruin it all.

But still…my heart is shattering within my chest. Angry tears stain my cheeks. I can't believe this. How could he? How could he? What kind of monster does something like this?

"You never loved her, did you? She was nothing but a waste receptacle for your revenge."

Uriel's expression remains impassive. "Your mother is human. I loved her like I love all God's creatures."

"Bullshit. Look around you, you sick fuck. Is this your definition of love?"

A smile plays across Uriel's lips as he raises a hand and snaps his fingers. As if they have been woken from slumber, the body-snatching lesser demons all begin to rise. Most of them sport cuts and bruises, but for the most part, they're all ok. They don't move; they simply stand, waiting for direction from their leader. An archangel is controlling lesser demons. How?

"We did not brutalize them. You and your friends did. See how easy violence is for you? How you take pleasure in inflicting pain? You must have rejoiced when you defeated them."

"But I didn't kill anyone," I retort.

"Oh?" Uriel takes a simple step forward, challenging my claim. "Are you sure about that? Because that little boy you sent to step in front of a bus did not survive. But you knew that. You saw the way his brain seeped out after his skull was smashed like a melon. You saw the way his mangled, lifeless body was drained of its blood. Tell me, Eden. Did you cry for him? For his poor parents who lost their young son? Or did you simply walk away with a sense of victory and pride swelling in your chest?"

I open my mouth to respond, but no sound comes out. I'd tried to block it out all these years. I told myself that it didn't count—he had deserved it for assaulting me. He was the bad one, not me. I was just defending myself.

"You see, Eden? There will be casualties in the war

between good and evil. Your mother, unfortunately, was one of them."

"Really, Uriel?" Lucifer interjects, facing him. "You've resorted to killing defenseless human women? I'm disappointed."

"Defenseless? She awakened the Legion of Lost Souls. The beast who will unleash Hell on Earth. I'd say she was anything but defenseless."

"And you expect us all to believe that you had no influence in that decision?" Lucifer takes a step towards him, yet still keeps a healthy distance from his estranged siblings. "This is exactly what you wanted. If this world were ravaged with evil, you'd be justified in your quest to destroy mankind. Father would have no other choice but to see reason. Wipe the slate clean and start over. That's what you want, isn't it?"

"Humans are flawed. Sinful. You and Samael saw to that."

"And that's why it was *your* job to protect them!"

I don't truly understand why, but Lucifer is furious. Since the beginning of time, he's taken pleasure in the corruption of humans. And now he wants to save them? That's what he wanted all along? I don't know if I can believe that. I'm not sure I should. But here he is, pleading on behalf of all mankind.

"Belial, you made your choice," Uriel reasons, as if anything about him or his sycophants is rational. "This realm is doomed and has been for much too long. They are slowly but surely executing their own extinction. It is our job as the guardians of the realms to keep them from succumbing to self-destruction."

"By killing them," Lucifer deadpans.

"Yes. It will be quick. Unlike what would happen if Samael had his way."

Lucifer heaves out an impatient breath. "You don't know what *Legion* would do. How do you even know he even wants to destroy this world?"

A dramatic pause, and Uriel smiles, his eyes dimming with sadistic satisfaction, and a sick sensation churns in my gut. He knows something. He has information about Legion.

"Tell us what you know," Lucifer demands, exasperated with these stupid games, as are the rest of us. "And make it quick. We all know you like to hear yourself talk, Uriel, but we'd like to be done with this before the Rapture. Unless you really *don't* know what the fuck you're talking about."

Uriel barks out an unsuspecting belly laugh that both startles and disgusts me. "Why don't we ask *Samael* and see what he has to say about all this. I have no reason to lie to you. But if you don't believe me…"

Again, the ground shakes underneath our feet, but it's accompanied with an odd tug within my torso. As if my insides are reaching out to something—someone—and whatever is on the other side is pulling in response. Like I am one half of an unseen whole, tethered by space and time. I stumble back, unsure, almost disoriented by the feeling. I can feel him, as I always have. I can taste his essence on my tongue. I can smell his scent of midnight jasmine and kindled earth. I can hear him growling my name in my ear as if he's pushing deep inside me, claiming my womb as well as my heart.

Legion. His name echoes inside my skull.
Legion. His name is slashed across my skin.
Legion. His name is an edict, a threat, a prophecy.
And he's here.

Earth will perish in fire, and he will spark the flame. And

if it means we can be together, if it means I can save him from himself, I'll only be too eager to strike the first match.

He appears before us in plumes of black feathers that disintegrate into tendrils of onyx smoke. Tall, broad, and as beautiful and cold as Death itself. His expression is stony and unreadable, and his eyes—those eyes that were birthed from the brightest stars in the universe—seem flat and dead. What has happened to him? Where did he go?

But as if his refusal to even acknowledge us wasn't hurtful enough, he stands with them. The Seraph. He's betrayed the Se7en and his sacred oath. He's betrayed me.

"Don't look so distraught, my dears," Uriel cajoles smugly. "Did you think I was the only one who wanted to end mankind? I mean, certainly Belial has shared his own little insurance plan, considering he's been planning human extinction since his fall from grace. I thought you would be grateful, brother, seeing as I'm saving you the trouble and sparing your little pets. And my daughter."

I frown but don't dare take my eyes off Legion. How can I?

"Lucifer…what is he talking about?" I whisper harshly.

"I'll tell you later," he murmurs back.

Of course, Uriel hears every word of our quick exchange. "Why don't you tell her now, brother? Tell her how the one you now know as Legion was created to be the destroyer of this world. How scripture may depict the great dragon as the Devil, when in fact, it is just you that is pulling the strings, being the master manipulator as Legion does the dirty work. And tell her how you assembled a backup plan in the event he fails. Because he will fail, won't he? You just needed a scapegoat. The real threat isn't Legion—it never has been. You protect the threat now like precious chattel, keeping her close to you, infecting her with your influence before she was even born. You even ensured that she would be joined with the other little pieces to your twisted puzzle."

Now I pull my gaze away from Legion and turn to face Lucifer, who looks more pissed off than I've ever seen him. I can literally see Hellfire in his eyes. "Tell me. Now."

But he doesn't. Not really. But it's enough for me to know that my presence here—with the Se7en, with Lucifer—was not by chance. "You needed to be protected."

Again Uriel laughs, just as he plucks a dark wooden case from out of thin air. It's over a foot-long and inscribed with ancient symbols that are not of this world. I know what it is before he even opens it, and judging by the low hisses from the Se7en and the way the air seems to be mystically charged, I'm not the only one.

"I believe you all were looking for this," my father boasts as he relinquishes the blade studded with blood rubies. "You probably thought I wanted it to kill all of you. Well, fortunately for you, I no longer need to. There's only one who needs to die today. I can't and won't leave anything to chance. This world will fall, and he will be the first of many. However, his death is not a tragedy. It is a reprieve."

On that note, every skin-walking lesser demon cheers with rousing exuberance. Uriel turns towards Legion, and my heart stops. He's going to use it. He's going to kill him. And Legion isn't even trying to resist it. It's as if he wants this. He wants Uriel to end his life.

"Stop!" I cry out. "Please. You can't let him do this. Legion, look at me."

At the sound of his name on my lips, Legion seems to snap out of his trance momentarily, and he does what I ask. He looks at me, his eyes suddenly clear and bright. And a dozen nights spent with me sleeping against his chest as he kissed away my nightmares plays out across his features. The times he watched me with a smile teasing his sensual lips…the moments I stared in awe as he laughed as if the world wasn't bearing down upon his shoulders. Every touch of his skilled fingers on my humid skin as he sexed me into sweet submission. I see them all reflected in his pained gaze. I feel them stirring in my chest. He remembers. He isn't gone for good. He's still in there.

I slowly step forward, and surprisingly, no one impedes my advance. My eyes stay locked on his, urging him to come forth, just as Lucifer commanded that lesser demon. Come forth and come back to me.

"Legion, please…" I begin, my voice steady and soft. I don't want to spook him. "You don't have to do this. Whatever he wants, whatever he's promised you, it's a lie."

"What I promised him, girl," Uriel snaps, his tone harsh. "Is a life free of the guilt and pain of carrying around countless lost souls. Souls that have tortured him for centuries."

I ignore his words and keep reaching out to my beloved. "We can get through this together. I don't blame you for anything. I don't hate you. You did nothing wrong."

Legion's appears to sober even more, as if he's just now realizing where he is and what he's allowing to take place. He takes one step towards me.

"He doesn't care about you. He doesn't care about me. We

are your family. All of us here. And if you do this...we all will die."

He takes one more step closer, prompting Raphael to do the same, a look of panic in his eyes.

But I don't let up. I keep moving towards him, even as the lesser demons grow more and more agitated. Even as Uriel seethes with contempt. If he wants to kill Legion, he'll have to go through me. He's already killed his human wife. He won't hesitate to slay his own daughter.

I can tell Raphael is confused as he looks to Uriel for guidance. This wasn't part of the plan. They didn't bet on Legion being strong enough to fight his inner demons. They probably told him that his sacrifice would be rewarded—that he was carrying out God's plan to rid the world of error. But they knew they weren't bargaining with their former brother. They knew he was trapped within himself, shrouded in shame and sin, and they used it against him.

"Remember the first night we slept in the same bed together?" I ask, conjuring a memory I had kept close to my heart. "And I woke up on the floor, screaming and crying after having a nightmare? You picked me up, pulled me into you, wrapped your arms around me, and whispered that I was safe...that everything would be ok because you were there. I didn't tell you, but that was the first time I realized what true safety and security were. You had told me you were sent to assassinate me, yet I knew that I could trust you. I felt it. I knew you'd never hurt me as long as you could help it."

"Shut up, girl," Selaphiel hisses.

But I don't shut up because I don't even hear her. She doesn't exist in this moment. None of them do. It's just him and me laying in a sea of dove grey sheets, marveling at the way our bodies fit together.

"I dreamt of you some nights. They may not have been my memories, but they felt like it. And in those dreams, you were so tender, so devoted, just as you've always been. No one has ever looked at me the way you do. No one has ever made me blush with just a single crooked grin or a feather-light brush of your fingertips against my skin. I didn't know what it meant to be truly cared for before you. You made me want to hope. To dream. To want. And all I want is you."

"Stupid child," Uriel spits. "You know not what you speak. He does not care for you."

I ignore my father's lies and soldier on, moving closer still. Moving closer to the demon who awkwardly deemed himself my boyfriend, even though he was so much more.

"And when you took me to Colorado Springs, and the Dark King did that spell...I never told you this, but I remember. After the veil was shattered and I found out I was Nephilim, I remember that night. I begged you to kiss me...to make love to me. But you didn't. You made me feel so...good. But you refused to kiss me because you said the first time you kissed me, you wanted me to remember it always. You wanted me to touch my lips the next day and smile at the memory. You refused to take away my free will."

The brown-haired male archangel is getting antsier. He's jumpy, nervous to the point of agitation. "Stop this, Uriel!"

"You have no idea what that meant to me. While so many people—mortal and immortal—have used me, manipulated me, you refused to take advantage. That's when I knew... that's when I knew I was falling in love with you. I was just too scared to admit it." Only feet separate us. I can already feel the heat of his body waft over me.

But I never get to touch him. I don't get to hold him. The chance to kiss his lips and proclaim my love while he wraps me in his chiseled arms is stolen from us. And all hope to bring him back—to save him from himself—is lost.

"Enough!"

Uriel, so stupid and careless, darts between us, the blade raised up over his head. I'm not even sure what I see but something dark and malevolent dims the stars in Legion's eyes just a split second before he grabs Raphael and yanks him in front of him, using him as a shield. The Redeemer slices through Raphael's chest and the angel screams, the sound so loud and high-pitched that it brings me to my knees. I cover my ears to salvage my hearing, desperately trying to stay conscious as the screeching noise rattles my skull to the point of excruciating pain. The others behind me have fallen too, as well as the lesser demons. Beams of blinding, brilliant light seep out of Raphael's every orifice, and I'm forced to turn and cover my eyes before they're burned from their sockets. I'm screaming. At least I think I'm screaming. I don't know anymore. I can't even be sure I'm not dead myself.

When the light behind my eyelids begins to dim, I dare to turn around and see what is left of the brown-haired archangel. But the only thing that remains is a pile of ash and tendrils of white smoke.

And The Redeemer at Legion's feet.

But the stars have been extinguished. Not even a single twinkle in the dark, dead depths of his eyes. And as he stares down at me, his gaze as black as night, I know that we've lost him.

He isn't Legion.

He isn't even a rogue soul seeking mischief.

He is *many*.

TWENTY-SEVEN

THE LEGION OF LOST SOULS PICKS UP THE BLADE, weighing it in their hand. And a slow, serpentine smile slithers onto their mouth.

I think I cry out, begging them to stop, but I can't hear my voice. With my ears still ringing, everything sounds like I'm submerged in water. I'm drowning again. Just like I did as a child at my mother's hands. Just like I did at that church at my father's hands.

In the next stutter of my racing heart, Legion whips the blade around to draw a deep gash over Uriel's chest, just over the space that would contain his angelic heart. Horror contorts his ethereal face as he looks down to witness the first streams of blinding light seeping from his torn flesh. Yet, somehow, he grabs ahold of Selaphiel and they both disappear, leaving no more than a tendril of white smoke in their wake.

But Legion isn't done. We are surrounded by enemies—enemies that they have set their sights on. Five angels still stand at the perimeter, and before they can flap their white wings and flee, Legion flings out darkness and shadows and hellfire, turning their bodies into ovens. The angels cry in excruciating agony as their blood boils and their internal organs literally cook inside of them. The smell of burning flesh…I have to swallow down bile and press my head to the cool concrete just to stay conscious. I can't look at them. Even if they were fooled into thinking Uriel was doing God's work, even if they had come with the intent to kill us all, I can't look as they are burned alive.

I tell myself I'll get up once the screaming stops, but it never does. However, it's not the angels that are shrieking in anguish. I pry open one eye to find that Legion has moved on to the lesser demons, ripping them limb from limb faster than they can realize what's happening. They are killing them. All of them. Legion is killing the humans.

I struggle to push up on shaky legs; my limbs reduced to Jell-O. Then a warm hand grips my arm to help me upright and pulls me into his chest.

"He has to be stopped," Lucifer says. And for the first time *ever*, he looks…scared.

The Se7en, Adriel, Niko, and Crysis are also on their feet, fighting through the pain in their skulls and the stench of death that still permeates the air. Luckily, the Alliance was smart enough to escape while we were all distracted by the Seraph. Thank God. Legion would rip them apart, no matter what side they fought for.

"He's gone…" Adriel whispers, the prelude to a sob in her

throat. "He's gone for good this time."

"No, he isn't," Cain growls. He looks to his brothers and sister and gives a stiff, authoritative nod. "Surround them. Carefully move in, but no sudden movements."

"Let me help," Nikolai offers. There's blood dripping from his ears.

Cain shakes his head. "You're not one of us. They'll kill you on sight."

"They?" Niko frowns with confusion.

"That isn't one demon," Cain explains. "That's every lost soul Legion has ever collected. They *are* the legion."

I look to Lucifer. Maybe—just maybe—they will listen to him. "You have to do something. Please? You have to stop them before they murder all those people. For me...do it for me."

Lucifer glances across the courtyard, at the carnage and blood that's smeared all over what used to be the heart of downtown Chicago. He looks reluctant, but thankfully, he nods.

"I'll do what I can."

He closes his eyes, centering his power. Compacting all his darkness so he can hurl it out over the pandemonium, covering the chaotic scene with his influence. Every remaining lesser demon falls, forced into a manufactured sleep. And then, one by one, they begin to fade away, carried by a wind of dark magic.

Legion spins around to face us, their face streaked with blood, their hands stained crimson. The Se7en move towards them with slow, measured steps to assure them that they don't intend to hurt them. However, every gun is drawn, and every blade is unsheathed. Surely, Legion would not hurt them, but they still have The Redeemer. And this isn't the Legion I know. I don't know if he's even in there at all.

But if there's a chance…if there's any hope that I can help bring him back, I'll do it. He would never want this. Even when he had to slay those Alliance members at the gas station, he took no pleasure in that. It fucked with his head. It made him feel like a monster stripped of any chance of redemption.

He may not come back to me, but I owe it to him to help him find his way back to his faith. Before me, all he wanted was to find redemption and gain God's favor as he had when he was in Heaven. I know he thinks that all hope is lost now; how can a fallen angel find his way back home? But I know his heart, and it is the most beautiful, purest thing I've ever had the pleasure to love.

The Se7en close in, hoping to trap Legion before they can dematerialize and get away. I doubt we'd be able to track them then so there's a good chance we'll never get another chance like this again. They're crouched down, eyes darting around the space like a feral animal. They're afraid. Disoriented. They don't know what's happening any more than we do.

"Hey," I say softly, my palms raised to show I'm no threat. "Can you hear me?"

Legion's lifeless gaze falls on me with a look of curiosity and delight. "We do." Their unified voices will star in my darkest nightmares for the rest of my days. Various tones and pitches, some distorted. Like dragging claws across a chalkboard. Yet, they speak as one.

"Good." I nod to show my satisfaction. I don't want to be condescending, but I want them to know that I am not a foe. I accept them. "Will you talk to me?"

"We will." A dozen spiders crawl up my spine.

"Thank you. I need you to let me help you—all of you. I know you're all angry and maybe a little afraid. All I want to do is make things better. Will you help me do that?"

Legion pauses for a beat, taking in Lucifer standing behind me, before saying, "We won't go back. We're never going back."

"You don't have to go back," I assure them. "I'm not here for that, I promise."

The Se7en are getting closer. I don't know what they mean to do, but I'm giving them a welcomed distraction. I can't imagine Legion would go quietly even if they asked.

"What is it you want then, girl?" they sneer.

"I want to talk to the one that was once called Samael. Can you find him for me?"

"Samael is gone."

"I don't believe he is. I think he may be lost. Can you find him for me? Please?"

"We will never go back."

"I promise—I'll do whatever I can so you never have to. Just please…let me talk to him. Just once. I just…I want to say goodbye."

The Se7en are almost in striking distance. This may work. We may be able to save him.

"Ok," Legion says. "You may speak to him. But he will no longer rule this body. Don't come back for him."

I blink back anguished tears and nod, no intention of keeping that promise. A quick glance to my right then my left to ensure everyone is in position.

Legion blinks, and for a moment, I think they've dozed off. But when their eyes reopen, I see silver stars and moonlight. I hear the wings of a raven and the scent of jasmine-kissed night air whispering across my skin. I feel fire kindling my skin, warding off the bite of winter winds.

He's here. My Legion. He's come back to me.

I rush to him against all my better judgment and throw myself into his arms, despite the blood that cakes his skin and clothes. I don't care. I need to feel him, smell him. I need to know that he is not lost forever.

Hesitantly, he bands an arm around me and holds me close. The other hand contains The Redeemer, which he keeps off to his side, as if he's afraid to have it near me.

"Legion…" Big, fat, ugly tears roll down my cheeks.

"It's ok, baby, I'm here now," he whispers in my hair between kisses. His voice is his again—gravelly and deep. It's the most beautiful sound I've ever heard.

"I thought…I thought I had lost you. You left me."

"I had to. I didn't want to hurt you again. I'd rather die than ever lay a hand on you."

I tear my face from the warmth of his chest and look up at his anguished expression. "But you didn't. That wasn't you then. And…and I'm fine—"

"I could have killed you."

"You wouldn't have. I trust you."

He shakes his head before diverting his eyes to the blood-stained ground. "You shouldn't."

I reach up to cradle his face in my palms, compelling him to look at me. He needs to see that I'm sincere. He needs to believe in *us* just as I believe in him.

"You're stronger than them. I've seen it—I've felt it. I need you. The Se7en needs you. And believe it or not, this world needs you. You have committed your existence to fighting for the greater good. I'm asking you, begging you, please...fight for us. Fight for you and me. I love you. Do you hear me? I love you, Legion. And I won't stop fighting. I'll never stop fighting to bring you back to me."

I don't know what happens, but apparently, I've said something wrong. Because the earth begins to tremble and the noxious smell of sulfur fills my nostrils. And I hear them... whispers. A thousand voices, many of them speaking in a tongue I don't understand, and they're angry. The lost souls have returned, and they want him back.

"No!" I beg, holding on tighter to him.

Legion's eyes go wide as the silver stars begin to die in his terror-stricken gaze. "Eden. Eden, I have to go."

In the distance, I hear Cain and the others shouting for me to move back...to get away from him. No. I can't. I can't let go. I'll never let go of him.

"Please stay with me," I cry into his chest, squeezing him tighter. "I can't do this without you. I need you. Please."

"I can't." He lifts my chin so I'm forced to see that only a few glimmering stars remain. "I love you. So much. So much that I'd move Heaven and Earth to keep you safe. So much that I'd rather die than subject you to a life of pain and ruin."

I gasp as he lifts The Redeemer and holds it out to me. "I want you to use it. Kill me. You are half Seraph. If anyone here has a chance of stopping me, it's you. This is what you were made for, Eden. I need you put an end to this suffering."

I shake my head and try to step back, but he won't loosen

his hold on me. He's growing more frantic, more anxious by the second. The voices hiss louder, demanding blood in exchange for our deception.

"Come with us," I shout over the roar of lost souls. "We can help you. We'll find another way."

Legion shakes his head. Another star implodes in his glassy eyes. "There is no other way. I can't change what I am. And this realm will never be safe as long as I'm alive." He tries again to push the blade into my hands, desperately pleading, "Do it. Kill me. Please. Kill me."

Everything around us begins to dim as if we're being wrapped in a cocoon of darkness. Violent winds howl and whip around us, trying to push us apart. I try to hang on even tighter, but they're stronger than I'd imagined. I can't do it alone.

"Get her out of there!" Cain calls out. He's closer now, but it's hard to hear through the wailing wind tunnel. I'm not ready yet. I'll never be ready to say goodbye.

Legion strokes my cheek with the back of his hand. "Eden…" A single tear rolls down his beautifully pained face.

The last star is distinguished. The howling winds still. And darkness falls.

"Now!" Cain roars.

The Se7en close the distance, attacking from all sides. But it's too late. Too late for them to pull Legion back from the darkness. Too late for me to pry myself out of their clutches.

The demon assassins don't even get within an inch of them before the lost souls send a blast of scorching energy to propel them back several yards. The Se7en are back on their feet within seconds, racing forward even faster, weapons at the ready. I try to struggle out of Legion's grasp, but they seem intent on keeping me, probably to punish me for my deceit.

"Please, let me go. I'm sorry." My palm tingles as a glowing orb is already forming.

"Such a pretty girl," they sneer in those unnatural, skin-crawling voices.

The sphere grows hotter, radiating with holy light. I don't want to use it, but I will.

"What do you want from me?" I don't want to know—hell no. But I need to keep them distracted long enough for the Se7en to find an in. Long enough for them to grab them so I can—

Too late.

It happens inhumanly fast. So fast that I can't even believe it's happening at all. But as the Se7en approach, Legion whirls their body around, taking me with them. I didn't see what they were doing. I couldn't even detect the movement. But by the time I realize what they'd done, it's already too late. There's no coming back from this.

There are screams, violent, agonized cries all around me, yet I'm too stunned to make a sound. No... *No...*

Jinn's dark eyes go wide with horror as he looks down to where the hilt of The Redeemer is protruding from his torso. Then, slowly, as if the movement pains him, he lifts his head to face what was once his brother, his leader, his friend. And now, his murderer.

Jinn, his lovely brown skin going ashen as The Redeemer staves the life from his body, parts his pale lips. And in an accented tone that sounds like a beautiful melody, the mute demon utters, "*And if he trespass against thee seven times in a day, and seven times in a day turn again to thee, saying, I re-pent; thou shalt forgive him.* I...forgive you...brother."

Phenex, face furious and streaked with tears, catches his closest friend from behind, pulling him from further harm. Legion has broken them all. Those wayward souls have permanently fractured the Se7en.

And just the way they came, Legion explodes into plumes of shiny, black feathers, shadows, and smoke.

Legion is gone. My mother is dead. Jinn is down. And the Se7en will never be the same.

I was created for a purpose. And when I met him, I thought my purpose was Legion.

But not to love him. Not even to save him.

My purpose was to kill him.

And I failed.

I look down at Jinn, my friend, drowning in his own blood, while his brothers and sister weep over his still, lifeless body.

Now I understand. Now it's as clear to me as those stars that once mesmerized me under the midnight moon.

Kill one to save a million.

For the Se7en, for the safety of all mankind, I vow on my life that I will not fail again.

TWENTY-EIGHT

LUCIFER

H E PACES THE FLOOR OUTSIDE HER BEDROOM DOOR, contemplating what to say. But the words have been stolen, snatched from his tongue and replaced with the bitter taste of regret. Shame. He feels shameful for possessing these thoughts…these *emotions*. And odd. Human sentiments hold no purpose in his existence. Yet, here they are, infecting him, changing him. And it was seriously driving him fucking mad.

Lucifer couldn't fuck his way out of this. He couldn't snap his fingers and be done with the discomfort of feeling. Eden had gotten under his skin, and as much as he enjoyed pressing all her pretty little buttons, he couldn't stand to see her in pain.

She didn't say a word on the journey back to Irin's house.

Nikolai was able to scrape together his last ounces of strength to flash Jinn back, so the ride back was tense, to say the least. He knew she blamed herself for this; she thought she could save the unsavable. And he and the Se7en were so desperate that they allowed her to try. They let her sacrifice her heart and her sanity because they believed she was the key to his salvation.

But he knew better.

He knew and still let her try because he needed her to see it for herself. What kind of monster was he? How could he shatter her into a million pieces for his own selfish desires because he was too stubborn, too afraid—*fuck*—to lose her?

And now here he is, reduced to a pathetic, sniveling coward outside her door, wondering what he could possibly say to make this better for her. Wondering if she would ever see him for more than the architect of all that was wrong and ugly in her life. She would be right to hate him, but he didn't care. Anything was better than seeing her crumble. He would rather burn in Hellfire for a thousand years than let her endure one more second of hurt.

He sucks in a breath. Spits out a curse. And knocks on the door.

He doesn't expect her to answer. When they arrived back at the mansion, she still hadn't uttered a single word. The others rushed to the infirmary, reciting silly little prayers to a negligent God, but she went straight to her room. Eyes glazed, shoulders limp…it was like she was in a trance.

Lucifer had no business following behind her. He was all the way fucked up to even think she wanted him anywhere near her after what she had just endured. But as her bedroom door creaks open, he holds his breath, thanking his Father for giving him this one small miracle.

"Eden…"

She doesn't say a word. She simply steps back to let him in. The irony of this simple gesture does not go unnoticed. Twenty-four hours ago, he would not have even bothered to knock. He took what he wanted, when he wanted. He didn't give a fuck about social norms because that shit didn't apply to the lord of the fucking underworld. But now…now her cold welcome is a gift. And he's only too eager to accept.

The room is in disarray with clothing strewn everywhere. She's washed the blood from her skin and changed her shirt, but she's back in the fighting leathers and boots from earlier.

"How are you?" he asks, shutting the door behind him. Stupid. What kind of question is that? "Are you hurt at all?"

"No." Her voice is icy enough to send a chill up Lucifer's spine. She slings a backpack onto the bed and starts stuffing it with clothing and weapons. She swiftly strides to the bathroom, retrieving some first aid items, and sticks those in there too.

"Going somewhere?" Lucifer asks, trying to sound casual.

"I'm going to find him."

"Who?"

"Legion."

"Eden, he's gone. He isn't coming back."

She slams down the backpack and glares daggers in Lucifer's direction. "Don't you think I know that?"

"Then why do you want to find him?"

"Because…" She shakes her head, unable to finish the thought. He knows it's too painful to be back in that courtyard,

312

bearing witness to that brand of unspeakable evil.

Lucifer knows that evil all too well. He created it. He nurtured it. And in pettiness and boredom, he unleashed that evil unto the world.

What would Eden think if she knew it was he who manipulated the monster that Legion had become? How would she feel if she knew that all of this was his doing?

Granted, this was all before he truly knew Eden, light years before he had grown to...*care* for her, a sentiment he was still struggling to digest. But if she had grown privy to his misdeeds—if she knew that she was the most crucial part of his devious plan—she would never forgive him, let alone speak to him again. And as fucking petty and human as that was, he couldn't risk it. He had already lost his brother. He couldn't lose her too.

"I'm going with you."

Eden pauses from her packing, looks at him and frowns. "What?"

"I'm going with you. You want to find him. Believe it or not, cupcake, I'm not just a pretty face."

She shakes her head. "I don't have time for games, Lucifer."

"Who said anything about games? You know the Se7en won't help you, and who would blame them? I'm all you've got."

"Crysis?"

"He's already gone back to join the Alliance to help rebuild the city."

"Nikolai?"

"I...released him. He earned it. He should be with his family."

She purses her perfect mouth, contemplating her options. She has none.

"Fine. But if you're coming with me, no funny business. You will not lie to me. You will not try to mindfuck me. And you won't question me about anything I may have to do. Got it?"

"Got it."

Lucifer turns towards the door under the pretense of packing his own bag. Honestly, there's nothing he truly needs. Only her.

"Luc?" Eden calls out before he hit the doorjamb.

"Yes?" He turns to face her, more eager than he intends.

"Uriel…he said I was part of your insurance plan. The most important piece to your puzzle that will bring ruin to the Earth in the event that Legion fails. What does that even mean? And what role do I play in all this?"

Lucifer's violet eyes fall to the floor, his expression blank and his brutally cold guise sliding into place. He never meant to drag this out for as long as he did, but here they are. And either way he plays this, she may very well hate him for the rest of her days, however long that may be.

Still, she'd understand. She'd do anything for the people she loves. Maybe one day he'd be included in that category.

Maybe.

He fixes his face with a crooked grin, the one he knows makes her breath still and her cheeks heat against her will, then gazes up at her through hooded eyes churning with a thousand tiny galaxies.

"I'll tell you on the way."

Can't wait for the release of Se7en Sinners 4?

Download the Dark Light Series now and get more from Nikolai, Dorian, and Gabriella.

ACKNOWLEDGEMENTS

I am so incredibly fortunate to have a team of amazing people in my corner. Next month (October 2017), I will celebrate five years of writing and publishing, and as cliché as it sounds, living out my dream. I am humbled that so many have stood by me through this journey. I could not have made it this far had it not been for their support.

Mo Sytsma: In so many ways, you are my better half. You are so much more than a PA. You're my therapist, my beta reader, my publicist, my editor, and my friend. Thank you for not giving up on me over the years. Real talk, this ship would sink without you.

MAUD: Everything you all touch turns to gold. Thank you for seeing my vision and bringing it to life. Kristina and Steven Lowe, you both are beautiful inside and out, and I am so grateful to have you on the cover, as well as in my life.

Hang Le: Cover artist extraordinaire! There's a reason why you're one of the most sought after cover artists in the business. You get me. You know what I want even before I do. Your talent is boundless.

Stacey Blake: Once again, you have made my words and these pages absolutely gorgeous. You are a lovely soul, and I am so glad to know you and call you my friend. Thank you for putting up with my procrastination!

Susan Mika Reyes: You have such an amazing eye for beauty, and I am proud to have your work displayed on my books! Can't wait to see you again so we can make some magic. I know incredible things are in store for you.

Kara Hildebrand: You are such a beautiful person, and I am so glad to have your eyes on this book, as well as several of my previous works. You never disappoint. Thank you for everything.

Christina Collie: All your bitching paid off! I finished! Thank you for pushing me everyday and offering your advice. You are a true friend.

Madeline Sheehan: Thank you for your amazing support. You have no idea how much you inspire and motivate me to keep going.

Rosa Saucedo: I know I did you sooo dirty, lol! But thank you! I needed you to keep pushing me. Feel free to berate me into writing books any time you like.

Sunny Borek: As usual, you're always there when I need you, whether it's to vent or request your beautiful edits. Thank you, friend.

Jonesin' for S.L. Jennings and Unicorn Squad: If I could individually name every single one of you here, I would. You all are amazing. I would be nothing without your undying love and support. Unicorn kisses for all of you!

Bloggers and readers: This community is what it is because of you. You are woven in the pages of every book I've ever published. Thank you for reading and sharing my stories, and helping to breathe life into the characters we cherish so much.

My family: Number twelve is in the books, and it's all because of you. It's all FOR you. I love you.

-S

About the Author

Most known for her starring role in a popular sitcom as a child, S.L. Jennings went on to earn her law degree from Harvard at the young age of 16. While studying for the bar exam and recording her debut hit album, she also won the Nobel Prize for her groundbreaking invention of calorie-free wine. When she isn't conquering the seas in her yacht or flying her Gulfstream, she likes to spin elaborate webs of lies and has even documented a few of these said falsehoods.

S.L.'s devious lies:

SE7EN SINNERS SERIES
Born Sinner
End of Eden
Wicked Ruin

INK AND LIES

TAINT and *TRYST* (Sexual Education novels)

FEAR OF FALLING and *AFRAID TO FLY* (Fearless novels)

THE DARK LIGHT SERIES
Dark Light
The Dark Prince
Nikolai (a Dark Light novella)
Light Shadows

Meet the Liar:

www.sljenningsauthor.com
www.facebook.com/authorsljennings
Twitter: @MrsSLJ
Instagram: instagram.com/s.l.jennings
Sign up for the newsletter: http://bit.ly/SLJ_Newsletter

Made in the USA
Monee, IL
20 June 2023

36453670R00179